AN INEXPLICABLE WOMAN

A Tabitha & Wolf Mystery: Book 4

Sarah F. Noel

Copyright © 2023 Sarah F. Noel

All rights reserved

The characters and events portrayed in this book are fictitious. Any similarity to real persons, living or dead, is coincidental and not intended by the author.

No part of this book may be reproduced, or stored in a retrieval system, or transmitted in any form or by any means, electronic, mechanical, photocopying, recording, or otherwise, without express written permission of the publisher.

ISBN: 9798867345099
Cover design by: HelloBriie Creative
Printed in the United States of America

*To my dear friends Mike & Charlotte, who helped me research
Brighton while keeping me well-fed. And to my godson, Toby
(who really is lovely).*

*Last, but definitely not least, my good friend
Chris Bailey, who is a good sport.*

CONTENTS

Title Page
Copyright
Dedication
Foreword
Prologue — 1
Chapter 1 — 2
Chapter 2 — 7
Chapter 3 — 15
Chapter 4 — 23
Chapter 5 — 30
Chapter 6 — 37
Chapter 7 — 44
Chapter 8 — 51
Chapter 9 — 56
Chapter 10 — 63
Chapter 11 — 72
Chapter 12 — 80
Chapter 13 — 88
Chapter 14 — 100
Chapter 15 — 110

Chapter 16	117
Chapter 17	128
Chapter 18	137
Chapter 19	147
Chapter 20	154
Chapter 21	160
Chapter 22	168
Chapter 23	176
Chapter 24	184
Chapter 25	193
Chapter 26	200
Chapter 27	208
Chapter 28	215
Chapter 29	225
Chapter 30	233
Chapter 31	240
Chapter 32	253
Epilogue	259
Afterword	265
Acknowledgement	267
About The Author	269
Books By This Author	271

FOREWORD

This book is written using British English spelling. e.g. dishonour instead of dishonor, realise instead of realize.

British spelling aside, while every effort has been made to proofread this thoroughly, typos do creep in. If you find any, I'd greatly appreciate a quick email to report them at sarahfnoelauthor@gmail.com

PROLOGUE

His large hands around her beautiful, graceful throat looked wrong. He knew he should have released her there and then, but instead, he squeezed harder. It only took a moment or two for her to stop resisting and go limp. He could have stopped then, but instead he squeezed for a bit longer, just to be sure.

CHAPTER 1

On the journey to Scotland, Wolf had marvelled at their excess of luggage. But now, as he looked around at the even greater throng of titled personages, servants, children and pets, and all the attendant bags and boxes they were leaving Scotland with, he wondered how he had let himself be bullied into allowing this travelling circus to accompany him to Brighton.

Of course, he couldn't imagine what he might have done differently. Despite what he might wish otherwise, it was hard to imagine that Tabitha would have agreed to be left behind. So already, that was two people and two servants. Then, of course, the dowager, sensing an investigation, had insisted on joining and bringing her granddaughter, Lady Lily, along. Given that the Dowager Countess of Pembroke had travelled to Scotland with her maid and her butler, Manning, and that Lady Lily had her maid, that was another five people (though in an act of surprising thoughtfulness, the dowager had allowed Manning to go off and finally have a real holiday while they were in Brighton).

In addition, there was Bear, of course. Under normal circumstances, Wolf would have welcomed his old friend's company. But Wolf's original intention had been to travel alone to Brighton and that his friend, former thief-taking partner, then valet, and now personal secretary, Bear, with Lord Langley, would escort the dowager, her granddaughter, Lily, and Tabitha back to London. But once the dowager and Tabitha had decided to accompany him, their burgeoning group had been joined by Maxwell Sandworth, Lord Langley and his valet. Because Langley wasn't going back to London, this also meant that rounding out their group was Melody, Tabitha's four-year-old ward, her brother Matt, known as Rat, and her mischievous puppy, Dodo. Oh, and Melody's nurserymaid, Mary.

Wolf didn't understand why Langley needed to accompany them to Brighton. Maybe that wasn't wholly accurate; he knew why: Langley wished to avoid his mother. Wolf shook his head as he considered that Langley was a grown man, a Peer of the Realm, and, to top it off, he worked for British Intelligence. Yet he was scared of his own parent! Langley had been left in charge of Melody when Wolf and Tabitha had been summoned to Edinburgh by the dowager but had followed them up to Scotland when his mother had turned up to redecorate his London house. Rat, who had been working as a servant at Pembroke House, had also been brought along because it seemed the boy would now live with Langley and be educated and trained to help him in his intelligence work.

As they descended from the train in Brighton, Wolf did a quick count of heads: minus Manning, that was eleven adults, two children and a dog. He wanted to ensure they all arrived together at The Grand Brighton, the palatial hotel they were almost taking over. It was lucky it was off-season, and all the hotel's suites had been available at such short notice. As it was, while the dowager was getting her own suite, Tabitha and Lily were sharing, as were Wolf and Bear. Surprisingly, Langley had offered to share with the children.

Wolf looked around at the large group and the huge number of bags and hat boxes and wondered how his life had changed. While his thief-taker life had sometimes been hard, there had been a simplicity to it that he sometimes missed. He and Bear had owned not much more than the clothes on their back and often didn't know where their next meal was coming from. But they'd been free to come and go as they pleased. They owed nothing to anyone, and no one had any expectations of them. Now, he was a landlord and business owner with many employees and tenants who relied on him. In addition, there were all the people living and working at Pembroke House, not the least of whom was Tabitha.

Wolf's relationship with his deceased cousin's widow was complicated, to say the least. They had scandalised society when she continued living at Pembroke House after Wolf had ascended to the earldom. Initially, she had stayed to help him manage the household. But then, she'd stayed because he'd wanted her to. Over the last few months, as she'd helped him navigate high society and played a pivotal role in solving three murders, Wolf's feelings for Tabitha had intensified. He wasn't sure what she felt in return. His one abortive effort to declare his feelings had ended abruptly when she rebuffed him.

Looking at Tabitha standing on the railway platform in Brighton, Wolf was as confused as ever about what, if anything, might happen between them. He had long ago decided she was the most beautiful woman he'd ever known. Her thick, wavy chestnut hair and gold-flecked hazel eyes were merely the more superficial aspects of that beauty. Over the few months he had known her, Wolf had fallen in love with the intelligent, compassionate, proud, independent woman. As he had this thought, Wolf caught himself; was that what this was? Was he in love with Tabitha? Then he thought back to that disastrous attempt at declaration; if he hadn't been about to declare love, what had he intended to say? Of course, the moment had been so spontaneous that he'd never had a chance to consider his words or intentions. So, perhaps Tabitha's brusque curtailing of the conversation had been for the best. At least then.

Wolf's realisation of his feelings for Tabitha made this trip to Brighton even more fraught; he had been summoned by his first love, Arlene, now Lady Archibald. He didn't know what she needed from him. But how on earth would he navigate this situation, particularly with his entourage in tow?

Bear interrupted his thoughts, "Let's see if we can rent sufficient carriages to transport this unruly group."

"We may need multiple trips. Go out front and see how many

you can hail. At the very least, let's get the dowager countess, Tabitha, Lady Lily, and the children in a carriage. From what I remember of that one case we did in Brighton, it's not a long walk from here to the hotel; you and I can stay to get everyone ferried over there and then stroll over. After such a long train ride, I'd like to stretch my legs."

Bear nodded in agreement and walked out of the station to see how many carriages were available for hire. He managed to find more than they'd hoped, and the dowager, her granddaughter, Tabitha, the children, and Langley easily fit in two with some of the luggage. The servants and the rest of the luggage would follow along when the carriages returned.

With the main party dispatched, Wolf and Bear began the fifteen-minute walk down to the seafront. It was a crisp but sunny autumn day, and the English Channel sparkled ahead of them as they strolled down Queens Road.

They didn't talk for the first few minutes. Bear was a man of few words, and Wolf had always appreciated that they could be in each other's company without the need to fill the silence with empty chatter. But finally, Bear asked, "What do you think she wants?"

Wolf didn't have to ask who "she" was; there was only one person Bear could be referring to.

"I have no idea. I did hear that her husband died a year or so ago, so I doubt it's anything to do with that."

Bear snorted derisively at the word husband, saying, "Yes, her husband died. I'm sure it wasn't soon enough for Arlene."

"Bear, please, let's not rehash this. I know you never liked Arlene and believed she threw me over for a title and a fortune, but I don't view her actions so harshly. Back then, I had nothing to offer her. We could barely feed ourselves sometimes, and I was in no position to take a wife. So, when she caught Archibald's eye, and he offered for her, she made the pragmatic choice. Women rarely have the luxury of marrying for love."

"That she accepted Archibald's offer is not what I hold against her, and you know that. She's a scheming, conniving woman who played with your affections."

Wolf sighed; he didn't want to debate this with his dear friend. Bear would never forgive Arlene for what he saw as a betrayal of his friend, but it had been so much more complicated than that. "Bear, we will never agree on this. I only ask that you put your animosity aside for long enough to help me with whatever she needs. And if you can't, I will handle it alone."

Bear laughed, a deep rumble of a sound, "Alone? Good luck with that. Between Lady Pembroke and the dowager countess, I doubt you will be doing much alone. And by the way, what will you tell Lady Pembroke about Arlene?"

"Well, to begin with, it's Lady Archibald now, not Arlene. But yes, I must tell Tabitha something. I'm just not sure what. What I do know is that I need to tell her at least a version of the truth before they meet. She's too astute not to realise there's a history between us, even if Arlene doesn't make it clear."

"Have you considered that Lady Archibald might be eager to pick up where you left off? She's now the widow of a baron with a fortune of her own, and you're a very wealthy earl. I wouldn't be surprised if summoning you down here was no more than a ruse to trap you in her web again."

Wolf sighed; a similar suspicion had often crossed his mind during the long train ride down.

CHAPTER 2

The train journey from Scotland had been long, and by the time they were in a hired carriage and making their way down to the hotel, the sun had started to set. Tabitha had never visited Brighton or any seaside town, so she had no idea what to expect. But as they made their way down Queens Road and the sun had started setting over the English Channel, Tabitha's breath caught at the view. Boats bobbed on the sea, and she could see West Pier and the still-under-construction Brighton Palace Pier jutting out into the sea. As they approached the seafront, she saw people strolling along the promenade. It was too chilly for anyone to be in the water or on the pebbled beach, but the seafront still made for a scene of carefree holiday fun.

Tabitha had got the dirty end of the stick and had ended up in a carriage with the dowager, who did not view the scene before them as Tabitha did. "My goodness, I can't imagine what Lady Willis was thinking visiting Brighton. Surely, there are less gaudy places she might have taken the sea air. There is something so incredibly common about all of this."

Tabitha sighed; she could foresee many such criticisms over whatever time they needed to spend in Brighton. It had been bad enough hearing the older woman make cutting comments about Scotland and its people, often in front of Scots. But to be back in England and still hearing how nothing was up to the dowager's impossible standards was so irritating that Tabitha snapped, "If that is how you feel, Mama, perhaps you should go back to London on the first train tomorrow."

The dowager sniffed indignantly, "That tone is quite uncalled for, Tabitha. As much as you might wish me gone, I have no intention of leaving. Despite my crucial assistance, without which you wouldn't have solved any of these recent cases, you insist on keeping things from me and attempting to investigate behind my back."

It was fortunate that the inside of the carriage was quite dark, because Tabitha couldn't help but roll her eyes. It was true that the dowager was often a very useful source of information, well, gossip, really, particularly when it came to the predilections and secrets of the upper echelons of society. And it was also true that the woman's flair for causing a scene had come in handy on more than one occasion. However, to say that her help had proved crucial was the kind of hyperbole the dowager was wont to indulge in.

Despite her involuntary eye rolling, Tabitha said nothing, and the dowager continued, now building to the state of high dudgeon she most enjoyed, "And so if you think you can send me back to London like a naughty child sent to bed without her pudding, you are sorely mistaken. I will not be left out of this investigation; I can assure you of that."

"Mama, we don't even know if there is an investigation," Tabitha pointed out. "All we know is that an old friend of Wolf's is in need of his help. There is no reason to believe there is anything mysterious or nefarious about her situation."

Tabitha wasn't sure who she was trying to convince, herself or the dowager. The truth was that Wolf had been very tight-lipped about this friend, this female friend, and what help she might need. Who was this woman from his past who could so easily command his assistance? It had been clear he'd wanted to travel to Brighton alone, and his evident discomfort at having them all join him made Tabitha very suspicious. And, if she was honest with herself, a bit jealous.

During their last day in Scotland, as arrangements had been made for their travel to Brighton, Tabitha noticed that looks passed between Bear and Wolf whenever this Lady Arlene

Archibald had been mentioned or alluded to. If she had to put a word to Bear's looks, it would have been disapproval. Yes, that was the word; it seemed as if Bear disapproved of their detour to visit Lady Archibald.

Before she could contemplate this further, the dowager continued, "Of course, there's something afoot! A mysterious woman from Jeremy's past tracks him down to send him a telegram pleading for help. He then drops everything to rush to her side, in Brighton, of all places. You don't need the nose of a bloodhound to sniff out an adventure here. It has all the makings of the worst kind of populist potboiler, for heaven's sake!"

The dowager had taken to being part of their investigations with a rather alarming enthusiasm. Tabitha wasn't sure how she'd so quickly moved from being a social pariah her mother-in-law wouldn't deign to acknowledge, to someone whose presence the woman insisted on dogging. Luckily, the carriage ride was brief, and Tabitha was saved from further debate as they pulled up to The Grand Brighton.

The hotel reminded Tabitha of an elaborate wedding cake with multiple levels of delicate white icing. This impression was reinforced as they entered the lobby: delicate, intricate, floral plaster friezes adorned the ceiling and cornices. Green-marbled columns were dotted throughout the lobby, each topped with more intricate castings. As their group made their way to the front desk, Tabitha looked up at the grand, wrought iron staircase decorated with more floral patterns. The Grand Brighton was aptly named.

Moving the large and unruly group with all their luggage from the carriages, through the hotel and into assigned rooms was achieved with all the patience and servility one might expect of a luxury establishment; even the dowager couldn't find fault. The rooms were large and comfortable. There were two-bedroom suites with a shared sitting area assigned to those of the party sharing, and a one-bedroom for the dowager. She was assured it had an excellent view and was one of their most sought-after rooms. Tabitha could only hope it met the woman's exacting standards.

Shown into her suite, Tabitha could see nothing to complain of. Everything was the height of fashionable, tasteful, expensive luxury. The furnishings were silk, the wood gleaming mahogany. Each bedroom was large, and the beds looked exceedingly comfortable. So comfortable that Tabitha was sorely tempted to take to hers and miss dinner altogether.

Ginny, her maid, followed Tabitha into the room accompanied by a porter with the luggage on a handcart. As always, Ginny had been organised enough to ensure a small, separate bag with enough clothes and accessories to dress Tabitha for dinner that night. Tabitha was happy to see that her bedroom had a private en-suite bathroom with a large, inviting bathtub.

Seeing Tabitha look longingly at the bathtub, Ginny said, "Why don't I run you a nice, hot bath? It's been a long trip, and I'm sure that's just what's needed before you face dinner."

Tabitha felt guilty; it had also been a long train ride for Ginny. Who was running Ginny a bath? But she knew that Ginny accepted her lot and had no complaints about her life as a lady's maid. If anything, Tabitha was a far more generous and thoughtful mistress than most. "That would be wonderful," Tabitha replied gratefully. She added, "I know you are unlikely to take me up on this offer, but please don't feel obliged to unpack everything tonight. It can all wait until tomorrow."

Ginny chuckled, "As you say, I won't take you up on the offer. But I appreciate that you made it, m'lady. Most wouldn't."

Ginny went to run the water, and Tabitha sat at the ornate, gilded dressing table, unpinned her hat and removed her gloves. She unbuttoned her sturdy, comfortable travelling ankle boots, removed the jacket of her travelling suit and placed it neatly on the bed for Ginny to deal with later.

Tabitha sat at the dressing table and looked at herself in the mirror. Why had she insisted on accompanying Wolf? While it was true that the first person to seize on the idea of joining him had been the dowager, quickly followed by Langley, there was little doubt that if she had declared she was instead going home to London, it would have been easier for Wolf to rebuff the others. But she hadn't; why?

It hadn't been long ago that she had the epiphany that she would never remarry and put herself in the power of another man. Even though she knew in her heart that Wolf was nothing like his cousin Jonathan, she still couldn't put aside the trauma of her two-year marriage and give up the independence and freedom she now had as a wealthy widow. And when she had that epiphany, she had acknowledged that if she were unwilling to become Wolf's wife and certainly unwilling to be his mistress, then someone else would eventually. Wolf was a young, handsome, wealthy, titled man. Undoubtedly, many women would be keen to become the next Countess of Pembroke.

Yet, even though she rationally knew all this and told herself she had made her peace with it, the truth was that as soon as she had heard of this Lady Arlene Archibald, the flames of jealousy had licked at her heart. Wolf's willingness to drop everything and run to this woman's side, and her certainty that he would do so, made clear there had been something between them once. Why had she insisted on accompanying Wolf here? Did she have some masochistic need to torment herself with the vision of him in the company of a woman who clearly meant a lot to him? To reinforce the knowledge that, whatever this Lady Archibald was or wasn't to him, he would eventually love and marry someone else?

Sighing at her irrational behaviour, Tabitha pulled the pins out of her hair and decided she needed a bath and an early night. At this point, she was here. To suddenly leave Brighton would only court comment in their little group. Hopefully, whatever Lady Arlene Archibald needed from Wolf would be quickly and easily accomplished, and they could return to London in a few days. Of course, she reflected as she removed her jewellery, this was only a temporary respite to the quandary she had created for herself. But for now, she was too bone weary to think beyond a bath, dinner, and a good night's sleep.

Lord Langley had decided to eat in his suite with the children, so dinner was a slightly reduced party of the dowager, Wolf, Tabitha, Lily, and Bear. Tabitha was relieved that the hotel's food and service matched the grandeur of its fixtures and furnishings. She was too tired and her emotions too fraught to handle the dowager having things to find fault with. Of course, excellent food and service didn't guarantee she wouldn't complain, but it at least lessened the chances.

Over the fish course, Wolf finally mustered up the courage to announce to the group, "I have sent a note to Lady Archibald saying I will call on her tomorrow morning." He paused, "Alone." In truth, Tabitha was relieved to hear him say this. Her evident need to torture herself did not extend to witnessing whatever lover's reunion might occur.

While soaking in her bath, Tabitha had realised that, while she might not be able to come up with a credible reason why she suddenly needed to return to London, she could at least control how involved she became in this case, whatever it turned out to be. She was sure there were things she could find to do in Brighton with Melody and Rat for a few days. And, if helping Lady Archibald stretched to more than a few days, then perhaps it would not be as obvious if she decided to return home.

Tabitha may have been secretly relieved to hear that she needn't accompany Wolf to meet Lady Archibald, but the dowager was not as sanguine at this news. "Jeremy, I believe I've made myself quite clear; I will not be sidelined in our investigations any longer."

Tabitha could see the effort it cost Wolf not to roll his eyes and sigh. Instead, he took a deep breath and said with all the patience he could muster, "Lady Pembroke, we don't even know if this is an investigation. All I know is that an old friend has asked for help. The reason for this request might be entirely benign."

The dowager's snort of disbelief perfectly expressed her feelings on the likelihood of this being the case. Wolf continued, "And, if there is a more compelling reason for Lady Archibald requesting my presence in Brighton, I can hardly ambush her with a large crowd of strangers in tow." He said this last part almost pleadingly; surely even the dowager could see the sense in his words.

Wolf had underestimated the woman's sense of self-importance, "Of course, I would not expect you to take all of them with you," the dowager said, waving her hand to indicate their dinner companions. "And, what use would any of them be anyway?" she added. Tabitha wondered if she was included in this general dismissal of the group. Probably.

The dowager continued, "But I have proven my worth many times over. One can only guess how much sooner you might have solved the case in Scotland if you hadn't been determined to keep me in the dark about the details." Tabitha was amazed at this comment. The ego of the woman was quite staggering at times. Ignoring the stunned look on the faces of at least some of her companions, the dowager ploughed on, "I think we can all agree that, going forward, it will be far more efficient and effective if I am brought in on a consultative basis from the very beginning."

Wolf felt he had to intervene at this point, "Lady Pembroke, firstly, I have no desire to continue to investigate anything. As I believe I have said previously, I left my thief-taking days behind me when I ascended to the earldom. I only became involved in the case in Edinburgh at your request. As far as I'm concerned, I will help Arlene however I am able to and then return to London never to investigate a crime again." Tabitha couldn't help but notice Wolf's slip in referring to Lady Archibald by her given name. That was telling.

The dowager had either missed that slip or was too incensed by the rest of his words to comment, "Jeremy, I'm not sure that it is for you to decide that our investigative collaboration is at an end. Need I remind you that I am the titular head of this family."

Now Wolf couldn't hold back a sigh, "Lady Pembroke, it is not for me to dictate how you spend your time, and if you feel that your calling is to investigate crimes, then I wish you well. But I don't believe that even you can command my time in such pursuits."

Tabitha felt this was a masterful checkmate; whatever key role the dowager had decided she had held in their past investigations, even she had to realise that she had neither the skills nor the contacts to continue alone. How would she even find possible investigations on her own? Indeed, Wolf's move did seem to stop the dowager in her tracks, at least momentarily. But was this really checkmate? Tabitha could see the woman scheming, replaying every move to find a way to clutch victory from the seeming jaws of defeat. She was too nimble and masterful a strategist to give up at the first obstacle put in her way.

Finally, the dowager seemed to have decided on a tactic, "If you insist, then visit this friend of yours alone, Jeremy. Let us see whether there is even an investigation to bicker over. If there is, we both know you will need my help sooner rather than later. And if there isn't, let us leave that for another day."

Glancing at Wolf, Tabitha realised he had been lulled into the intended sense of security; he thought he'd won this skirmish. Had he learned nothing over the last few months? The dowager was gathering her forces and saving her strength for another day. And that day would come, of that Tabitha had no doubt. And the wily woman would be even stronger and more assured when it did. Tabitha was half tempted to advise Wolf to hang out his thief-taking shingle again just to appease the dowager and stop her scheming, because she would never take no for an answer.

CHAPTER 3

Wolf was determined to be up and out before the rest of his group had breakfasted. He didn't want to allow anyone the opportunity to change their mind and insist on joining him. He had Arlene's address, and the hotel porter's directions made clear it was a very walkable distance from the hotel. Wolf realised he'd left very early in his haste to be out before the dowager was up. Despite his history with Arlene, perhaps because of it, he didn't want to arrive at a totally indecent hour for calling, which made a leisurely walk even more appealing.

Leaving the hotel, Wolf crossed the street to walk along the promenade. It was a chilly but sunny morning, and the salty breeze coming off the sea was bracing. Wolf walked in the direction pointed out to him and was quickly at the still-under-construction Brighton Palace Pier. He stopped and looked out at the sea. The pebble beach stretched before him. In the distance, he saw a couple sitting on it, playing with a young child.

Taking a few deep breaths, Wolf thought about what might have been with Arlene. Could they have been that young, carefree couple playing with their child? He'd been so young when they'd met, barely a few months after he had stormed out of his father's house, swearing to make his way in the world. He had only recently met Bear and started having some success as a thief-taker when Arlene's father had hired them to retrieve some sensitive papers. It felt like he and Arlene had fallen in love at first sight. It had been the kind of blithe, easy, thoughtless love that only comes to the young. A love that didn't consider practicalities and saw no obstacles that it couldn't overcome.

Arlene's grandfather, Thomas Jones II, a wealthy plantation owner in Grenada in the Caribbean, had owned her grandmother, Hana, one of his house slaves. After emancipation, they married and eventually moved back to England. Arlene had been raised and educated as a lady by her grandfather. Even though to many, if not most, in society, Wolf would have married below him by taking Arlene as a wife, to her grandfather, Arlene was a cultured heiress in love with the wastrel son of a second son. Arlene and Wolf may have thought their love could conquer all, but her grandfather had very much disagreed with that sentiment.

Bear might think Arlene had toyed with Wolf's affections with no real intention of marrying the penniless, title-less young man, but Wolf knew it had been far more complicated than that. Life with him would have been hard under any circumstances, but for a young woman with her skin colour, those challenges would have been exponentially harder. Being a rich, titled, coloured woman was a very different proposition than being one who was the impoverished wife of a nobody. And Arlene's grandfather had made it very clear that she'd be cut off without a penny to her name if she married Wolf.

Wolf began to walk again, and thought about how he'd felt about Arlene. With the hindsight of maturity, his love had been a young man's hot, rushed passion; careless, thoughtless of any consequences. When Arlene had announced her engagement to Lord Archibald, Wolf had flown into a blind fury, cursing her in a way he was ashamed to recall. But would he have married her? Could he have? In truth, the only way he could have married Arlene was to play the prodigal son and return to his father's house, content to be a lawyer or some such career.

For all his protestations of love for Arlene, he'd never actually contemplated giving up his life as a thief-taker and doing the only thing he really could have to win her grandfather over – if that would have even worked. As much as he'd thought he couldn't live without her then, he hadn't been prepared to give up his freedom and independence to have her. Now, ten years later, he was honest enough to look back at the callow youth who claimed so much for his love but showed little willingness to sacrifice for it, and acknowledged it had been a superficial, immature kind of love at best. What kind of life would they have made together?

As Wolf continued to walk along the promenade, he thought about the girl Arlene had been. She had been beautiful, of that there was no doubt. He had wanted Arlene from the first moment he laid eyes on her. Her hypnotic eyes were green, framed by dark, lustrous lashes. Her cheekbones were high, her lips full and just waiting to be kissed.

But beyond her beauty, what had drawn him to Arlene? Wolf honestly couldn't remember. Was she witty? Kind? Intelligent? He remembered that she was a shameless flirt. She loved nothing more than to tease Wolf out of his senses. Those few weeks when they could sneak away to meet, Arlene would leave Wolf out of his mind with lust as she ran away laughing. But was it love? Wolf thought about his feelings for Tabitha. With Arlene, he'd felt he would die if he couldn't have her. With Tabitha, it felt very different. Was it better? Worse? He shook his head, trying to dispel such thoughts. Whatever he felt for Tabitha seemed not to be reciprocated, so what did it matter how it compared to his feelings for Arlene all those years ago?

After about thirty-five minutes, he arrived at Sussex Square in Kemptown. The graceful symmetry of the sweep of Georgian townhouses circling the landscaped square made clear that Arlene was living amongst the great and good of Brighton. Counting the house numbers as he walked the crescent, Wolf came upon one of the largest houses in the middle of the street. While some houses were entirely painted white stucco, Arlene's home mixed this with blonde brick. Tall, sash windows with highly decorative, wrought-iron balconies framed the imposing portico guarded by two ornate columns on each side, leading to the stately front door. Everything about this house and its neighbours screamed taste, elegance, and money. Arlene seemed to have achieved her heart's desire: admittance to refined, genteel society.

Wolf paused before the door; he could still turn back. He could send a note saying he regretted being unable to attend Lady Archibald at that time. He could return to the hotel, gather Tabitha and their unruly group, and return to Pembroke House. What would he tell Tabitha? Would he lie? Would his unwillingness to face Arlene in itself say more than any words? Suddenly, exhausted by his internal battle, he forced the issue by ringing the bell and setting in motion whatever that choice would bring.

A tall, well-muscled, very dark-skinned butler answered the door. Wolf was curious if this choice of staff extended throughout Arlene's household. Arlene's light skin tone, eye colour and features were such that she might pass as perhaps a Spaniard, if she chose. As a younger woman, she had chosen to take advantage of this racial ambiguity. It seemed that the security that marriage, a title and wealth afforded may have made her less concerned about signalling her true heritage.

The butler showed Wolf into a well-appointed drawing room. Sunlight streamed through the windows, highlighting the bright, modern, but sophisticated furnishings. Wolf had only been seated for a few minutes when the door opened, and the mistress of the house swept into the room. Ten years had done nothing to diminish Arlene's beauty. If anything, her face had lost its childish softness and matured into sculpted features. With her long, graceful neck, straight nose with its gently flaring nostrils, and regal bearing, Arlene commanded any room she chose to enter. Her almond-shaped, green eyes locked with Wolf's, and Arlene slightly inclined her head, silently asserting her belief he would soon be more in thrall to her than ever.

Wolf was so caught up in her gaze that he found himself lost for words. They might have stood in silent communication for some time if Arlene hadn't broken the spell, saying, "Wolf, you came!"

Despite his thoughts of fleeing just a few minutes before, Wolf found himself saying, "Of course. Did you have any doubt?"

Arlene moved into the room and came towards him, taking one of his hands in hers, laughing lightly, "We did not part on the best of terms, and so I wasn't sure. I am so glad to see you do not bear me any ill will."

Arlene had been looking down at their entwined hands as she said this, but now, she looked up and into his eyes. He'd forgotten the spell those eyes could cast over him. Suddenly, he was twenty years old again, and all he wanted to do was to pull Arlene into his arms and kiss those luscious, pouting lips. Wolf could see a knowing, even slightly mocking look come over Arlene's face; she realised the power over him she still possessed. She moved a little closer, still holding his hand. She was so close that Wolf could feel her breath on his face as she whispered, "I have missed you, Wolf. And I believe you have missed me."

There was no doubt in Wolf's mind that he could have, if he wanted to, kissed and taken her then and there. His mind was fuzzy with desire, and it would have been the easiest, most pleasant thing in the world to sweep the years away and give in to the sweet temptation. A noise behind Arlene was the only thing that saved him, as a dark-skinned maid bustled into the room with a tea tray and broke the spell. A brief look of irritation at the interruption flashed over Arlene's face, but then she broke her grasp on his hand and stepped away to sit on a pale, pink silk sofa.

The maid set the tea tray down, curtseyed and left the room. Wolf indicated he did not need tea, but Arlene poured herself a cup. After what felt like an age of pouring and stirring, she finally took a sip and put the cup and saucer back on the table before her. "Truly, I appreciate that you came so quickly. I realise you have many responsibilities now as an earl. And, of course, there are your responsibilities to Lady Pembroke, your cousin's widow." At this, Arlene looked up at him with a challenge in her eyes, "Did you think that all the London gossip didn't eventually make its way down to Brighton?"

In truth, Wolf hadn't considered what Arlene might know

about his current living situation. He answered with a sharpness of tone he regretted immediately, "I'm not sure what gossip you may have heard regarding the countess, and I don't really care. My domestic arrangements are nobody's business but my own."

Rather than being taken aback at his words, Arlene replied with a smile of almost feline self-satisfaction, such that Wolf almost expected her to lick her lips; it seemed she was pleased with her ability to provoke him. What game was the woman playing? Wolf regretted not turning back when he'd had the chance. He needed to ignore Arlene's efforts to bait him. "Arlene, what is it that you need? You made quite an effort to track me down in Scotland, and, as you've pointed out, I came immediately. I hope it was for something more serious than merely to prove that you still have the ability to command my attention."

Arlene's downcast eyes as Wolf chastised her might have fooled another man into believing he was witnessing contrition. Still, Wolf had experienced enough of Arlene's flirting, teasing, and playacting ten years ago that he recognised the role she had now assumed. As quickly as his desire for her had reasserted itself more than a decade later, so did his distaste at her lack of sincerity and candour. Wolf stood, realising that he did not have to stay and be part of whatever pastiche of a knight rescuing a distressed female he was being drawn into, "Arlene, if there is nothing else, I will bid you good morning and be on my way."

Suddenly, Arlene looked up at him, her beautiful eyes filled with tears, a seemingly genuine look of distress on her face, and pleaded, "Please don't go, Wolf. I know I have not begun this as I should, but I need your help."

Wolf wished he had the strength to ignore Arlene's anguish, or apparent anguish, but he didn't. Sitting back down, he asked, "So, let us begin again. What do you need from me?"

"I need you to find the person who murdered my dearest friend, Danielle."

Whatever Wolf had expected to hear, it wasn't this. "Murder? I think you need to start at the beginning."

Arlene began to tell her tale; she had first met Danielle after the death of her husband, the baron, two years before. "My husband's estate is in West Sussex, and we spent most of our time there during our marriage. He had no taste for London society, and I was barely tolerated by it. After his death, ownership of the estate passed to his heir, a nephew. I had no love for the house and was happy to take the money left to me and move here.

"However, though Brighton society may be less harsh to someone of my skin tone, any acceptance is mostly superficial. While I did not marry my husband for love, John was kind, and doted on me. Our life in the country was quiet but not unhappy. I'm not sure what I hoped to find when I moved into town, but I was lonelier than ever. People knew enough about my heritage that I could not pass as I once had, and the whispers and suspicious glances wherever I went quickly wore me down. I even struggled to staff my household and was lucky to be able to find enough servants whose skin colour either matched mine or were desperate enough for work that they didn't care.

"And then I met Danielle. We met by chance at the library. I'm unsure which of us was the most surprised to see another smartly dressed, dark-skinned woman. I invited her for tea, and we were friends from that moment."

"Was her background," Wolf paused, unsure exactly how to phrase the question delicately, "similar to yours?"

Arlene laughed, "No, her grandfather had never owned her grandmother. Though it's always possible that such an arrangement existed somewhere in her history. She is American, well, her father, Jonas Mapp, was. He was quite a famous Shakespearean actor who moved to London when he was in his thirties. He died when she wasn't much more than a child. According to Danielle, he was considered not only a fine actor for a man with his skin colour but one of the finest of his time. He married a Swedish opera star, and Danielle was the result of that short-lived marriage.

"Danielle inherited both of her parent's talents and was a

wonderful actress and singer. She had the voice of an angel. She had been living in Brighton for some time and working at the Theatre Royal here, performing regularly in light operettas."

"If she was as good as you say, why hide away in Brighton?" Wolf asked. He didn't know much about the theatre, but even he knew that London was the epicentre of Britain's theatrical and operatic world.

Arlene smiled and shook her head, and then she answered as if talking to a sweet, well-meaning, but silly child, "For much the same reason I am hiding away here; life is not easy for women with our skin tone. As talented as she was, and as much as some theatre companies courted her, there was always some bigotry, sometimes explicit, often subtle, but no less hurtful. Eventually, when it was clear what the cost would be to emulate her father's success, she decided to take a Brighton theatre company up on its offer and see whether it would be easier to be a large fish in a small pond."

"And was it?"

"To some extent. Her enormous talent quickly made her a star in Brighton, and that kind of fame brings a certain insulation. Brighton society feted her, and having her attend and sing at a soiree became quite the coup."

CHAPTER 4

Wolf had ended up spending more than an hour with Arlene. He walked back slowly to the hotel, trying to make sense of the feelings the visit had stirred up and the story Arlene had told. The run of Danielle's latest hit had finished a few weeks before, and the night of the final performance was the last time anyone had seen the actress alive. She had just disappeared. Then, a few days later, her body had been found stuffed into a trunk used to store props; she had been strangled. A stagehand named Robert, or Bobby Charles, who Danielle had some kind of history with, had been arrested and accused of the murder.

Wolf considered Arlene's rationale for why the Brighton Borough Police inspector had arrested the wrong man. At least in her telling, Robert Charles was a hulking giant of a man, slow-witted but very gentle. Danielle had always been very kind to him, and Robert had worshipped the actress. Arlene felt the police had shown little appetite for investigating the crime. She claimed that they had quickly arrested Bobby only because the colour of his skin was the same as the victim's, and now considered the case solved. But, in truth, she had no more solid reason for believing in Robert Charles' innocence than the police had in his guilt.

Wolf could imagine the scenario the police had constructed: Danielle's kindness to the stagehand was misconstrued, and when his advances were rebuffed, the large man easily strangled her and hid the body. Arlene believed the police had seized on Robert as the culprit because of his skin colour, but was she defending him for the same reason? When he had probed as to other possible suspects, it became clear that Arlene's knowledge about her friend's life and social circle was surprisingly flimsy. But then, Wolf reflected, it wasn't surprising that Arlene was as self-absorbed in her friendships as she was in her romantic relationships.

He had been so deep in thought that Wolf found himself back in front of the Brighton Palace Pier before he realised it. He wasn't ready to return to the hotel yet, so he sat on a promenade bench looking out at the sea. His thoughts and emotions were so tangled up that he felt a headache coming on. Was he going to take on this case? Was there even a case to take on? He had made no promises to Arlene despite her increasingly emotional pleading.

Wolf had been pulled into the last three investigations against his will, to one extent or another. The first had been at the behest of Mickey D to fulfil a debt Wolf had carried over from his thief-taking days. The second and third had been to help the dowager. But he had no obligations to Arlene. Moreover, agreeing to help her might imply to Arlene and Tabitha that he continued to feel tied to his former love. And if he did agree at least to look into Danielle's murder to see if he believed Robert Charles to have been unfairly accused, what did he do about Tabitha and the dowager? As insistent as Tabitha had been to be involved fully in every aspect of their prior investigations, would she want to be part of this case? He could only imagine the oil and water mix Arlene and Tabitha would make. And then there was the dowager.

While the older Lady Pembroke continued to surprise, most notably in her acceptance, even embrace of the former Whitechapel street urchins, Melody and Rat, Wolf had his doubts as to how she would feel about the Earl of Pembroke proving the innocence of a Negro. After all, when Arlene spoke of being rebuffed by London society because of her skin colour, she was talking about women the dowager called acquaintances, if not friends.

Wolf was so absorbed in these reflections that he didn't notice someone approach and sit beside him. Looking up, he was surprised to see he'd been joined by Lord Langley. "I came out for a post-breakfast walk and saw you sitting here. I assume you called on Lady Archibald this morning." Langley paused, then continued with surprising compassion in his voice, "I suspect you might have a rather complicated past with the baroness. I hope the meeting went smoothly."

Wolf paused before answering; it was still somewhat bemusing that Maxwell Sandworth, Earl of Langley, had gone from being an adversary in two of his previous investigations to being almost an extended family member now, or so it seemed. It had been one thing to provide shelter when Langley had turned up unexpectedly in Scotland with Melody and Rat in tow. But that the man had continued to be part of their group as they travelled to Brighton and was now speaking to Wolf as if they were old friends was something Wolf couldn't quite get his head around.

Langley had also surprised Wolf with his affection for Melody and his genuine concern for Rat. However, despite getting to know the man better and even being grateful to him for his help in the last case, Wolf still couldn't totally shake the cold, somewhat reptilian impression the man often left.

Nevertheless, Langley seemed to be an established figure in Melody and Rat's lives, and the children had somehow become Wolf's responsibility. So, Wolf realised he might as well accept that Langley was now a fixture in his own life for the foreseeable future, and so he answered truthfully, "Yes, Lady Arlene Archibald and I have a complicated past. She was my first love. But I was a penniless thief-taker living in Whitechapel at the time, and she was an heiress. I had nothing to offer her, so she married an older, wealthy baron. I may have railed against her choice then, but I came to a more mature understanding of its sense many years ago."

Langley smiled sympathetically; he had experienced his own heartbreak many years before under not dissimilar circumstances. "What does she want with you now?" he asked.

Wolf told him the entire story, even hinting at the emotional turmoil caused by their reunion and his doubts about investigating. Langley didn't interrupt, and when Wolf was finished, he sat deep in thought for a minute or two. Wolf appreciated a listener who didn't jump to judgement and comment; it was one of the things he most valued about Bear. And so, he left Langley to his contemplation and fell back to his musings as he looked back out at the sea.

Finally, Langley said, "Pembroke, I know that we got off on a bad footing, to say the least, but I want you to know how much I admire you." This statement surprised Wolf, and he looked over at the older man, who laughed, "Yes, I'm sure that was not what you expected me to say. Suffice it to say that your cousin, Jonathan, was not a good man. I'd heard rumours for many years about the kind of brother, son, and then husband he was. But I had more personal experience of his greed and selfishness multiple times. He used his wealth and privilege purely for self-serving ends and was utterly unconcerned about his workers and tenants. It has long been clear to me that you are cut from a very different cloth.

"As an aside, I encourage you to take up your seat in the House of Lords as soon as possible. I am sure that inheriting the earldom and the estate has been rather overwhelming. To say nothing of the various investigations you've been pulled into. However, the Lords needs men of integrity and compassion. And it is clear you are such a man."

This unexpected praise touched Wolf. Before he could answer, Langley continued, "What has also become clear is how highly you value justice. True justice. Cassandra confessed to the truth of her husband's death, and we will both be forever grateful to you and Lady Pembroke for your sensitivity and compassion towards the dowager duchess."

Wolf inclined his head in acknowledgement. In truth, he had long held the perhaps radical view that a legal remedy to a situation and justice were often far from the same thing, even if there was sometimes a grey area. In the case of which Langley spoke, there had been no such ambiguity. Wolf had convinced Tabitha that justice would not be served by the Dowager Duchess of Somerset being arrested and convicted for the very justifiable murder of her son, the duke.

"There is much injustice in the world, Langley. It is hardly my lot in life to remedy it all," Wolf protested, realising where Langley's argument was leading.

"Indeed, there is. And by your telling, it is far from clear that this case is a mistrial of justice. However, the man I have come to know and respect would not walk away until he was sure. There is a world of difference between all the faceless victims of injustice out in the world and one who has been specifically presented to you. I believe your doubts about investigating are less about the case's merits and more about the discomfort you feel at the injection of your first love into your new life."

Wolf looked away. Of course, Langley was correct. But acknowledging the situation didn't make it any less difficult to face. Langley continued, "Now I know the full story, I can see why you were keen to make the journey to Brighton alone. If you wish, I will find a way to persuade both Lady Pembrokes to return to London with me, leaving you here to deal with this situation however you feel best."

At this statement, Wolf barked out a hollow laugh, "While I appreciate the offer, Langley, good luck persuading the dowager countess to leave once she smells blood."

"Leave her to me. I have known the older Lady Pembroke my entire life and have the measure of the woman. Just say the word, and I assure you we will be on the next train to London."

"It's almost worth taking you up on the offer just to see how you manage it. And perhaps I will take you up on it. I just need to think more about what I want to do."

As Wolf said these words, he heard voices behind them and heard his name being called, or a version of his name, "Wolfie, Uncle Maxi, we've come to see the sea!"

Turning his head, Wolf saw Tabitha with Melody, her

nursemaid, Mary, Rat, and Melody's puppy, Dodo, crossing the road and approaching them. Once they were safely on the promenade, Tabitha released Melody's hand, and the adorable four-year-old girl with the red-gold ringlets and delightful spray of freckles across her nose ran towards the two men on the bench. Realising that a choice had to be made, Melody looked between the two men but clambered into Langley's lap in the end.

Wolf wasn't sure whether this clear preference should hurt him, but he thought about how much time Langley had spent with Melody recently and realised she was far more comfortable with him. Given Wolf's initial reluctance to form any relationship with the child and how, even now, he wasn't entirely sure how to act around a four-year-old, this preference was hardly shocking. Nevertheless, despite his rational thoughts on the matter, Wolf was surprised that he was still a little hurt.

"Uncle Maxi, Tabby Cat said there will be donkeys I can ride…"

At this, Tabitha interjected, "Melly, dear, I said that there might be donkeys and that perhaps you can ride one."

Clearly, such conditional statements were indistinguishable from concrete promises to a young child, and Melody giggled happily at the prospect of such fun. "And then we are going to have fish and chips for lunch just like we used to have with Ma and Pa."

At this, Wolf raised his eyebrows. He couldn't imagine the sophisticated, elegant Tabitha eating fish and chips out of newspaper on the seafront. She raised her eyebrows back; there was plenty the man didn't know about her. As it happened, she had never had fish and chips, but it had sounded delicious when Ginny described it, and she was almost as eager to try the food as Melody.

"Does the dowager countess know about these plans?" Wolf asked mischievously.

"She does not," Tabitha conceded. "However, she left straight after breakfast with Lily to pass judgement on the modistes of Brighton. I heard the hall porter also suggested somewhere they might have lunch. There was also a rather worrying conversation about an armoury."

"An armoury? What on earth is she up to? I worry that she may have perceived my comments yesterday about investigating on her own as a throwing down of the gauntlet," Wolf admitted.

Langley chuckled, "I'm not sure why the dowager countess needs a weapon of any sort. No sword could ever be as sharp as her tongue." Wolf and Tabitha acknowledged this statement's truth but were still concerned about what the older woman was up to.

Melody squirmed on Lord Langley's lap as the adults talked, finally pleading, "I want to go down to the water."

Standing quietly, slightly behind Tabitha, Rat said, "Me an' Melly ain't never seen the sea."

"Melly and I have never seen the sea," Langley gently corrected. Since the earl had taken Rat under his wing, at least part of the boy's education was correcting his Whitechapel cockney speech.

"Yeah, sorry, guv. I mean, m'lord, Melly and I have never seen the sea," the boy repeated.

Nodding in approval, Langley said, "Then why don't I accompany you and Melody, and of course Dodo, down to the water? Though I must warn you, it is very cold this time of year, so I doubt that paddling will be happening."

Melody jumped down off Langley's lap in great excitement. Mary looked less excited at the prospect of walking down the pebbled beach to the water's edge. However, the little group set off with Melody holding Langley's hand and chattering away. Dodo wasn't happy about the pebbles, so Langley picked the puppy up and carried her down to the water's edge.

CHAPTER 5

Tabitha took the seat Langley had vacated and watched the little group make their way down to the water. "He's really very good with the children," Tabitha observed. "I'm not sure when I've ever been as surprised by anyone as I've been by Lord Langley recently. How did we misjudge him so badly?"

Wolf turned away from watching Langley and the children and looked at Tabitha, "Did we misjudge him? Let's not forget that he did abduct Melody. The fact that it was in the service of British Intelligence and that the child perceived the visit as a delightful holiday at the home of an indulgent uncle doesn't detract from what he did."

Tabitha sighed. Casting her mind back to her abject terror at the time of what might have happened to Melody, she knew Wolf was right. Realising that untangling the conundrum that was the Earl of Langley was not something that might be achieved in a brief conversation, she decided that she and Wolf had more immediate things to discuss. "Shall we take advantage of the children's absence and walk for a while?" she asked.

Wolf realised that this conversation could not be put off any longer. He stood up and offered Tabitha his arm. They began to walk towards the West Pier. Looking out at the decorative iron structure with its pavilion buildings and amusements, Tabitha thought about how much fun it would be to bring Melody and Rat back during the summer months. Tabitha's mother had never been one to encourage fun activities and had made every effort to curb Tabitha's natural exuberance as a child. That was not the kind of childhood she wished for Melody to have.

Tabitha and Wolf walked past West Pier in silence. But it was not a companionable silence but rather one fraught with the tension of unspoken words and emotions. Finally, realising he must be the one to speak first, Wolf said, "I met Lady Archibald, then plain Arlene Johnson, when I was a young man. I had only recently stormed out of my father's home, found my way to London, met Bear and begun my thief-taking career. Arlene's father hired us to retrieve some papers."

Wolf paused; he knew these were not the details Tabitha wanted to hear. "Arlene and I fell in love." Wolf considered that statement and revised it, "Well, we were very young and believed we were in love."

"And now you don't believe it?" Tabitha asked gently but insistently. She wasn't sure why she needed to know this. After all, hadn't she once believed herself in love with Jonathan? More than most people, she understood the vacuity of youthful infatuation.

"I'm not sure what I felt," Wolf admitted. "When I was in the middle of it, my emotions felt raw and true. But now, I look back and, well…" Wolf wasn't sure how to phrase his thoughts clearly.

Taking pity on him, Tabitha interjected, "Speaking from experience, I can say that the feeling of being in love when one is an immature, unworldly young person, fresh to such exalted emotions, is very different in depth and intensity to what one might feel at a later stage in life with more experience and sagacity."

Given that Tabitha was still only twenty-two, Wolf was tempted to tease her at such a characterisation of herself as a woman long in the tooth. But he was too caught by the notion that she might know what a more serious, mature love might feel like. He cautiously glanced at Tabitha, but her head was turned away from him, and he could read nothing in her face. Unwilling to probe any deeper meaning in her words at this time, he merely agreed with her pronouncement. However, he did want her to understand more of his history with Arlene. "I was a penniless nobody at the time, and Arlene was a wealthy heiress. Very understandably, her father forbade any marriage between us."

In a moment of pettiness that she immediately regretted, Tabitha asked, "And Lady Archibald's love wasn't strong enough to withstand a loss of income?"

"Tabitha, you know as well as anyone that while even money can't protect a woman, a total lack of it leaves her particularly exposed. And Arlene would have been even more vulnerable than most women." Tabitha had some very petulant thoughts, which she was soon grateful she had kept to herself as Wolf continued, "Arlene is of Caribbean heritage. Her grandmother was a slave."

Wolf wasn't sure what he expected Tabitha's reaction to be. Would she be shocked? He quickly realised he hadn't given her enough credit for the compassion and kindness that he otherwise knew was at the heart of everything she did. "Ah, I see," Tabitha said. "Yes, then she could not lightly take on a life of poverty when she otherwise had the opportunity to wrap herself, at least somewhat, in the protective cloak that wealth affords." While these words might have been said sarcastically, Wolf was relieved to hear them said with genuine empathy.

Tabitha wanted to ask about Wolf's feelings towards Arlene after their reunion that morning, but she knew she had no right to an answer. Beyond what explanation Wolf might or might not owe her, Tabitha wasn't willing to lift the lid of this Pandora's box. Instead, she asked, "Can I ask why Lady Archibald has summoned you now after all these years?"

Relieved to be on safer ground with this part of the story, Wolf explained Arlene's request. Tabitha didn't immediately comment, and once Wolf finished his story, they again walked in silence. Finally, Tabitha asked, "Do you intend to oblige her and take on this case?"

"It's not even clear there is a case. And anyway, as I was explaining to Langley when you came upon us, despite being thwarted in my determination to put my thief-taking days behind me recently, that has been my intention. I had no choice but to investigate the duke's death, and I would have refused the dowager's last two commands to investigate at my peril. But this is different. While I understand and sympathise with Arlene's distress at the loss of her friend, this does not translate into a willingness to take on an investigation."

By this time, they had walked far enough up the seafront that Langley and the children were barely visible in the distance, and so they turned and began the walk back. This gave Tabitha time to formulate carefully what she wanted to say. In truth, this was something she had been considering since they left Scotland, and she had thought about how best to phrase her suggestions for most of the long train ride. "Wolf, why are you so determined to give up a career you enjoyed and which you were successful at?"

"Is that a serious question? I was a thief-taker because I had to do something to earn my keep, and I fell into it when I met Bear. Yes, I turned out to have some aptitude for the career, but it's hardly one befitting the Earl of Pembroke, is it?"

Wolf was genuinely bemused by Tabitha's question. When he reflected on his years as a thief-taker with Bear, he remembered that time as often hard but mostly happy. He'd had his freedom and independence. For the most part, they took the jobs they wanted and turned down others that felt more morally ambiguous. This gave him a certain measure of comfort that he was helping people who deserved it, for the most part. Sometimes, he and Bear had been so poor that they had to take whatever work was thrown their way. On occasion, the money earned from such jobs caused the bread it bought to turn to ashes in his mouth. But luckily, those times were few and far between. Regardless, it was a job he did to survive, something he no longer had to worry about.

Tabitha continued, "I know that you feel quite overwhelmed by your duties and responsibilities as the new earl, but I do think that duty is the right word for how you view your new title; it is a burden you feel you must shoulder. But when we are investigating, you have a lightness of spirit about you that is markedly different from how you seem when you are working with your steward and man of business."

"Does anyone enjoy those chores?" Wolf asked.

"I think Jonathan did. Perhaps he merely enjoyed coming up with new ways to cheat his workers, tenants, and business partners. Still, I always got the impression that managing an estate and his various businesses energised him. In contrast, you seem depleted by such activities."

Wolf couldn't deny the truth of her words. The power, privilege and wealth that had been so unexpectedly thrust upon him just a few short months ago weighed heavily. "So, you're suggesting I hang out a thief-taking shingle at Chesterton House?" he asked, rather more sarcastically than he'd intended.

Tabitha chose to ignore his tone and replied, "Not at all. But what I am suggesting is that you no longer put up such resistance when investigations do come your way. Instead, embrace that you have a skillset that other people are grateful to employ. You no longer need the work in order to survive, so you have the luxury of only taking on cases you wholeheartedly believe in. And perhaps Lady Archibald's case isn't such an investigation. But you won't know this until you've at least looked into it somewhat."

It wasn't lost on Wolf that, contrary to how she usually spoke about investigations, Tabitha didn't speak of we and us but instead of what he alone might do. Nervous about addressing this head-on, he nevertheless asked, "And what of you? I know that you have found a sense of purpose in the investigations we've been a part of. Would you continue to work on any future cases with me?"

Her feelings about this particular case aside, it was true that Tabitha had enjoyed the intellectual challenge their investigations had brought. They had allowed her to stretch her mind in ways shut off to her outside the schoolroom. She had enjoyed the camaraderie and teamwork with Wolf and Bear and the feeling that she was making a meaningful contribution to their efforts. If she was honest, she was not happy at the idea that their investigation in Edinburgh might be the last.

"I would like to continue to be a part of any future investigations," Tabitha admitted. "While I know that the dowager countess can be more of a hindrance than a help in investigations, being part of these cases has relieved the boredom that is so often the lot of women of our status and so I am wholly sympathetic to her. While I am so happy to have Melly in the nursery and am genuinely grateful that you desire my continued presence to help manage your household, investigating has provided me with an opportunity to use my mind. And I would miss that."

Wolf considered Tabitha's words. When he first inherited the earldom, he'd assumed there was an expectation that he would throw himself into his new responsibilities and give up everything about his old life. But no one had ever expressed such an expectation; it was entirely self-imposed. If anything, the dowager, a veritable doyenne of society, continually made clear that she wished the continuation of such investigations. Of course, her wish was that they continue with her full participation. But regardless, it was obvious she did not disapprove.

"Then, perhaps I will agree to look into the murder and consider whether I believe there to have been a miscarriage of justice with the arrest of this Robert Charles," Wolf conceded. Tabitha didn't reply, but a light squeeze of his arm implied her approval.

They walked the rest of the way back, talking of other things: Rat's new life as Langley's protegee, Lady Lily's ongoing preparations for her coming out, and what the dowager could possibly want from an armoury.

Returning to the bench, Tabitha and Wolf spent a delightful half an hour watching Langley playing with the children on the beach. He'd shown them how to skim pebbles into the water. And then, inevitably, Melody had insisted on paddling, even though the water must have been frigid. Lord Langley had taken off his jacket and waistcoat, rolled up his trousers, removed his shoes, and joined Melody in the water. Watching this sight, Tabitha shook her head and said, "It is so sad that Lord Langley never had the chance to raise Anthony. It's clear what a wonderful father he would have made."

"Particularly relative to the man who actually raised the duke," Wolf pointed out.

"Indeed. That makes it even sadder for both of them. Watching him with Melody and Rat, I find myself suddenly genuinely happy that he can be a part of their lives. I admit that when he first requested that he spend time with Melly, I was very unsure of the wisdom of such a relationship."

"To be fair, you had a good reason to worry."

"I did. But I am delighted to have those worries proved unfounded. In fact, I believe the children's lives are richer for having him be a part of them. And there's no question of the joy they bring him. I realise I was not a fan of Lord Langley's in the beginning, but I was wrong in my initial assessment of him. He's not the easiest man at times. But he is a decent and honest one, and I think he has a bigger heart than most people give him credit for. I'm glad that he has found such joy with Melody and Rat."

CHAPTER 6

Eventually, Tabitha determined there had been enough paddling, and the children and puppy were herded back into the hotel to warm up and change their clothes. While they were gone, Wolf talked to the hall porter, Mr Joseph Champion, about the best place to sample fish and chips.

"Well, m'lord, there's a little fish an' chip store down by the walkway under the Lower Esplanade, by the new pier. But you'll be getting your food in newspaper, and there's nowhere to sit. Perhaps a better alternative for folks such as yourselves is a nice little restaurant that's opened just a few minutes' walk away. They have real tablecloths, and it'll be more appropriate, if you get my drift. But the fish and chips is very good." As he said this, the portly hall porter tapped his belly, as if his girth was sufficient to recommend the quality of food served.

Left to his own devices, Wolf would have been happy to have eaten his fish and chips out of newspaper, sitting on the beach, but he couldn't envision Tabitha doing so comfortably, and agreed with the hall porter that the restaurant would answer their needs.

As Wolf was talking with Mr Champion, Bear came into the lobby. Wolf gave Bear a quick update on his conversation with Arlene, or at least some of it. Bear was on his way out to purchase some new art supplies and thanked Wolf for the invitation to join them for lunch but assured him he would find somewhere to eat when he finished his shopping.

Finally, Tabitha, Langley, the children and Mary were all assembled in the hotel lobby. Wolf gave a quick summation of his conversation with the hall porter, and with everyone in agreement, they set off for lunch.

As promised, the restaurant wasn't far and proved to be a charming, sunlit establishment with red-checkered tablecloths and a cheery owner. Tabitha had begun eating the fish and chips as genteelly as possible, cutting each chip into delicate little bites. Seeing her do this had caused Rat and Melody much amusement, and even Langley surprised her by saying, "When in Rome, Lady Pembroke," as he folded a slice of buttered bread in half and filled it with chips. Nothing would persuade Tabitha that there was any other way to eat her fish except with a knife and fork, but she did venture to try the chip sandwich. The thick-cut chips, just salty enough, combined with the buttered bread, had sounded, and even looked, quite awful. But they'd tasted wonderful.

Tabitha had eaten many fine meals over her twenty-two years. Still, she had to admit that there was something particularly satisfying about the combination of lightly fried batter over white, flaky cod. She'd watched the children, Wolf, and even Langley liberally pour malt vinegar over their food. It was hard to imagine how the acidity of vinegar could enhance the flavour of a meal, but Tabitha was game and had poured a little over a piece of her fish.

"Oh my, but this is delicious," she exclaimed with such surprise that everyone, including Mary, couldn't help but smile.

"We'll have you eating jellied eels in no time," Wolf declared. Tabitha looked at him in shock, but he just smiled back at her and said, "Don't worry. I'm just joking. I'm no great fan of eels, even on my hungriest day." Relieved, Tabitha poured more malt vinegar over her fish and chips. She wasn't quite ready to douse her food with it as she saw Rat and even Melly doing, but she was definitely sold on the flavour combinations the meal had opened up to her.

As Tabitha savoured the delicious fish and chips, she reflected on how appalled her mother would be to see her enjoying fried food doused in malt vinegar and then sandwiched between slices of bread slathered with butter. Tabitha's mother, a woman almost as harsh in her judgements and inflexible in her standards as the dowager, had more than once during Tabitha's childhood made the statement, "You are what you eat!" This was not a comment on the health benefits of one food over another but an observation that to be refined, one must only partake of refined food.

By her mother's exacting, if rather irrational, standards, food such as fish and chips were eaten by commoners not because they were tasty, cheap and filling but because the meal was inherently rough and uncouth. Such food would be inedible to the refined palates of the aristocracy. This golden rule had first been expressed when Lady Jameson had caught the seven-year-old Tabitha sneaking down to the kitchen where Mrs Rowling, their cook, had fed the little girl some of the savouries and puddings she made for the staff for their meals.

Picking up her chip sandwich again and taking a far more enthusiastic bite this time, Tabitha observed wryly, "It is a very good thing that the dowager countess isn't here. I can only imagine what she would say about us eating this food, and with our hands, no less."

Wolf enthusiastically finished the last of his food and then said with a smile, "I think we should make it a goal of this trip to bring the Dowager Countess of Pembroke here to eat fish and chips before we leave. Even if she can't be persuaded to pick up a chip sandwich."

Langley chuckled, "I, for one, would pay good money to see that. In fact, I will make a wager with you. I will wager ten shillings that you cannot achieve such a thing."

Tabitha raised her eyebrows, "A ten-shilling bet is hardly an inducement to either of you," she pointed out.

"Ah, but I truly hope that I lose this wager. And it's hardly rational to bet too much against my own wishes," Langley explained.

Previously too absorbed in eating his meal, Rat now piped up, "I bet her ladyship would eat here if Melly asked her to."

"A very astute observation, young man," Langley said. "There you go, Pembroke. The lad has already given you an advantage in this wager by suggesting a very likely way to win."

"In that case, I accept the wager," Wolf said. The atmosphere so far had been very convivial, but Wolf needed to move onto a more serious topic, and so said in a lowered voice, "I am going to the police station when we are done here. I want to find out what I can about the arrest of this Robert Charles. Perhaps even have the opportunity to interview him."

In the months since he inherited the earldom, Wolf had come to appreciate how his title opened doors for him. Previously, he had been welcomed into Pentonville Prison by its obsequious warden, and even offered the man's office for a private interview of a prisoner. He hoped that this magic trick of servile deference, due to nothing more than the serendipity of birth, would continue to hold. Even so, Wolf was grateful when Langley said, "Let me come with you. As you saw in Scotland, my ability to get a swift authorisation from the Home Secretary can come in handy."

"And if one earl turning up at the police station is awe-inspiring, just imagine what toadying two earls might engender," Tabitha teased lightly. Wolf glanced at her, but despite her carefree tone, Tabitha seemed determined not to make eye contact with him. He realised that, yet again, she seemed to have willingly excluded herself from this investigation. Previously, if Wolf had suggested that he talk to a suspect without her, Tabitha would have pushed back as strenuously as possible. Wolf was surprised to realise how disappointed he was that she was so willing for him to investigate without her. Confirming his suspicion, Tabitha said to Melody, "Perhaps there is a Punch and Judy puppet show somewhere along the promenade. What do you think of us trying to find it this afternoon while Wolfie and Uncle Maxi are working?"

Melody seemed unsure what entertainment was being proposed, but Rat said excitedly, "Oh, m'lady Tabby Cat, I once saw a Punch and Judy show in London." He turned to Melody and said, "You were there too, but you was, I mean, were, just a little one. It's so funny." Tabitha found Rat's obvious effort to curb his cockney speech, particularly around Lord Langley, peculiarly touching. Perhaps it was because she suspected it spoke to the boy's uncertainty about the continuation of good fortune that had moved him and his sister from living on the streets of Whitechapel to living in Mayfair mansions; he was determined to do everything in his power to please his saviours.

After such an endorsement by her adored older brother, Melody's excitement at the proposed afternoon's entertainment could barely be contained, and she bobbed up and down on her chair. Even Mary seemed excited by the prospect.

Their meal at an end, Langley proposed that he and Wolf make their way to the police station immediately. Wolf enthusiastically agreed; he had no desire to run into the dowager and have to explain this possible investigation until he had a clearer picture of what they might be dealing with.

As the waitress cleared their plates, Tabitha asked where they might find a Punch and Judy show. The young woman thought about the question, "Well, in the summer, you'll usually find Old Bob doing a show on West Pier. But I'm not sure he'll be about this time of year. His arthritis is right bad when it gets colder. But most afternoons, Young Bob, no relation, does a show in the Royal Pavilion Gardens."

Tabitha thanked the girl, gathered up Melody, Rat, and Mary, and wished Wolf and Langley luck at the police station. The waitress had given clear directions to the Royal Pavilion, and it was a very short, five-minute walk to reach the magnificent gardens of the outlandish, regency seaside pleasure palace that King George IV had built for himself when he was still Prince of Wales.

As they approached the Pavilion, Melody exclaimed, "It's a princess' palace!" Tabitha couldn't argue with that characterisation; all domes, minarets and intricately detailed carvings, the Pavilion was a magical-looking place. Tabitha couldn't understand why Queen Victoria disliked it so much.

Even in late autumn, the gardens were almost as beautiful as the building and, left to her own devices, Tabitha could have happily wandered along the paths. Tabitha didn't know much about plants and wished she had Lily with her to name the shrubs that were still flowering, even at that point in the year. She was particularly delighted with a flower that seemed to be everywhere in shades of pink, purple and cream. Tabitha decided she would ask Lily to come back with her another day. She was sure the young woman would be even more delighted with the gardens than Tabitha herself was.

They quickly caught sight of the Punch and Judy show with its red and white stripe-painted little wooden theatre, under which the puppeteer would hide and work his magic. They seemed to have timed their visit well; children were starting to gather in front of the theatre, and a chalkboard announced that the next show would begin in five minutes.

Tabitha watched Rat take Melody's hand as the two excited children ran forward to join the others already sitting waiting. It was such a simple scene, but it brought tears to Tabitha's eyes to watch Rat joining the audience just like any other excited child in anticipation of a puppet show. He was only a child, but this was sometimes easy to forget. Rat had been forced to grow up so quickly, first as the child of impoverished parents in Whitechapel who had to help add to the family coffers from a young age. And then, when their parents died, as Melody's caretaker and protector. And then, when Rat joined their household, it hadn't been as a child in the nursery as his sister had, but as a member of the household staff. While this had been almost entirely Rat's decision, Tabitha berated herself now for allowing that to be the choice. Even now, as his circumstances were, no doubt, improving enormously as the hand-selected apprentice to Lord Langley, Rat was hardly embarking on a normal childhood.

Tabitha made a mental note to talk to Langley about how Rat was treated and how he spent his days. She was thrilled that the earl intended to educate the intelligent lad and prepare him for a solidly middle-class career. Still, she wanted to ensure that he also had plenty of opportunities, like that afternoon, just to be a ten-year-old boy playing in the park.

CHAPTER 7

Leaving the restaurant, Wolf admitted that he had no idea where the Brighton police station was, but to his surprise, Langley knew exactly where they were going. "Let's just say, knowing these things is part of the job," Langley said cryptically at Wolf's evident surprise. He continued, "It's not far from here on Bartholomew Square. It's housed in the town hall."

They walked in silence for the first couple of minutes until Langley said, "I meant what I said before. If you want me to take everyone back to London, I will find a way to manage that. Let us talk to this Robert Charles, get a sense of whether there is a case here, and then you can decide what you want to do."

"Thank you, Langley. I greatly appreciate the offer," Wolf said sincerely. The only man Wolf had ever really trusted totally was Bear. On inheriting the earldom, Wolf hadn't expected to find any like-minded men amongst his new peers, and indeed, during his early social forays, he'd felt like a fish out of water. However, during two recent investigations, he'd come to know, like and trust Anthony Rowley, the Duke of Somerset. Now, he realised that Maxwell Sandworth, Earl of Langley, was becoming another man he trusted. No one was more surprised at this than Wolf. He'd always believed himself a good judge of character, but his first and even second impressions of Maxwell Sandworth couldn't have been more wrong. Perhaps, as a member of British Intelligence, Langley projected a dislikeable persona precisely to keep people at a distance.

As promised, the walk to Brighton Town Hall was brief. The

building itself was a stately, imposing Georgian-era building with a plethora of neo-Grecian columns, more than enough to strike the appropriate deference into the hearts of all who entered. The police station was located in the building's basement and did not continue the rest of the building's architectural majesty. The ceilings were low, and the walls windowless. While police stations were rarely pleasant places to be, this one had a particularly oppressive atmosphere.

Langley had indicated to Wolf that he should take the lead, and so Langley was the one to approach the constable behind the desk. Wolf couldn't make out most of what was being said in hushed tones, but he did catch the words "Home Secretary". If two earls weren't enough to force compliance from the Brighton Borough Police Force, Wolf imagined that invoking the name of the Home Secretary would be.

After a few more moments of discussion, Wolf's assumption seemed to prove correct as the constable walked around the desk and beckoned them to follow through a door and down another dank, depressing corridor. He knocked on a door with a small nameplate with Inspector Maguire printed on it, and from within came a harsh bark of "Enter."

The constable opened the door to reveal yet another depressing room. However, this office had one tiny, barred window near the ceiling. But it didn't do much to alleviate the unpleasant ambience, barely adding any additional natural light to a room that was otherwise illuminated by gaslight, even though it was the middle of the day.

"Inspector Maguire, these two lords have questions about the Danielle Mapp murder. One of them has a letter from the Home Secretary." This statement was said in such a sarcastic tone that it seemed the constable wasn't even convinced about their titles, let alone about Langley's authorisation, whatever it was. Wolf did wonder why the man had then brought them through. His next statement clarified his motivation, "It's more than my job's worth to question such things, so I've brought them to see you."

Inspector Maguire was surprisingly young, with close-cropped black hair, much shorter than the current fashion, and startling blue eyes. The man's expression made clear his irritation at being interrupted, and his scepticism that Wolf and Langley were indeed who they claimed to be.

Over the months since he had inherited the earldom, Wolf had come to realise that much of the deference that such a title inspired in people came from the arrogance and air of authority with which he carried himself. Given that these were not his natural character traits, when needed, Wolf had done his best impersonation of his grandfather, the old earl. An imposing, supercilious man, the old earl had behaved as if his authority and rank would always get him what he wanted, and he was rarely disappointed. Wolf had personal experience of Lord Langley's ability also to adopt a haughty, imperious persona when it suited him, and so wasn't surprised when Langley strode into the office uninvited, did not offer his hand to the inspector, and sat down at one of the chairs in front of the desk. Wolf thought of his grandfather and followed Langley's lead.

If the inspector was surprised or offended at this behaviour, he was shrewd enough not to show it. Malcolm Maguire hadn't risen to the rank of inspector in the Brighton force quicker than any man before him without having a keen awareness of how to play the political game. If these men were who they claimed to be, the superintendent would want them treated as respectfully as possible. In fact, Superintendent Ross, always keen to impress Chief Constable Brown, would want to be notified as soon as possible so that he could take credit for anything positive that might come out of this meeting. Of course, anything negative would immediately be held against Maguire.

"Constable Richards, thank you, that is all," Maguire said, waving his hand to dismiss the other policeman.

Richards shut the door behind him and was tempted to listen at the keyhole. But then he realised that he only had a few minutes left on his shift and better not be found anywhere other than at the desk when his shift replacement turned up.

Malcolm Maguire studied his visitors for a few moments.

They certainly looked the part of earls: expensive, well-fitting clothes, the flash of a signet ring on the pinkie finger of the older of the two, and an overall look of well-being. And there was something in their bearing that spoke of generations of authority. "What can I do for your lordships this afternoon?" he asked in a polite but still cautious tone.

"We would like to talk to you about the murder of a young woman, Danielle Mapp, and the subsequent arrest of a Robert Charles," Langley stated with a cool directness.

"And why would a pair of earls, down from London if I had to guess, care about such people?"

Wolf couldn't help but ask curtly, "Why wouldn't we care? Because of the colour of their skin?"

Maguire's eyes narrowed a little at the question but replied calmly but with a definite edge to his voice, "Because one is an actress in a tuppeny, regional theatre, and the other is an even more insignificant stagehand. Not the kind of characters who usually get the attention of the great and good in our fair capital."

"We have been asked to look into the case by a friend," Wolf answered equally calmly.

"And who might this friend be?" Maguire asked with genuine curiosity. Truly, he was genuinely perplexed by why these two aristocrats cared about a sordid little murder in Brighton. The skin colour of the victim and accused only added to the mystery.

Langley, never a man to show more of his hand than necessary, snapped at the inspector, "That is irrelevant to our request. I have a letter from the Home Secretary stating that I be given all and any help and access I require. With no questions asked." Anticipating the other man's next comment, Langley added, "You, or your superior officers, are welcome to contact Whitehall to verify my credentials." As expected, such a statement removed the last resistance that Inspector Maguire had. No ambitious young police officer wanted to bring himself to Whitehall's attention in such a potentially negative way.

"What would you like to know?" Maguire asked.

Langley indicated with an almost imperceptible gesture that Wolf could now take over the questioning. "Let's start with the murder itself. Our understanding is that the victim, Miss Mapp, was found stuffed into a trunk, having been there for a few days. Is this correct?" Maguire nodded his assent. Wolf continued, "How had she been killed?"

"Strangulation, according to the coroner's report. Her neck had been squeezed so tightly that the murderer's finger marks had left visible bruises. I should add, in advance of likely future questions, it was clear from such marks that the murderer was a man with large hands."

"How was the body discovered?" Wolf asked.

"It seems that Miss Mapp had been murdered on the last night of the theatre's most recent show or shortly thereafter. There had been some kind of cast celebration planned that she had failed to attend. But, it seems it was not uncommon for her to excuse herself from such social gatherings. The cast and crew had a few days off before the start of the new show. So, it was also not unusual when no one saw or heard from Miss Mapp for a while. Then, a couple of weeks ago or so, preparations were beginning for the new show. The wardrobe mistress was going through trunks looking for costumes when she came across Miss Mapp's body stuffed into one of them."

"And what brought you to the conclusion that Robert Charles had committed the murder?" Wolf asked.

Maguire resented having his investigation challenged, and his displeasure showed itself in the tensing of his neck muscles. However, he was wise enough to try to keep this irritation out of his voice and replied, "My men and I made a thorough investigation and talked to everyone in the theatre company. There were eyewitnesses to Charles' infatuation with Miss Mapp, and one witness overheard a heated conversation when she rebuffed his advances on the day she was murdered. Moreover, he also didn't attend the party that night and had both opportunity and motive. As I said before, the murderer was a man with large hands, and Robert Charles is such a man. This is one of the more open and shut murder cases I've dealt with."

Wolf knew that he shouldn't bait the inspector, but he couldn't help himself and challenged, "And the colour of his skin had nothing to do with your certainty that he is the murderer?"

Inspector Maguire seethed at this accusation, and he was tempted to throw these high and mighty earls out of his office. But again, better sense prevailed, and he said in a tight voice, "I can assure you that Robert Charles was given the same benefit of the doubt as any Englishman would have been." However, even as he spat out these words, an ember of doubt that he had tried to ignore for weeks suddenly started glowing; while Malcolm Maguire may not have held Robert Charles' race and skin colour against him, the same could not be said of the superintendent. As far as he was concerned, they needed no more evidence than the known depravity and animalistic tendencies of such men. As soon as Robert Charles' race had become known, Superintendent Ross had pushed Maguire to make an arrest. The witness testimony had only compounded what Ross considered a clearcut case against Robert Charles.

While the specifics of the inspector's doubts were unclear, it was obvious to Wolf that his words had hit a nerve, and that perhaps Maguire wasn't as sure of his suspect's guilt as he claimed. Seizing on this moment of doubt, Wolf demanded, "We would like to speak to Mr Charles. Alone."

Yet again, Inspector Maguire's initial reaction, outrage that these two peers of the realm thought they had the right to storm into his office making demands, was quickly balanced by the reality of the power these two men commanded between them, particularly given their apparent ties to the Home Secretary. With his sense of self-preservation winning out over his temper, Maguire said, "He is in the cells downstairs. I'll have a constable escort you down. But I warn you that we haven't been able to get much sense out of the simpleton."

Wolf stood to leave and then asked as an afterthought, "Does Mr Charles have legal representation?"

Maguire let out a harsh bark of a laugh, "Do you think lawyers are lining up to do pro bono work for a man like Robert Charles?" he asked. "He's lucky he even got assigned the barrister he has, though much good Mr Jeremiah Jackson will do the poor bastard."

CHAPTER 8

While it had appeared that the police station was in the building's basement, it seemed there was yet another subterranean level. Wolf and Langley were led down some rickety, wooden stairs to the cells. A low ceiling, combined with no windows, immediately gave the space an oppressive, claustrophobic feeling, which wasn't improved by the dankness of the stale air. Inspector Maguire might have seen the wisdom in granting Wolf's request to see the prisoner, but he was damned if he was going to give the earl the courtesy of holding the interview in an office, and he'd enjoyed the thought of the two elegantly dressed aristocrats sullying their persons down in the cells.

Wolf and Langley were led to the second room off the narrow corridor. The heavy wooden door was unlocked, and they were shown into a small cell. The ceiling seemed even lower here, but Wolf was relieved to see there was one high opening, covered by bars, to provide at least some ventilation. The only furniture in the cell was a sturdy-looking wooden bed with no mattress, pillow or blankets. Wolf wondered if this was the treatment that all prisoners received or if Robert Charles was being singled out.

The accused man was lying on the bed, in the foetal position, facing the wall. He didn't make any movement as Wolf, Langley and the constable entered the cell. "Hey, Charles, you've got company," the policeman said harshly. When there was no response, he went over to the bed and roughly shook the man. "I said, you've got company."

Finally, there was movement from the body on the bed.

Robert Charles sat up and looked at the three men in confusion. Even with its small window, the cell was very dark, and Wolf couldn't see much of Robert Charles other than the outline of his body and the whites of his eyes. Still, it was obvious that he was a large man, almost as tall and muscular as Bear. Wolf could see why he'd make a good stagehand.

Looking around the bare, dark cell, Langley said imperiously, "Constable, find us two chairs and bring a lamp." Whatever the policeman thought about being bossed around in such a tone, he kept to himself. He left the cell to return with two stacked chairs and a gas lamp. "Leave us," Langley demanded, not even thanking the man for the chairs.

The constable turned to leave the room, muttering, "If some damn fool toffs want to be left alone with a violent killer, who am I to argue?"

Wolf closed the cell door and then took one chair, with Langley taking the other. With the gas lamp providing some illumination now, Wolf could see just how young Robert Charles was, probably not even twenty. "Mr Charles, we have been asked by a friend of yours, Lady Arlene Archibald, to help you if we can." Wolf had no idea if Robert knew Arlene and the confused look on the man's face indicated that he didn't. Wolf said, "Well, Lady Archibald was a good friend of Miss Mapp's and is an old friend of mine."

Still, the prisoner said nothing. Wolf continued, "Lady Archibald believes you are innocent of Miss Mapp's murder and has asked me to help prove that. Will you let me help you?" The other man nodded but still had not spoken a word. Wolf wondered if he was, in fact, a mute. Testing that theory, he asked, "How long had you known Miss Mapp, Danielle?"

Finally, Robert seemed spurred to speak and said in a slow, deep voice, "Miss Danny was Bobby's friend. She's been Bobby's friend for a long time."

Glad that they seemed to be getting somewhere finally, Wolf asked, "And how did you meet Miss Danny?"

Robert said with certainty, "Miss Danny was Mammy's

friend." Now that the man was speaking, Wolf thought he heard a slight American accent. He remembered that Danielle's father had been American and asked, "Bobby, did you travel on a big boat across the sea when you were younger?" The man nodded but said nothing more.

Wolf realised he was going to get limited historical information from Bobby and instead asked, "Do you like working in the theatre?"

The large child-like man nodded his head again, but this time, he did add, "Mr Bailey is my friend. He's my best friend." Wolf had no idea who Mr Bailey was and asked. Bobby answered, "Mr Bailey is my best friend. He owns the theatre."

Wolf filed away this information and asked, "Did you start working at the theatre at the same time as Miss Danny?"

With what sounded like a sob in his voice, Bobby answered, "We moved to Brighton when Mammy died. Miss Danny promised she'd look after me." Wolf had never asked Arlene how old Danielle was, assuming that they were about the same age. While it wasn't impossible to believe that a man as young as Bobby Charles might form an infatuation with an older woman, it sounded as if he looked up to her as more of a mother figure. Of course, that still didn't rule out the possibility that he'd killed her.

Aware that there was only so much useful information to be gleaned from Bobby Charles, Wolf thought carefully about his next question. He asked in a very gentle voice, "Bobby, did you hurt Miss Danny?"

At this, the enormous young man became very agitated and started to rock himself back and forth on his bed, repeating over and over, "Bobby loves Miss Danny".

Wolf glanced over at Langley, and they shared a look; was this an admission that there had been a spurned infatuation or merely grief at the loss of the closest thing to a familial relationship the man had? Whichever it was, it seemed there was not more to be had from Bobby Charles at this point. Wolf stood, followed by Langley, and they made to leave the cell. Wolf took one last look at the accused man, still rocking back and forth on his hard prison bed. He couldn't decide if this was an outrageous miscarriage of justice based on nothing more than the colour of the victim's and accused man's skin, or a clear-cut case of a giant of a man with the mental capacity of a child striking out in anger.

The constable was waiting for them in the corridor, and they indicated that he could remove the chair and lamps and lock the door. They could make their own way out of the police station.

A few minutes later, as they left the town hall behind them after asking for directions to the Theatre Royal, Langley vocalised Wolf's doubts, "I consider myself a good judge of people, but I have no idea if Robert Charles is the innocent victim of aggressive and intolerant policing or an example of the most obvious suspect being the correct one."

Wolf turned slightly and looked at the older man he had somehow grown to think of as a respected confidant, "Do you think I should investigate?"

Langley paused for a moment before answering, "From what I know of your previous cases, particularly the first one, you were asked to investigate murders where initially you were unsure of the innocence of the accused men."

"Well, in the first case, he hadn't been accused yet, but your point is well-taken."

"How is this different?" Langley asked. "Is the difference here that the person asking you to take on the investigation is Lady Archibald, with whom you have a complicated history?"

"Well, that's definitely a part of it," Wolf acknowledged.

"Are you worried that if you stay in Brighton to investigate this, old feelings may be awoken, and that may complicate your relationship with Tabitha, Lady Pembroke?" Langley asked, cutting to the heart of the matter and surprising Wolf with his insight.

In fact, Wolf's surprise at Langley's perceptiveness was such that he could think of no better answer than the truth and replied, "Yes. That is exactly what I'm most worried about."

Langley stopped walking, causing Wolf to stop as well, and surprised Wolf again by putting his hand on the younger earl's shoulder and saying, in a voice filled with compassion, "I know what it is to love a woman you feel you can't have. Of course, I don't understand what stands in the way of any romance between you and Lady Pembroke, but it is clear there is some kind of real or perceived barrier, at least on her part. But, for anyone with eyes, it is clear there are strong feelings on both sides. I have waited over twenty years for a chance to be with the woman I love. I doubt you will have to wait as long, but you may need to be a little patient. However, running away from your past is unlikely to be the answer. Face your history with Lady Archibald head-on and be honest with Tabitha."

"It's just... well, it's only... sometimes, her actions and words are inexplicable. She wants nothing to do with this investigation, even though usually I cannot get her to stand down, no matter the danger. The space between us has never felt wider and harder to bridge," Wolf tried to explain.

"Again, if I might offer some advice as one who is older and perhaps has gained some wisdom over the years. Is it possible that Lady Pembroke's coolness is a reaction to how unusually tight-lipped you have been since receiving the telegram from Lady Archibald?"

Wolf thought about these words. He hadn't been intentionally distant since receiving the summons when they were in Scotland. But the shock of hearing from Arlene after all these years and his nervousness at a reunion might have caused him to retreat into himself. Perhaps Tabitha's reserve over the last few days was nothing more than a reaction to his own. "Thank you, Langley. You have given me much to consider," Wolf said with utter sincerity.

CHAPTER 9

Rat and Melody had enjoyed the Punch and Judy show so much that Tabitha promised they would return to see it again at least once while they were in Brighton. Tabitha enjoyed the easy walk back to the hotel. She realised that she didn't have many opportunities to walk around London; it just wasn't the done thing. But here, away from the prying eyes of gossipy neighbours and the strictures of London society, she was able to enjoy the walk down to the seafront, glancing in the windows of some of the more interesting-looking shops and feeling the bracing sea breeze on her face.

Rat and Melody happily ran up and down the street as Tabitha and Mary strolled at a more leisurely pace. By the time they reached the hotel, Tabitha was sure she looked a fright, her cheeks flushed from the exercise, and her hair windswept from the sea breeze. Her first thought was to go to her room and make herself look more presentable. But, as she made her way through the lobby past the tables set up to her left for afternoon tea, an unmistakable voice reached her, "Tabitha. Tabitha!" Looking over, she saw the dowager and Lily sitting at a table with a striking, darker-skinned woman. The dowager gestured for Tabitha to join them.

While her first instinct was to pretend she hadn't seen or heard them, Tabitha realised the dowager would not be fooled, and so asked Mary to take the children back up to Langley's room and to have some refreshments sent up. Tabitha then did the best she could to smooth her hair down, took a deep breath, and went over to the group.

"Tabitha, you'll never guess who this is," exclaimed the dowager, gesturing to the beautiful stranger. And now that she could see the woman up close, Tabitha realised that beautiful was a far more apt description than merely striking. The woman had the most arresting green eyes that were focused on Tabitha with a curious intensity. Her curly hair was a very dark brown, almost black, with dark copper highlights, and her smooth skin a shade that could have connoted a variety of parentages, including southern European. Except she wasn't Spanish or Italian, was she? With a shock, Tabitha realised that this must be Lady Arlene Archibald herself. What on earth was she doing here, in their hotel, having tea with the dowager countess?

Suddenly, Tabitha was even more aware of her own rather dishevelled appearance. Any doubts as to how windblown she looked were quickly dispelled when the dowager exclaimed, "What on earth happened to you, Tabitha? You look as if a tornado swept you up!"

Tabitha had hoped to be able to avoid meeting Wolf's long-lost love while they were in Brighton. But short of total avoidance, she certainly had hoped to meet her under better circumstances. As if reading her thoughts, Lady Archibald gave her a very insincere smile and said, "Lady Pembroke, I had hoped to have a chance to meet you. Still, how much more fun is it to do so like this?"

Tabitha wasn't sure how fun she'd call it. Why had the woman come here? Was it to gain the upper hand over Tabitha by just such an ambush? If so, Tabitha was aware that the plan had succeeded. She was totally caught off-guard and at a disadvantage. But why bother? If Lady Arlene Archibald had Wolf in her sights again, she could hardly be worried that Tabitha was a rival for his affection. Could she?

The dowager indicated that Tabitha should sit and join them. She demurred, saying, "Mama, as you just pointed out, I'm windswept, which is hardly appropriate for taking afternoon tea in public."

"Pish posh. This isn't London, it's Brighton. It isn't as if royalty might come upon you. Or even members of the aristocracy. The worst that might happen is that some minor landed gentry see you looking like this," the dowager argued.

"Well, we are here," Tabitha pointed out.

"Exactly. This hotel should be grateful to be graced with our presence, even when we're not looking at our best!"

Tabitha was usually willing to accede to the dowager's whims in order to keep the peace. But this time, with Lady Archibald's amused gaze on her, Tabitha refused to back down. "I insist on going upstairs for a few minutes to at least fix my hair. Of course," she added, "if Lady Archibald has other places to be, I will understand if she can't spare the time."

Arlene gave Tabitha a dazzling smile, put her hand lightly on the dowager's arm, bent her head towards the older woman as if speaking to a dear friend and confidante, and said, "My dear Lady Pembroke, I am happy to wait while the other Lady Pembroke," she paused for a moment as if trying to choose the most delicate way to phrase her next thought, "makes herself look a little more presentable."

Even though Lady Archibald was doing nothing more than echoing her own stated wishes, Tabitha was irritated beyond belief. Who was this woman to judge Tabitha unpresentable? And how had she and the dowager become such bosom friends so quickly?

The truth was that the dowager, who would have been a general to rival Wellington if she had been born a man, appreciated that Lady Archibald seemed to have a taste for blood and a willingness to plunge in the knife that almost rivalled her own. While Tabitha and the dowager had been enjoying something of a detente recently, the dowager was not known for her forgiving nature and positively enjoyed the holding of grudges. Mean-spirited disapproval of Tabitha was a hard habit to shake. She couldn't help but enjoy Tabitha's discomfort and Lady Arlene's cattiness.

Tabitha was glad to find Ginny in her room, going through her dresses to find one for dinner that evening. Ginny raised her eyebrows at the state of Tabitha, who said, "Yes, I know how I look. I can't go into details, but can you do your best to make me look as presentable, no, as elegant and sophisticated as possible in not much more than five minutes?" Ginny raised her eyebrows even further but didn't question the request. Instead, she set to work. Casting a professional eye over the shirtwaist, skirt and jacket that Tabitha had gone out in, Ginny disappeared into the capacious wardrobe. She emerged victorious with a beautiful, mint green dress in her arms.

With Ginny's help, Tabitha was able to change her outfit, re-pin her hair, and be on her way downstairs in under ten minutes. Catching sight of herself in the mirror on her way out of the bedroom, Tabitha wondered again at what a marvel Ginny was.

Making her way back to the tea table at an unhurried pace, Tabitha noted that Lady Lily had wisely made her escape. Tabitha was sure that, having spent most of the day obediently following her grandmother around modistes, milliners, jewellers, and cordwainers, Lily deserved a reprieve and was probably already curled up in an armchair in the hotel library with a book. However, Lady Arlene Archibald had not left and seemed to be enjoying a cosy little chat with the dowager, who was all smiles.

Both women looked up as Tabitha approached. Lady Archibald's eyes narrowed a little, apparently not happy at Tabitha's much-improved appearance. Seeing Tabitha, the dowager exclaimed, "Ah, I'm happy to see you looking far more presentable. Do come and join us. Lady Archibald was just telling me the most amusing story about her encounter with Lady Willis last year in Brighton." Tabitha plastered a smile on her face and took the seat next to the dowager.

"Lady Archibald, how did you happen to come upon Lady Pembroke?" Tabitha asked with genuine curiosity.

"Oh, it's just the most amusing story," the dowager answered, even though the question hadn't been posed to her. "Lady Archibald had guessed that we'd be staying at The Grand and had come down to introduce herself to you. She was asking after

Lady Pembroke at the front desk when I happened by on my way to tea. After some initial confusion, worthy of one of Mr Wilde's plays, we both realised that actually she was looking for you. By that time, the least I could do was to ask her to join me."

Over the last few months, Tabitha had learned to underestimate the dowager at her peril. In fact, the woman herself had admonished Tabitha multiple times for attempting, incorrectly, to predict her reactions. Nevertheless, Tabitha was surprised at the dowager's easy acceptance of the dark-skinned Lady Archibald. Had she assumed that Lady Archibald was Spanish or Greek? Not that the dowager was known for her love of continentals. Realising that this was yet another example of the enigma that was her former mother-in-law, Tabitha gave up trying to unravel the conundrum. Instead, she gratefully accepted the fresh pot of tea the waitress had placed in front of her. Rarely had she had a greater need of the fortifying powers of a cup of Darjeeling.

Tabitha poured herself a cup of tea, added milk and sugar, and then took her first restorative sip. As she did so, she looked at Lady Archibald over her teacup. The woman was trying to strike a pose of indifference, but Tabitha was very observant and could see the little lines around her eyes as she strained for nonchalance. It was comforting in a way to realise that Wolf's first love was as uncomfortable as Tabitha was. However, unlike Tabitha, she had been the one to force this meeting. Why?

Tabitha didn't have to wait long for an answer. Just as she had taken a little Bakewell tart and was beginning to slice into it, Lady Archibald said with an air that aimed for but didn't quite achieve nonchalance, "Lady Pembroke, the rumour mills are all atwitter about your living arrangements. Wolf always did enjoy flouting society's rules, but I'm surprised that you don't care more for your reputation."

Lady Archibald's pointed use of Wolf's nickname wasn't lost on Tabitha, nor was the dowager's undisguised glee at Lady Archibald's full-frontal attack. She almost expected the dowager to rub her hands together in delighted anticipation of what was to come.

Tabitha's first instinct was to parry and thrust, sending back as barbed a comment as she had received. But what was to be gained by that? Indeed, Tabitha had a strong suspicion that was precisely the hoped-for reaction. Instead, she popped a bite of the Bakewell tart in her mouth and savoured the delightful treat. She then took another sip of tea. By the time she finally spoke, a good thirty seconds of silence had passed. "I am so sorry to hear of your dear friend's passing," Tabitha said. "That loss must be hard to bear."

Rather than answer, Lady Archibald just stared, confused as to these rules of engagement. For all the world, Tabitha's sympathy sounded genuine. Her ability not to rise to the bait Lady Archibald had thrown out was either indicative of a worthy adversary or a clueless dimwit. And Lady Arlene Archibald doubted it was the latter. Even the dowager was impressed by Tabitha's well-played deflection.

Lady Archibald took a leaf out of Tabitha's playbook and had a sip of tea and a bite of a delicious macaron while considering her next move. Finally, deciding she would not achieve her visit's objectives with anything less than very pointed questions, she said, "I'm sure you're curious as to why I have sought you out, Lady Pembroke."

Tabitha looked her in the eye and answered coolly, "Is there much to be curious about? You had a youthful romance with Wolf. Now, you find yourself a widow and have managed to pull him back into your orbit. You have heard about our living situation and are unsure as to the nature of our relationship and so decided to attempt to assess for yourself whether or not I am your competition." This statement was so shockingly frank and also entirely accurate that Arlene silently applauded the beautiful younger woman. She was a worthy opponent.

The dowager could no longer contain herself and actually clapped her hands, saying, "My my, Tabitha. Where have you been hiding this backbone all this time? This is going to be a very entertaining trip." Then, her eyes gleaming with mischief, she added, "Lady Archibald, you really must join us for dinner tonight."

Tabitha knew immediately what the wily old woman was up to; she wished to see how much more tension and drama might be created between Tabitha and Lady Archibald with Wolf present. Interestingly, Lady Archibald quickly shot down that suggestion, "Thank you, dear Lady Pembroke, but I am otherwise engaged for the evening."

Tabitha considered whether she believed this excuse, and she was correct in her scepticism; as much as Arlene had been unable to resist ambushing the woman she believed was her competition, she was nevertheless aware of how Wolf would react to this visit. He had made it very clear that his domestic arrangements were none of her business. Arlene had no wish for him to express his displeasure at her behaviour in front of Lady Pembroke. It was fortunate that he hadn't already happened upon their little tea party. Realising this, Arlene quickly made her excuses and stood to leave.

"We must do this again soon, Lady Archibald," the dowager exclaimed with genuine enthusiasm."

Tabitha wondered if Lady Archibald had told the dowager the details of the investigation she had asked Wolf to take on. Not wanting to open that particular Pandora's box, she decided that having excused herself from helping with the case, she could leave Wolf to deal with the dowager with a clean conscience.

CHAPTER 10

It was a very short walk from the police station to the Theatre Royal, which was located across the street from the Royal Pavilion Gardens that Tabitha had visited earlier with the children. It was a fine-looking theatre that appeared to have undergone quite recent renovations, its terracotta frontage clean and unspoiled. The doors were locked, and there wasn't anyone around at the box office. A street cleaner told them where the stage door was, and Wolf and Lord Langley walked back down the street and then around as they'd been instructed. Wolf was happy to see that the stage door was ajar, held open by a brick.

Letting themselves in, Wolf and Langley immediately found themselves in the heart of the theatre, standing in what must be the backstage area during a performance. Except that there was no scenery or curtains in place. Instead, they had the entire stage in front of them. Wolf could see the red velvet cushioned audience seats stretching up into the gods.

Wolf had not been to the theatre more than once or twice in his life and had never seen it from this view. It was fascinating. There were bright lights, and he found himself drawn to the front of the stage. Shielding his eyes from the glare of the lights, Wolf looked out and realised that two men were sitting towards the front of the stalls, deep in discussion. Realising they were now being watched, the men stopped their conversations, and the older of the two demanded, "Who are you, and what are you doing in my theatre?" he said in an accent that Wolf initially had a hard time placing, but then realised was from somewhere in the West Country.

As he spoke, the man stood up and walked towards the front of the seats. He was a large man, tall and rather heavyset, with a shock of white hair that he wore long as if he were a cavalier of old. He had a neatly clipped beard that was as white as his hair. Wolf suspected that he normally had quite a jolly countenance, but at that moment, he was looking anything but friendly.

Langley had come up behind Wolf, and he now answered, "I am Maxwell Sandworth, the Earl of Langley, and this is Jeremy Wolfson Chesterton, the Earl of Pembroke."

"And I'm the Queen's uncle," the man countered. But as he looked more closely at the men's fine clothes and observed their general air of well-being, it struck him that perhaps they were who they claimed to be. "Wait there," he said as he disappeared through a door to the side. A minute or so later, he reappeared on the stage and approached them. Holding out a hand, he said, "Actually, I'm Christopher Bailey, Kit to my friends. This is my theatre."

Now that he could see impresario Christopher "Kit" Bailey properly, Wolf could only marvel at the man's outfit. His trousers seemed to be made of crushed black velvet, and although he wore no jacket, he had on a waistcoat patterned with large pink flowers. To top off this ensemble, he wore a bright blue silk cravat. Trying not to stare, Wolf instead shook the proffered hand and said, "We're sorry we barged into your theatre uninvited, but you're actually the person we're looking for."

"Am I, indeed?" Kit asked suspiciously. He had experienced enough debt collectors and irate husbands in his life to be on his guard at such a statement.

"Yes. We have been asked to look into the murder of Danielle Mapp," Wolf explained.

Kit shook his head sadly, "Bad business that. Golden lads and girls all must, as chimney-sweepers, come to dust." Realising his words were lost on this audience, Kit added, "Shakespeare. But while we must all come to dust eventually, Danielle was taken far too soon. We lost our leading lady and our stagehand, to boot."

"In fact, we were just with Mr Robert Charles, your stagehand, who seems very attached to you," Wolf explained.

"Poor Bobby," Kit said, shaking his head again. "I can't believe that he would hurt anyone, let alone Danielle."

Wolf wasn't sure how to phrase his next question, "Is it possible that he didn't realise what he was doing? He seems quite childlike in his behaviour. Perhaps he had no idea of his strength."

Not answering this question directly, Kit said, "He wasn't born like that, you know. Danielle told me once that he was a perfectly normal child until he was about nine. His father had died when he was a baby, and his mother had taken up with an Irish labourer at some point. Nasty, drunken brute of a man. One night, he came home and thrashed Bobby to within an inch of his life, for who knows what infraction. His mother didn't think he would live, but Bobby was always a strong, healthy lad, and he did survive, but he was never the same again. Very sad."

Kit shook his head in sad contemplation of the vagaries of life. "But to answer your question, I don't believe that Bobby is capable of hurting anyone, even by accident. As I said, particularly not Danielle. He was very fond of her." Kit said this last statement with a knowing tone to his voice.

"He told us that Miss Mapp had been a friend of his mother's," Langley said.

"Yes, I don't remember the whole story. But his mother had somehow been involved with Danielle's father's career. I believe they both were from the same town, somewhere called Providence, in Long Island. No, wait, Rhode Island. That's it. Anyway, they were both Americans. At some point, Mrs Charles had come over to England to work with Mr Mapp."

"Fine Shakespearean actor, you know," Kit said, shifting the conversation. "I had the privilege of seeing him perform quite a few times. At first, he got cast as Othello, of course. But it was a measure of the man's talent that by the end of his life, he was just as likely to play Hamlet or King Lear. He even played Richard

III. Can you believe it? That a London audience would pay to see a man with skin as dark as coal as an English king! That's how good he was."

"Was Danielle as talented as her father?" Wolf asked, genuinely curious.

"Danielle's talent was different to her father's; she had the voice of an angel. Don't get me wrong, she was a fine actress, particularly in lighter roles, but it was her voice that was so electrifying. As soon as I heard her sing, I knew I had to entice her to join my company."

"We heard that her mother was a Swedish opera singer," Langley commented.

"Unfortunately, I never had the chance to hear her sing, but apparently, her voice was as pure and true as her face was beautiful. Something else Danielle inherited."

"Is there somewhere a little more private we could talk?" Wolf asked. While Kit's companion seemed to have disappeared and it didn't appear that anyone else was around in the cavernous stage area, Wolf preferred to ask his questions somewhere he was assured of privacy. Kit beckoned for them to follow him as he walked through a door off to the right of the stage.

They followed Kit through a warren of corridors, many filled with a variety of stage props, until he got to a door off to the side. Kit opened the door and invited Wolf and Langley to enter. Kit's office, because this was what the room seemed to be, was barely big enough for the three of them to fit in, but it was decorated as gaudily as the man himself. The three chairs that were somehow squeezed into the room were each upholstered in a different patterned fabric, with each one managing to be the worst possible match to the other two and all three clashing quite dramatically with the wallpaper that again had large flowers on it. Wolf thought that if he spent too much time in that room, he'd emerge with a headache.

Kit closed the door behind them, indicating that they should take two of the ugly chairs, and he took the third one behind the very messy desk. As he sat, he asked, "So you have my undivided attention, milords. How can I be of assistance?"

"It would be very helpful if you can take us through what you know of Danielle, her last days and hours and then whatever you know about how the body was found and Robert Charles' subsequent arrest," Wolf explained.

Kit sat back in his chair, laced his fingers together over his ample belly, and cleared his throat in eager anticipation of an excellent storytelling opportunity. Before owning the theatre company, Kit had enjoyed a long and reasonably successful career as an actor, and he still would stand in on occasion when necessary. He was a natural raconteur and enjoyed great notoriety for the yarns he would tell at the tavern on many an evening when the curtain had come down, and the money was all counted. "I first met Danielle several years ago. Or should I say, I first heard her sing. I had gone scouting for talent. The moment she began to sing, I fell under her spell, as did everyone else in the theatre."

"This was in London?" Langley interrupted.

Kit didn't appreciate hecklers in the theatre, and he didn't appreciate having his stories interrupted. As far as he was concerned, a tale needed to have the appropriate scene setting and then build its drama to the grand climax. If this meant that some facts had to be changed or moved around, well, that was all in the service of the narrative. An audience like this Lord Langley, who couldn't wait for the storyline to unfold at its own pace, was exactly what made Kit consider whether or not it was time to sell up and retire back to Somerset.

"Yes, London," Kit snapped. "May I continue?" Langley looked suitably chastened, and so Kit resumed his story, "As I was saying, I fell under her spell. It wasn't merely how she hit the notes; there's many a performer who can do that. Rather, it was the anguish and heartbreak she managed to imbue each song with. And when the song was a happy one, a tale of the glories of young love perhaps, you truly believed that she spoke of her own sweetheart. Why, I remember there was one song, towards the end of the show when she came out dressed as a milkmaid and sang about the joys of spring and the farmhand who had won her heart and then been tragically killed in a farming accident. Well, I tell you, there wasn't a dry eye in the house by the time the song was done. Now that's a rare talent."

Wolf could have done without the flowery descriptions, but he was worried that if they interrupted again, Kit might throw them out of his theatre. Nevertheless, he did steal a glance at Langley. Perhaps feeling Wolf's eyes on him, Langley turned his head slightly, and their eyes met for a moment, but it was long enough for Wolf to feel sure that Langley's patience was being stretched as thin as his own.

Kit had a showman's sense of when he might be losing his audience and realised that his visitors would need a somewhat pared-down and sped-up version of this story. "Anyway, I approached her the next day and made her an offer she couldn't refuse. She was to come down for a season, and we'd take it from there. Opening night came, and we received a standing ovation. Word quickly got around about the Belle of Brighton, as I advertised her, and suddenly, the show was sold out every night. One season stretched into two and then three. And before I knew it, Danielle had been the star of my theatre for almost five years."

At this last sentence, tears filled Kit Bailey's eyes, and he pulled out a large, purple handkerchief, wiped his eyes, and said, "I'm a soppy old sod, I know. But Danielle was a wonderful woman, a good friend, and she made this theatre what it is today."

Wolf felt that now there was a natural lull in the story, he could ask, "Did Robert Charles come to Brighton with her that first season?"

"No, Bobby didn't come down here until maybe a year or so ago. His mother died, and Danielle went up to London to fetch him down. She asked me to give him work as a stagehand. Well, you've met the lad. He's a fine, strapping fellow. He makes a good enough stagehand as long as he's given clear directions. He's a hard worker and never complains about long hours or late nights. Nothing is too heavy for him to haul. I grew quite fond of the boy myself. As I said before, he was always very gentle. Until, it seems, he wasn't." Kit said this last sentence with a heavy solemnity in his voice. "I had no idea I was harbouring a Caliban in my midst."

"We understand that on the last night of your recent show, there was some kind of celebration but that neither Miss Mapp nor Mr Charles attended. Were you there?" Wolf asked, happy that they seemed finally to be talking about the murder, however obliquely.

"I popped in for a few minutes just to toast the performers. But I had some business to take care of and so left after maybe only twenty minutes. So, it would have been possible for Danielle and Bobby to have shown up after I'd left, and I wouldn't have known. But my understanding is that they didn't attend."

Wolf thought about how he wanted to phrase the next question, finally asking, "Was everyone in the cast and crew as accepting of Danielle and Robert as you?"

"Ha! They knew where the door was if they had problems with my leading lady. Danielle was far too valuable to the theatre for me to accept anything other than that she be treated with respect," Kit exclaimed. Wolf considered the man's words; Kit's full-throated defence of Danielle seemed to be more about the value she held for him rather than any moral imperative.

"Our understanding from Inspector Maguire is that your wardrobe mistress discovered the body a couple of days later. That must have been quite the shock," Langley observed.

"Mrs Malloy hasn't been the same since. She says it's just about ruined her nerves. I may have to start looking around for a replacement. So now there's three people I have to replace," Kit lamented.

Kit didn't have much else of use to tell them. However, they still sat through at least one further burst of grandiloquence on Danielle's talents, followed by more handwringing about how Danielle's loss could mean the end of his theatre company.

When he could next get a word in, Wolf asked, "I believe Miss Mapp was unmarried. Did she have any admirers of note?"

"There were men aplenty, as you can imagine. Always sending flowers, sometimes waiting for her at the stage door. I'm not sure how seriously she ever took any of them. There was this toff recently who seemed to be around more than the others. Young, snot-nosed, arrogant ass. But I think Danielle saw him as nothing more than an eager pup. At least that's what she seemed to be saying the one time I came across him importuning her in her dressing room."

Now, this was some new, interesting information, Wolf thought. "Did you tell Inspector Maguire about this young admirer?"

"I'm sure I must have. Though, those coppers were so sure they had their man in young Bobby that I can't imagine they took much notice." Kit said these words sadly, visibly upset about the arrest.

"That brings me to the last thing I'd like to ask you, Mr Bailey," Wolf said.

"Kit, that's good enough for me. Mr Bailey was my father, and a right bastard he was."

"Kit, then. Inspector Maguire said he has testimony about Mr Charles' infatuation with Miss Mapp and that one person claimed to have overheard them argue. Do you know anything about who this witness might be?"

"Bobby loved Danielle; there was no doubt of that. But it really seemed to be more of the love for a mother figure. He had no one else, it seemed. But perhaps other people misinterpreted his affection. And as for an argument. I'm sure I have no idea. I've never heard Bobby raise his voice."

Feeling they had gathered all the useful information they were likely to out of Kit Bailey, Wolf asked, "Would it be possible for us to interview the members of your theatre company?"

"Of course! Anything to help ensure justice for our dear Danielle. Though I suggest you return another day. We are starting a rehearsal in a few minutes. After that, people won't be keen to hang around any longer than necessary. Why don't I let everyone know that you want to talk to them and ask them to come in earlier than usual tomorrow morning? Let's say ten o'clock. You can use my office to interview them. How's that?"

It was a perfectly reasonable plan, and so Wolf and Langley thanked the larger-than-life Christopher "Kit" Bailey and made their way back out of the warren of corridors to finally emerge back on the stage and then through the stage door out to the street.

CHAPTER 11

Wolf and Langley returned to the hotel unaware of the drama that had unfolded there not much earlier. By the time they entered the opulent hotel lobby, the dowager and Tabitha had retreated to their respective suites, the dowager to scheme and Tabitha to reflect on her meeting with Lady Archibald. Langley excused himself, saying he hoped to find Rat and continue the boy's new studies. Wolf considered whether he wanted to try to find Tabitha and discuss the day's interviews, but, remembering her stated determination to excuse herself from any involvement in this case, he instead went to his suite in search of Bear.

Wolf found his friend sitting by the window, using some of his new art supplies to make charcoal sketches of the seafront. Looking up as Wolf entered, Bear asked, "How was your afternoon?"

Wolf went and sat in the other chair at the small table Bear was sketching at, "Interesting. Very interesting." He briefly told Wolf about his visit to the Brighton police station.

"Do you think there's a case here, and if there is, will you take it on?"

"Honestly, I'm not sure if there's a case. I do think the Brighton police arrested Robert Charles based primarily on the colour of his skin and because of his size and limited mental capacity. Perhaps when we go back tomorrow to talk to the rest of the theatre company, I will hear more from this so-called witness that will make me re-evaluate that judgement. But of course, as we know all too well, just because an arrest is made for the wrong reasons doesn't mean that the wrong person has been accused."

Wolf paused and thought about the second, more fraught question, "As to whether I'll take the case, well, I will continue to investigate for now." Seeing a look cross his old friend's face, Wolf asked, "You think I'm doing the wrong thing?"

"I have no opinion on the merits of the case, but I do have an opinion on you giving Arlene an opportunity to get her claws back into you," Bear replied. He paused, "Did you know she was coming here today?"

"What do you mean?" Wolf asked in a panicked voice. "Arlene came here? How do you know?"

"Because I ran into Lady Lily on my way back from buying my art supplies. It seems she'd managed to escape the worst of it, but apparently, Arlene turned up here asking for Lady Pembroke and ended up having tea with the dowager countess." Reacting to the shock on Wolf's face, Bear hastily added, "I'm not sure what to make of this, but apparently, Arlene and the dowager countess quickly became fast friends. Perhaps like recognises like," he commented with great insight.

"So, Arlene never met Tabitha?" Wolf asked, mentally kicking himself; he should have anticipated that Arlene would pull a stunt like this. It had been obvious that morning that his old love was jealous of whatever she believed his relationship with Tabitha to be. He remembered only too well how territorial Arlene could be.

"Oh, they met," Bear said, confirming Wolf's worst fears. "Lady Lily only caught the initial meeting, but her comment on it was to meow and mime a cat's claws, so I doubt it went well."

Bear held back from saying the words, "I told you so." However, his face and tone expressed his feelings clearly enough that Wolf said, "Yes, yes, I know, you warned me. I believe I must go to Tabitha. Though, I'll be damned if I know what to say."

Wolf was about to stand, then stopped and said, "Doesn't Angie have some family living in Brighton?" Angie Doherty was the common-law wife of Whitechapel gang leader Mickey

D. Mickey D was Wolf's sometimes client, sometimes adversary, regular antagonist, occasional informant, and even once, blackmailer. While Wolf had very complicated feelings towards Mickey, he had nothing but genuine affection for the plump, rosy-cheeked, motherly Angie.

"I think she might have a sister down here. Actually, I'm sure it's a sister, a younger sister. She's married to a publican, I believe. I remember because the pub had a particularly amusing name, the Cock and Bull."

"Yes, I remember now. I want you to do something for me tomorrow and see if you can track this sister down. I really felt on the back foot in Edinburgh without our usual Whitechapel sources of information. I'd prefer not to repeat that experience in Brighton. Any relation of Mickey D's likely has some connections to the less salubrious members of Brighton society. Particularly if her husband owns a pub."

Saying this, he stood and made his way towards the door, "Okay, wish me luck. I have no idea what I'm going to say to Tabitha."

"Maybe the truth?" Bear suggested.

Wolf walked down the hallway and knocked tentatively on the door to Tabitha and Lily's suite. Of course, a single man entering the bedchamber of a single woman was normally quite scandalous. Still, at this point, he couldn't imagine they could scandalise the dowager any more than she already claimed to be by their living situation. And who else was there in the hotel who could pretend to be shocked?

The door was opened by Lily, who didn't seem at all surprised by Wolf's appearance. "I'm assuming it's not me that you've come to see," she said wryly. Lily indicated for Wolf to enter, turning as she did so to Tabitha, who was sitting on the light-blue upholstered sofa in front of the fireplace, and said, "I believe I have something I need to do in my room." And with that, she quickly exited through a door to the side.

Wolf closed the door behind him and hesitantly approached the seating area, "I apologise for this socially unacceptable visit, but I just heard from Bear what happened. I had to come and tell you how sorry I am that you had to endure it. May I join you?"

Tabitha inclined her head to indicate he should sit and said, "You have nothing to apologise for. I'm assuming you didn't send Lady Archibald here. But you are certainly welcome to join me."

Wolf sat in an armchair next to the sofa. "I didn't send her, but I should have anticipated that she would do something like that. I hear from Bear that she and the dowager countess seemed to have found a lot of common ground."

"Ha!" Tabitha said, "I'd rather characterise it as being thick as thieves. It was as if they each intuited the other's feelings towards me and gave life to the ancient proverb that the enemy of my enemy is my friend."

"I am so sorry you had to put up with that. Certainly, if I hadn't brought you down to Brighton with me, this could have been avoided," Wolf said.

"Wolf, you didn't bring me down here. I came of my own volition. And as you know, you couldn't have stopped me if you wanted to. In fact, I believe you tried and failed. And I assume you didn't direct Lady Archibald to seek me out. So, let us put the incident behind us. We were bound to meet at some point during this visit. At least now it is done."

Tabitha paused, unsure of whether she wanted to enquire after the investigation or not. Finally, her inherent curiosity won out, "Did you and Lord Langley make any progress today?"

"I'm not sure I'd call it progress, but we did talk to the police inspector in charge of the case, managed to talk briefly with the accused man, and even went to the theatre where the victim and the accused were both employed and talked to the owner. He's quite a colourful character, to say the least. He's invited me back tomorrow to interview the rest of the company." Wolf was very aware of his use of the personal singular pronoun. Under normal circumstances, this would be a red flag to a bull as far as Tabitha was concerned, and she would have immediately demanded her involvement. But she said nothing and merely nodded at his

75

narrative.

Tabitha was as aware as Wolf of her uncharacteristic reaction to hearing about his plans for the following day. But having met Lady Arlene Archibald, Tabitha was even more resistant to being involved in the investigation that the other woman had instigated. She realised it was childish and petty, but she felt somehow that by helping the woman prove her friend's innocence, she was providing succour that would not have been given to her if the tables were turned. Of course, she reflected, did she wish to be no better than such a woman? And was she willing to deny a possibly innocent man justice out of spite? But how was she denying him justice? Surely her ego wasn't so inflated such that she imagined Wolf with Bear and Langley by his side was unable to pursue an investigation without her assistance? These thoughts ran through her mind as Wolf talked as she tried, not wholly successfully, to convince herself of the merits of her behaviour.

As if it perfectly justified her reluctance to accompany Wolf to the theatre, Tabitha said, "I have promised Melly that we'll find her a donkey ride tomorrow. Rat is trying to pretend he's too grown for such a childish activity, but I suspect he is as excited as his sister at the thought. Then, in the afternoon, the dowager, despite having been in Brighton a mere twenty-four hours, has already lined up some social visits for us to make."

When the dowager had first lightly mentioned these plans after tea and her expectation that Tabitha would be one of the party, it had occurred to Tabitha that it wasn't beyond the old woman to have agreed to visit Lady Archibald without informing her. She had come straight out and asked the question. Despite some huffing, the dowager finally acknowledged that Lady Archibald wasn't on the list of planned social calls.

The dowager was preparing her granddaughter, Lady Lily, for her first season and considered Brighton society an acceptable practice ground before London. Tabitha found Lily a refreshingly direct and yet charming young woman. Highly intelligent, Lily wanted nothing more than to be allowed to study her beloved botany. But even though some young women were being admitted to universities around the country, the idea that one of Lily's rank would choose academic pursuits over an advantageous marriage was too preposterous even to consider as far as her family was concerned.

Wolf sat talking with Tabitha for a few minutes more, but the conversation was stilted and formal, quite unlike the comfortable banter and confidences they usually shared. Tabitha and Wolf both felt it, but each guessed at different causes for the sudden cooling of their friendship. Tabitha felt that Wolf's feelings of guilt at Lady Archibald's ambush were tied up with a renewed passion for his first love that he was unwilling to acknowledge yet. Wolf felt, well, he wasn't entirely sure what he felt. He knew Tabitha had withdrawn, but he didn't fully understand why. He knew it was bound up with Arlene. But was it merely distaste at the messy situation he had brought her into that had only been made more difficult by Arlene forcing herself onto Tabitha that afternoon?

Finally, rising and excusing himself, Wolf left the room shaking his head with confusion. Tabitha sat watching him leave, almost ready to burst into tears by the time the door closed behind him. Hearing the door, Lily came back into the sitting room. Seeing Tabitha looking so forlorn, Lily sat beside her, took her hand, and said gently, "I know it is none of my business, Aunt Tabitha, but it is quite clear what you and Cousin Jeremy feel for each other. It's even clear to me, and Mama always says I have no ability to read other people's emotions."

Unable to hold back her feelings any longer, a few tears rolled down Tabitha's cheeks as she said quietly, "Whatever interest I may or may not have held for Wolf cannot compare to the strong pull of first love. You saw Lady Archibald this afternoon, Lily. She is the most beautiful female I've ever laid eyes on. How could a man ever forget such a woman? And it is very clear that she has not forgotten him. Nothing is standing in the way of them being together now."

Lily snorted, "Well, nothing except that he is in love with you and not with her."

Tabitha smiled through her tears, "Lily, dear child, you are young and full of romantic notions. I know that Wolf cares for me, but it is as a friend." As she said this, Tabitha reflected on that moment in the carriage some weeks before when Wolf had been about to declare something. But what?

"I have no friends who look at me as Cousin Jeremy looks at you," Lily said knowingly. "And I'm not the only one who sees it. Grandmama believes he is in love with you as well!" she announced triumphantly as if laying down a winning hand in bridge.

"Lady Pembroke thinks no such thing," Tabitha said with certainty.

"Oh, but she does. She grumbles about it all the time. She talks about how he can do better and that his feelings must be because you've entrapped him somehow by managing his household. Or some such rot. Honestly, I'm not sure how this is news to you. Between you and me, I think she's jealous. I know it's quite disgusting to contemplate in someone of her advanced age, but I believe she may be somewhat infatuated with Cousin Jeremy."

Lily's statement did make Tabitha laugh. She also couldn't argue with Lily's statement. And this information did give her pause. But then she thought about the beautiful, poised, elegant woman who had sat opposite her at tea and had thrown down the gauntlet, clearly asserting her prior claim over Wolf. Regardless of what he might feel towards Tabitha, it was impossible to believe Wolf didn't have any residual feelings for the beautiful Lady Archibald. And if there was any chink in his armour at all, that woman would find it.

Beyond the conundrum that was Wolf's feelings towards herself, Tabitha couldn't forget her own resolution never again to marry. Tabitha knew Wolf was nothing like her deceased husband Jonathan, who was a cruel, violent man who tried to control Tabitha's every thought and action. Nevertheless, she couldn't imagine ever willingly putting herself under a man's control again, even the most benevolent husband. And she would never agree to be a man's mistress, of that she was certain. So why was she selfishly holding onto these pointless feelings for a man she could have no claim over? If she were a true friend, she would encourage him to return to his first love, and yet she couldn't find it in her to do so.

Dinner was a rather subdued affair that evening. Tabitha and Wolf still felt awkward in each other's presence, and Lily and the dowager were in the middle of an ongoing disagreement about whether Lily was able to visit the Royal Pavilion Gardens the following morning before their planned social calls in the afternoon.

"Grandmama, there is no good reason why I might not visit the gardens before lunch," Lily argued. The dowager's rationale was quite simple: she did not trust Lily not to get caught up "Obsessing over a plant and failing to return in time." In addition, she worried about what state Lily's hair might be in by the time she did return. For once, Tabitha had some sympathy for the dowager's point of view. It was not uncommon for Lily to get caught up in her botanical studies and lose track of time. And there had been many occasions when she had returned from her garden at home with leaves and twigs in her hair.

Having forbidden Lily to leave the hotel under sufferance of insisting on even more visits to the milliner's shops if she were disobeyed, the dowager sat in stony silence only matched in her self-righteous indignation by her granddaughter. Tabitha had managed to infuriate both granddaughter and grandmother by gently suggesting to Lily that perhaps she postpone her visit to the gardens by a day and to the dowager that she accept this compromise.

Lord Langley sat at the dinner table ignorant of most of the afternoon's melodrama but very aware of the tension between his various travelling companions. By unspoken consensus, everybody finished their meal as quickly as possible and retired to their various suites for the rest of the evening.

CHAPTER 12

By breakfast the following morning, Lily and the dowager seemed to have recovered from their tiff at least enough to have a civil conversation about which dress Lily would wear that afternoon. None of Lily's new clothes had been delivered yet. Until then, she had a very limited number of dresses the dowager would even consider acceptable.

Finally, having forced the necessary concessions out of her granddaughter, the dowager turned to Wolf and said, "Dear Lady Archibald told me all about your promise to rectify the gross miscarriage of justice that has been perpetrated on that poor young man."

There were so many things wrong with that statement that Wolf was momentarily stumped as to where to begin. That Arlene had somehow ingratiated herself with the normally highly critical and hard-to-please dowager sufficiently to have earned the moniker "Dear Lady Archibald" was shocking enough. Wolf shouldn't have been at all surprised that Arlene had somehow translated his ambivalence about investigating into a promise that he very definitely hadn't made. But perhaps the part of the dowager's statement that surprised him the most was her characterisation of Robert Charles as "that poor young man." It made Wolf wonder how much of the truth Arlene had revealed over tea.

"Lady Pembroke," Wolf said carefully, "Lady Archibald may have misrepresented my position; I promised nothing. It is unclear to me if there is even a case here. What exactly did she tell you about the accused man?"

There must have been something about the way that Wolf phrased that question because the dowager narrowed her eyes at him suspiciously, "Why do you all make these assumptions about me? You believe she couldn't have told me that the colour of his skin is akin to hers because if she had, I would never be championing his innocence. Isn't that correct?"

Her question was so prescient that Wolf was unsure how to answer. The dowager, taking his silence as an acknowledgement of the truth of her statement, continued, "Jeremy, it is bad enough that Tabitha presumes to know what I will say and do while always expecting the worst. But it cuts me to the quick to discover that you do not hold me in higher regard."

She continued, "Apart from anything else, if Her Majesty saw fit to be the godmother to that African princess, Sarah Forbes Bonetta, who am I to hold such prejudices? Tell me that."

Lord Langley, who had himself been at the receiving end of the dowager's ire many times during his life, came to Wolf's rescue, "Lady Pembroke, I'm sure that is not what his lordship meant at all. Rather, I believe his concern arises from nothing more than what we deduced from our conversations yesterday with the police and then the accused himself." Wolf flashed Langley a look of gratitude and then nodded in vigorous assent.

Whether or not the dowager believed Langley, she was sufficiently distracted by his words that she put aside her righteous indignation and leaned in, eager to hear more. Wolf was normally reluctant to share too many details of an investigation with the dowager for fear she would be too eager to participate. However, this time, he was so happy for the distraction Langley had provided that he immediately rushed to tell the whole story of the investigation to date.

When Wolf had finished, the dowager asked, "So you are going back to the theatre this morning to question everyone?" Wolf nodded, and she continued, "Then I will come with you and help." Somehow, Wolf hadn't anticipated such a statement and wasn't sure how to answer. Having only just got himself out of hot water with the older Lady Pembroke, he was loath to remind her of his previous transgression. The woman, likely sensing his hesitation, continued, "Tabitha has made it clear that she will not be involved in this investigation, and you can hardly be expected to question the entire theatre company alone."

Langley waded in again, "Lady Pembroke, I was planning to go along to be of assistance."

"And which one of you is going to question the women?" the dowager demanded with the gleeful anticipation of one producing their trump card. "It takes a woman to understand how to pry the truth out of another." It was unclear to anyone at the table that this was true. But Wolf had learned over the last three investigations that there were occasions when the dowager's particular talents could come in very handy. If nothing else, it would be quite entertaining to see what she made of Christopher "Kit" Bailey. And so, he quickly agreed that she should join the investigative party that morning.

Despite Tabitha's stated unwillingness to be part of this investigation, seeing Wolf, Langley, and the dowager depart for the theatre without her was quite dispiriting. Watching them head out to the hotel's carriage for the short ride to the theatre – but not so short that the dowager would consider walking – left Tabitha more confused about her feelings than ever. She'd been so sure that she wanted nothing to do with Lady Archibald's investigation, but back in her suite, Tabitha wondered whether she had cut off her nose to spite her face.

The carriage ride hadn't been long enough for Wolf to consider how best to utilise the dowager's particular skill set during the interviews. However, he also realised that the woman was a force unto herself, and it was highly unlikely he could manage her even if he wanted to. Wolf had directed the carriage to the stage door and asked the driver to return in two hours. Making their way into the theatre, the dowager paused, leaned on her cane and looked around her in genuine amazement. "I must say, I've done many things in my time, but I've never been backstage in a theatre," she exclaimed. "How very different everything looks from this vantage point."

No sooner had she said these words than a booming voice hailed them from across the stage. Looking over, the dowager asked in too loud a voice, "Who on earth is that bizarrely dressed man?"

Wolf realised, too late, that he hadn't warned the dowager about Christopher "Kit" Bailey, who was dressed even more outrageously that morning than before if that was possible. The black velvet trousers had been replaced with what could only be described as purple bloomers. Baggy around his hips and upper legs, they stopped at his knees, where they were gathered tightly. He again wore no jacket, but the waistcoat du jour was patterned in wide blue and yellow stripes, which contrasted garishly with the bloomers. To top off the outfit, Kit had replaced the cravat with a mint green silk scarf wrapped twice around his neck with the tasselled ends left dangling. Just as it was the day before, his long, white, flowing mane of hair was loose over his shoulders.

Arriving next to them, Kit looked the dowager up and down and said in a voice that mimicked her own, "Who on earth is this rude little woman?" Wolf almost choked, holding back a snort of laughter. Langley was unable to exercise such self-control and had to turn away and turn his snort into a sneeze.

Throwing her shoulders back and lifting her chin as if that might add more height to her barely five feet, the dowager said with all the haughtiness of a bloodline that could be traced back to knights fighting at the Battle of Bosworth Field next to Henry VII, "Rude little woman? How dare you. I am the Dowager Countess of Pembroke. And I am never rude, merely accurate."

Kit looked at her for a moment, and Wolf held his breath in anticipation as to how much worse this meeting might go. But then, the large man threw back his head and guffawed. The dowager, unused to being laughed at under any circumstance, poked her cane at him, "I cannot imagine what you find so amusing. It certainly cannot be anything I've said." But this just made Kit laugh even harder.

Finally, wiping the tears out of his eyes, he said, "What a

wonderful character you will make. I only wish it were still socially acceptable to stage *The Importance of Being Earnest*. What a marvellous Lady Bracknell I could make in your image. As it is, I may have to put on *A School for Scandal* and tinker with the Lady Sneerwell character."

It was rare, if not unheard of, for the dowager to be left speechless. She was used to being loathed, reviled, and feared. She was not used to being mocked to her face.

Realising how quickly this situation was spiralling out of control, Wolf stepped in and said, "Kit, thank you for allowing us to question your company. How many people are there in total?"

"Well, you're in luck. We have a core company of eleven in production, including myself and Mildred at the box office, and seven actors. We then hire temporary actors as a show requires. However, money has been a little tight recently, and we've been trying to make do with just our core company. So for both the last production and the one we're rehearsing now, it's just the seventeen of us, minus Danielle and Bobby, of course. Oh, and Mrs Malloy, who is still indisposed."

Wolf thought for a moment. While they could get through seventeen people more easily if they divided them up between them, he didn't trust the dowager, particularly in the mood she was now in, to pick up on the subtle clues that he or Langley would. But it was hard to imagine she would tolerate having her interviews overseen by Wolf or Langley, and so perhaps it was best for them to interview everyone together. It was a good thing he had told the carriage two hours. They'd be lucky to be done by then. Doing the maths in his head, he realised that gave them an average of seven minutes per interview. That would never work. And then there was the matter of how small Kit's office was.

Finally, Wolf bit the bullet and said, "Lady Pembroke, why don't you take Mr Bailey's office with Lord Langley and interview all the women, and I will find somewhere else to talk to the men." He expected the dowager to protest the division of labour, but perhaps she was still too stunned by Kit's irreverence towards her, for she merely nodded her acceptance of the plan.

Kit called over a middle-aged, homely-looking woman and told her to escort the dowager and Langley to his office and then stay to be interviewed. The woman didn't look very happy at this command but kept her thoughts to herself and led the others back through the door they had gone through yesterday.

"Actually, before I start my interviews, I'd like to see Danielle's dressing room and where the body was found," Wolf said to Kit. "Has anyone been through her room since the night of the murder?"

"We didn't have the heart. A new actress is coming to audition this afternoon for the understudy role, and Jackie will take the lead role Danielle would have performed. Either way, we'll have to clean out the room soon, but until then, it's untouched. I'll take you up there."

Instead of going in the direction Langley and the dowager had gone, Kit led Wolf off the other side of the stage, down a short corridor, to a painted white door with a brass plaque that said 1. Miss Danielle Mapp. Kit paused, his hand on the doorknob, "I haven't been in here since they found her body," he said sadly, shaking his head. He waited a moment longer, steeled himself, and then turned the knob.

The dressing room was smaller than Wolf would have imagined. And almost half of it was taken up with a large, green sofa that looked as if it had seen better days. There was a dressing table with a large mirror. The dressing table was covered with a mess of makeup, feathers, combs, and the other paraphernalia Wolf might have expected an actress to make use of. In a large mahogany frame, there was a photo that Wolf assumed was of Danielle. It looked as if it was a photo taken to advertise a play; she was very made up and had struck a saucy pose. Walking over and picking it up, he commented, "She was beautiful."

"Indeed," agreed Kit. "Talented, beautiful, and just a great girl."

There was a screen at the back of the room with a silk robe thrown carelessly over the top. There were a few hooks on the wall. One had a large picture hat on it, and another had a feather boa. Everything about the room felt as if its occupant had been in the middle of getting ready and had stepped out for a moment.

Even though Wolf hadn't known Danielle, he felt a great tide of sadness at the life cut short. The beautiful voice that an audience would never hear again. Sadness that Arlene had lost one of the few friends she'd ever had who really understood what she experienced.

"I'd like to come back before we leave and do a more thorough search," Wolf said. "But I don't want to hold you up. I imagine that your theatre company would rather I not interview them here. Is there another dressing room I might use?"

Kit nodded and led Wolf down the hall to the next dressing room, which had its own brass plaque that read 2 Merryweather Frost.

Wolf pointed at the plaque and asked, "Your leading man?"

"Yes. Good old Merry. Honestly, he's getting a bit long in the tooth to play a leading man. But he still has all his hair, is a strong tenor, and the ladies still love him, if you can believe it. Also," Kit confided, "he was more than happy to play against Danielle. And not every actor would be. If you know what I mean." Wolf knew exactly what he meant.

Merryweather Frost's dressing room was immaculate. Unlike Danielle's, the dressing table top was empty. There were no clothes scattered around the room, and the whole place had the feel and scent of cleanness about it that had been missing next door. As if reading Wolf's thoughts, Kit said, "Neat as a pin, isn't it? That's Merry, never a hair out of place or a spot on a piece of clothing. His favourite saying is, 'There's a place for everything and everything in its place.'"

Wolf thought about all the gossip that flew around London about the most famous actors and actresses and asked, "Was Danielle Mr Frost's leading lady off the stage as well?"

Another loud guffaw and Kit replied, "I said that the ladies love him. It doesn't mean he loves them back, if you know what I mean." And he tapped the side of his nose with his forefinger and winked as he said this.

"Before I forget, you were going to show me where the body was found," Wolf remembered.

"Ah," Kit said, all merriment evaporating. "It's down the end of this corridor, in fact."

He led Wolf back out of the dressing room and further down the corridor, past three or four other dressing rooms, which Kit informed Wolf were shared by the rest of the cast.

At the end of the corridor, there was a rather tattered-looking burgundy velvet curtain that was partially hiding what was revealed as a large alcove when Kit drew it back.

"We use this for short-term storage. For larger items or things that we haven't used for years, we have additional storage in the basement. You can see a couple of trunks pushed to the back. They have costumes in them. There was a third trunk, just like them, at the front here. She was found stuffed into that. We had to get rid of that trunk; theatre folks are very superstitious."

"And it was the wardrobe mistress who found her?" Wolf confirmed.

"Yes, Mrs Malloy. But you won't be able to interview her today. As I told you, her nerves haven't been the same since. She's been staying with her daughter in Hove to recover. Her assistant is helping out, but if she doesn't come back soon, I will have to replace her."

Wolf asked for and was promised Mrs Malloy's and Danielle's addresses. Kit promised to provide them before they left the theatre that morning.

There was nothing more to see, so Kit led Wolf back to dressing room number two and left him sitting on the chair in front of the dressing table while he went to find the first person to send in for questioning.

CHAPTER 13

The tall, elegant man sent in first was obviously Merryweather Frost. Everything about him screamed, leading man, from his velvet smoking jacket to his perfectly styled and pomaded hair, which looked suspiciously black for someone his apparent age. Merryweather entered the room, looked at Wolf sitting in front of his dressing table, and asked caustically, "So, will I be perching on that uncomfortable sofa while you interrogate me from above?"

Wolf ignored the question and instead said, "Thank you for taking the time to talk with me, Mr Frost. I'm not sure if Kit told you who I am and how I became interested in Miss Mapp's death."

"He mentioned that a couple of swells were playing at private investigators and had come to see him yesterday. I'm assuming you are one of them."

Merryweather said this with such derision in his voice that Wolf was half tempted to offer to swap seats with the man just to get the interview back on track. However, he knew the power he would be giving up by taking the lower chair, and he wasn't ready to cede that yet. Instead, he changed his tone and body language very subtly to shift into his best Peer of the Realm persona. "Yes, I am the Earl of Pembroke, and my colleague is the Earl of Langley. We have been asked to look into Miss Mapp's death by Lady Archibald. Does that answer your question?" Wolf said this with his tone dripping with as much condescension as possible, and it seemed to have the desired effect: Merryweather visibly wilted in the face of so many titles and sat on the sofa.

Nevertheless, he ensured it was evident how uncomfortable it was for him to fold his tall frame accordingly.

The rest of the interview went smoothly enough, but wasn't particularly informative. Merryweather echoed much of what Kit had said, Danielle was supremely talented. Moreover, she was a pleasant castmate who never lorded it above the rest of the company. Beyond these general platitudes, Merryweather seemed to know little about Danielle's life outside of the theatre, and like Kit, he reserved most of his grief for how her loss would affect the theatre company's success.

Two hours later, Wolf wasn't sure whether he'd gleaned any useful information from anyone. He certainly hoped that Langley and the dowager had more to report than he did. To a man, the male members of the cast and crew seemed genuinely shocked and saddened by Danielle's death. Wolf didn't get the sense that anyone was being anything less than truthful. Everyone had left the theatre about thirty minutes after the curtain went down on the last night of the show, and no one had been overly surprised when Danielle didn't join them for the celebration.

By the time Wolf finally left the theatre, the dowager and Langley were already in the carriage, and she was tapping her cane in impatience at having to wait for him. "Jeremy, what on earth were you doing back there that took so long? Langley and I managed to interview a couple of actresses, that dowdy woman from the box office and the assistant costume girl, in less than an hour. Then we had to wait in that terrible office until the carriage arrived, and then wait for you!"

Wolf didn't point out that he had interviewed more than twice as many men as they had women. He also didn't point out that questioning witnesses called for thorough, thoughtful questioning and wasn't a race to see who could finish first.

None of the men he had questioned had admitted to being the person who claimed to have heard Danielle rebuff Bobby's advances or even claimed to believe he was infatuated with her. He asked the dowager and Langley if they'd had more luck.

"Strangely, no," Langley admitted. Of course, it's possible that the costume mistress was the witness in both cases."

"Yes, we will have to pay her a visit," Wolf agreed. "Did anyone strike you as evasive or guilty in any way?"

The dowager said, "Yes," at the same moment that Langley said, "No."

Looking between them, Wolf ended up turning to the dowager and asking, "Why do you say yes?"

"Well, it was less what she said or even how she said it. But clearly, the younger actress, Janice or some name like that, who always took the lesser roles but acted as Miss Mapp's understudy as well, has the clearest motive to want her out of the way," she answered as if her logic was unimpeachable.

"Well, putting aside whether or not that is the strongest motive, we know that the murderer was a large man, not a small, young woman," Wolf pointed out.

The dowager harrumphed her displeasure at being contradicted, then said, "Jemima, or Jeanette, whatever her name was, could have hired someone to do the actual murder."

Wolf sighed; he could see that the dowager was hellbent on chasing down this particular rabbit hole. "Lady Pembroke, if I may make two observations: it has been my experience in my more than ten-year career investigating crimes that while one should never close off any avenue of discovery prematurely, it is also usually the case that the simplest explanation turns out to be the correct one. So, let us not write off the young actress yet, but also, given her size and gender, put her towards the bottom of our list of suspects, at least for now."

Another harrumph indicated the dowager's reluctant acknowledgement of the wisdom of Wolf's words.

Before they had a chance to discuss the interviews any further, they were back at the hotel. They agreed to freshen up and meet back in the restaurant for lunch and a further debriefing. As Wolf went up to his suite, he wondered if Tabitha was in the hotel somewhere and if he would bump into her.

Despite all of Wolf's failed attempts to protect her by

keeping her at arm's length in investigations, it felt deeply wrong not to have Tabitha involved now. He knew that it was her choice, but Wolf still felt as if he was at fault somehow. More than anything, he missed her insights and observations and knew the investigation would be poorer for her lack of involvement. He supposed he could set up their usual board of clues; they had brought the corkboard with them from Scotland. There was nothing about the innovative method of reviewing the investigation's elements that necessitated Tabitha's involvement. It just felt very wrong without her.

Wolf didn't bump into Tabitha, but he did meet Bear coming out of their shared suite. "Did you have any luck tracking down Angie's sister?" he asked his friend.

"Actually, I did. I was just going down to get something to eat. Do you want to get rid of your outerwear and join me?" Bear answered.

"I do. In fact, I'm regrouping with the dowager countess and Langley to discuss our interviews at the theatre this morning. You can join us."

Wolf noticed Bear's slight hesitation in agreeing and understood the man's concern. When Wolf had first ascended to the earldom, Bear had nominally functioned as his valet. It had always been a rather thin pretence, initiated merely to explain Bear's presence at Chesterton House. But it quickly became clear that, as the new earl, Wolf needed a real valet, and Thompson had been hired. By that time, Bear was a well-established member of the household, and Wolf would have been happy enough just to have him continue to live there as his friend. But Bear was too proud a man for that, and so he had become Wolf's private secretary.

The shift in status had gone largely unremarked on amongst the servants. Still, Wolf knew that Bear was sensitive to how others, particularly the dowager countess, might feel about a man who was recently a servant now dining with her. Even though this wouldn't be the first time, it was evident that Bear was ill at ease on each occasion.

Acknowledging this unspoken discomfort, Wolf said, "You know, in many ways, she's not as fierce as she'd have us all believe. And she can be surprisingly open to people at times. Look at how much she enjoyed having Mickey D and Angie as dinner guests! And she became bosom buddies with Arlene over a cup of tea, for heaven's sake. She has never said anything about your new status. So let us give her the benefit of the doubt until she does. At which point, I will make clear how I expect you to be treated." While these words only went so far in addressing Bear's worries, he did agree to join the threesome for lunch.

If the dowager had any thoughts on Bear's appearance, she kept them to herself. However, at the mention of his errand for that morning, she put down her knife and fork and gave him her full attention. "Mrs Doherty has a sister living in Brighton? What a fascinating coincidence. And you managed to find her?" Of all the many ways the dowager had managed to subvert expectations recently, her positive delight in Mickey D and Angie's company as dinner guests in her home had definitely been the most surprising. In fact, she had referred to them as "A breath of fresh air," compared to, "The crashing bores of the aristocracy."

Politically savvy enough to seize the opportunity, Bear turned and directed his answer to the dowager, "Yes, milady. I remembered that she and her husband ran a public house here in Brighton. I had some memory of the name of the place, so I asked the hall porter this morning, and he directed me to an establishment with that name. It's not far away, down The Lanes, in fact."

"I was shopping in The Lanes yesterday with Lily! The dowager proclaimed. "I found the most wonderful armoury there." This reminded Wolf that they had forgotten to ask what she needed in an armoury. But not wanting to distract from Bear's narrative, he made a mental note to bring it up later.

Bear continued, "It's a lovely old place, with the best steak and ale pie I've ever had. Jeannie, that's Angie's sister, is as good a cook as Ang is."

Wolf considered for a moment how he wanted to phrase his next question. He realised now that perhaps he should have had this conversation with Bear in private. Finally, he threw caution to the wind and asked, "Was she receptive to helping us? And more to the point, do you think she and her husband have similar connections here in Brighton to Mickey D and Angie in Whitechapel?"

"Well, I didn't come out and directly ask what their connections are to the more criminal elements of Brighton society. However, it was clear from the look of the regulars filling their establishment that they are familiar with some of the lowlifes in town. And it seems that word of the favour we did Mickey and Seamus recently had made its way down here. Jeanie and her husband Paddy were very welcoming and seemed inclined to help."

Bear paused, then added, "I almost forgot. In a particularly lucky coincidence, their public house is where the theatre company drinks and where they celebrate the end of the shows."

"That is a lucky coincidence," Wolf agreed. "Were you able to ask them anything about the company or that night?"

"Unfortunately, they were too rushed off their feet to talk any longer, but I said we'd go back later after the lunch rush was over."

"I've never been in a public house," the dowager exclaimed excitedly.

Wolf looked sharply at her. Surely, she didn't expect to accompany him to a working man's drinking establishment. The dowager noted his look and said, "I have good reason to believe you've taken Tabitha into such places. Is there a reason she may go where I may not?"

As it happened, Wolf had never been comfortable with Tabitha accompanying him to public houses either. But he was even less comfortable with the idea of taking the ageing dowager countess. However, he had learned that the woman would not be dissuaded once she had decided on something. Moreover, any attempts Wolf made to persuade her would likely make her even more obdurate. She seemed to believe that places such as public houses were merely playgrounds for her to adventure in. Perhaps experiencing one for herself would do more to bring home reality than any cautionary words. And so, he replied, "Of course, you may accompany us, Lady Pembroke."

Langley raised his eyebrows in surprise but said nothing. But then, remembering the dowager's afternoon plans, he said, "Aren't you supposed to pay some afternoon social calls with Lady Lily today?"

"Pish posh, social calls. Tabitha may go with her. I have far more important things to take care of, it seems."

Wolf had one more bit of information, even if he wasn't sure how it was relevant, "It seems that on the Saturday afternoon before a new show's opening on a Monday, one of the theatre company's traditions, one might almost say superstitions, is to go out to a place called Devil's Dyke. Apparently, they do this regardless of the weather."

"Why on earth would they go to such an awful-sounding place?" the dowager asked.

"I heard versions of this from Merryweather and his understudy in passing. It seems that years ago when Kit had first taken over the company, they had all gone there for a picnic on the Saturday before opening. Theatre folks are a superstitious bunch, and apparently, one of the many that they live by is called Blessings from Above. The claim is that if a bird flies into the theatre, it is good luck. On the day of the picnic, a bird came and did something. I can't remember if it perched somewhere or was just nearby. Anyway, that first show was a huge success, and from that point on, this has been an unbreakable tradition."

"What absolute poppycock!" the dowager exclaimed.

"That may be. But I've heard more absurd things in my time. Bear in mind a large part of the hold such superstitions have over people is their belief in whatever the thing is. So, if the company decided that visit to Devil's Dyke somehow brought them good luck, Kit would be foolish to try to refute such a belief. Anyway, they will all be there on Saturday. At this point, I'm not sure what we would gain by joining them, but it's something worth filing away."

"Why did they bother telling you about that?" Langley asked.

"In both cases, we were talking about how Danielle's death would impact the upcoming show. Both of them worried about the emotional toll her death has taken and what bad luck the others might construe from the murder. It seems that, given this, Kit feels it is particularly important to get this Blessing from Above." The dowager snorted but said nothing else on the topic.

The group ate a light lunch and discussed the other interviews, none of which had yielded any relevant information. They were just finishing when Tabitha entered the restaurant with Rat and Melody. The little girl noticed the diners first and rushed up to the table, chattering excitedly, "Uncle Maxi, Wolfie, Granny, I got to ride a donkey. Her name was Mandy, and she was so sweet. I got to feed her a carrot, and then I went on her back all by myself. The man said that girls my age don't usually ride by themselves, and he thought Rat should ride with me. But I told him that I'm almost five and didn't need to be held." Her audience smiled; it wasn't hard to imagine the strong-willed Melody imposing her desires on a hapless donkey owner.

"Melody dear, that all sounds wonderful," the dowager answered. "I do hope that, after touching that animal, you washed your hands before eating lunch." This last observation was directed at Tabitha, who chose to ignore the implied criticism of her parenting skills.

Seeing the dowager happily ensconced with Wolf, Bear, and Langley, Tabitha felt more left out than ever. Why had she assumed that when she removed herself from the investigation, the dowager would somehow be excluded as well? In fact, Tabitha's absence was likely to spur the older woman to entwine herself even more deeply. Watching their cosy dining group, Tabitha was reminded of her childhood when, as the youngest of four daughters, she was regularly left out of conversations and games. Except, this time, Tabitha knew that she had excluded herself rather than having been left out. But she was unable to control her irrational response and said in a voice that was far sulkier than she intended, "Come, Melly. We shall take our lunch over by the window and leave them to their important conversations."

As Tabitha moved away with the children, the dowager looked at Wolf and rolled her eyes. The irony of this almost made him laugh out loud, given that usually she was the person over whom eyes were being rolled.

Langley, who was sitting next to Wolf, leaned over and said quietly, "Go to her."

Wolf had no idea what to say to Tabitha and wasn't convinced there was anything that would make the situation better, but he felt he had to try.

By the time Wolf approached the table by the window that Tabitha had chosen, she and the children were all seated, and she was looking at the menu and explaining the various options to Melody. Except for the fish and chip lunch the previous day, neither Melody nor Rat had ever eaten in a restaurant before. Rat looked particularly uncomfortable and kept running his finger around the collar of his shirt, one that Langley had purchased for him before leaving London.

Watching Rat squirm, Tabitha said gently but firmly, "Rat, do try to sit still and not fidget."

"It's just, well, I ain't…" the boy caught himself, "I have never eaten somewhere this nice before. I mean, I ate with Lord Langley at his house, but that was in the nursery with Melly, and there weren't all these knives and forks. What are they all for anyway?"

Tabitha laughed, and her face lit up in a way that Wolf realised he hadn't seen since he had received Arlene's telegram. But then, Tabitha caught sight of Wolf coming towards her, and her face immediately shuttered up again. "Lord Pembroke, how can I help you?" She said with a formality that pierced his heart.

Wolf didn't want to create a scene in front of Melody and Rat, so he ignored her use of his title, but he did ask if he could join them for a few minutes. Tabitha indicated that he might, and he sat down opposite her. Still, he had no idea how to break the ice. He thought about Langley's advice from the day before, took a deep breath and said, "Bear has discovered that Angie, Mickey D's wife, has a sister who lives in Brighton and runs a public house with her husband. He went there earlier, but they didn't have time to speak to him. We plan to return later. Apparently, the dowager plans to join us. I know that you do not wish to be involved in the investigation, but is there any way I could persuade you to accompany us and help manage her?"

Wolf knew this was a pretty thin excuse; the last person the dowager would listen to was Tabitha, but he played the only card he believed he had. Wolf could see Tabitha internally debate her answer as he watched a mix of emotions play out on her face. Finally, she said, "I believe I can manage to help you in this small way." Then her features softened, and she said with a new lightness to her tone, "I certainly don't want to miss witnessing Mama in such a setting. I may be dining out on that story for some time to come."

"There is only one problem," Wolf confessed. "Lady Pembroke has decided that she is prepared to forgo her afternoon social calls in favour of accompanying us but plans for you to still accompany Lily in her stead."

Tabitha snorted derisively, "That was her plan, was it? She sets up these visits that no one but she wants to make with people none of us know, and then she excuses herself and leaves me to make strained conversation with total strangers. I don't think so." Tabitha paused, then said wickedly, "You may tell Lady Pembroke that I will join you this afternoon, and so will not be available for social calls."

Wolf's first impulse was to question why he needed to be the bearer of that news. But looking at the tilt of Tabitha's head and the slightly mocking, questioning look on her face, he realised he couldn't fail this test and said, "Of course, I'll be happy to pass that news along." He looked at the large grandfather clock in the corner of the room, "It's thirty minutes past one already. I believe that if we are to miss the evening rush, we need to leave here in no more than an hour. Can you manage that?" Tabitha assured him that she and the children would get something light to eat, and she would be ready to meet them all in the hotel lobby in an hour.

"Then let me leave you to your lunch and go and relay this information to Lady Pembroke," Wolf said. He walked back to the other table, aware that all their eyes had been on him the entire time. He sat back down and said in as nonchalant a voice as possible, "Tabitha will accompany us to see Jeanie this afternoon."

"She can't do that," the dowager exclaimed. "Tabitha must make the social calls we'd agreed on."

Wolf knew that the dowager alone had been the instigator of their planned afternoon visits but chose not to point that out. Instead, he mustered his nerve and told the dowager, "Then I suggest that you send around your calling card explaining you will not be able to visit. Either that, or you could change your mind and accompany Lady Lily after all."

The dowager's face turned a beet red, her mouth pursed in anger, and her eyes became hard as steel; she was not used to being thwarted and certainly wasn't used to being told what to do. She tapped her fingers on the table, conflicted as to her next move. This was a chess game she wasn't used to playing. Finally, with her voice far calmer than her manner suggested, the dowager decided, "I will send my cards saying that I am fighting a slight head cold. No one wants to entertain guests who are sniffling into their tea. I will go and make arrangements with the hall porter now. Though I must say, this is all very inconsiderate and selfish on Tabitha's part."

The dowager rose from the table and made her way back to the hotel lobby. When she was safely out of earshot, Langley said, "Well played. What did you say to the other Lady Pembroke that persuaded her to join us?"

"I'm not entirely sure," Wolf confessed. "But I believe that what finally won her over was anticipating the Dowager

Countess of Pembroke in a public house and all the humour that might arise from observing such a situation." Langley and Bear chuckled.

The hotel was barely half a mile from the Cock and Bull public house, but Wolf anticipated the dowager's unwillingness to walk. She had very strong views about the kind of people who felt it necessary to perambulate the streets. And so, Wolf left to ensure the carriage would be available for their use. The three men had agreed that with the dowager and Tabitha both going, there wasn't room in the carriage or a need for Langley to accompany them as well as Bear. He was happy to spend the afternoon working with Melly on her reading and Rat on his studies.

CHAPTER 14

An hour later, Tabitha appeared in the hotel lobby. Wolf wasn't sure how she had managed to order and eat lunch with the children, then return to her room in time to change and meet him so promptly. In fact, she was earlier than the dowager, who caused them to leave a full fifteen minutes past their planned departure time.

Tabitha had changed into her plainest, simplest dress and short jacket and had removed all of her jewellery. She understood the importance of not standing out when visiting an establishment like the Cock and Bull. However, the dowager seemed to have a very different idea. Very different, in fact. As the dowager approached them from the lobby lift, Tabitha and Wolf's eyes met. Tabitha's look said, "How could you fail to suggest an appropriate outfit?" and Wolf's very shamefaced look replied, "I'm an idiot." In fact, rather than dressing down, the dowager seemed to have gone out of her way to look as rich as possible. She was wearing diamonds that were more appropriate for a ballroom than an afternoon visit anywhere, let alone a working man's public house and a very fine-looking fur stole.

"Mama, diamonds may not be the best choice for this afternoon's visit," Tabitha said carefully.

"Why on earth not? I want these people to know who they are dealing with. Nothing says wealth and power like diamonds. Anyway, Mr Doherty has assured me that I might walk through Whitechapel in diamonds in perfect safety."

"This is Brighton, not Whitechapel," Tabitha pointed out.

"I do not doubt that Mr Doherty's influence stretches at least as far as the south coast," the dowager insisted. "And anyway, we have Mr Bear with us. He will stay close to me, and no one will dare lay a hand on my person."

While she was probably correct, it was an unnecessary risk and could put their entire interview in jeopardy. Wolf stepped in, "Lady Pembroke, I must insist that you return those diamonds to your room. The key to a successful interview is that people be put at ease and not feel at all threatened. Rubbing their noses in how much richer and more powerful you are to them will not be at all helpful."

The dowager gave Wolf a long, hard look, "Jeremy, you have been very domineering recently and have now taken the liberty of telling me what to do twice in one afternoon. I do not like this behaviour. Not. One. Bit." However, she did turn back to the lift, returning five minutes later without the diamonds but still wearing the stole.

Bear had chosen to go on ahead; the carriage might be large enough for four people, but not when one of those people was his size. Wolf agreed. By the time the dowager returned to the lobby and they were underway in the carriage, Bear would likely beat them to the public house.

Again, the carriage ride was so brief that it had barely been worth the effort to get in and out of it. However, there were some battles not worth fighting, Wolf thought as he handed the dowager down the carriage steps. She descended with condescension worthy of the Queen herself deigning to visit the tenements of London.

The Cock and Bull looked as if it had been standing for hundreds of years; its bricks painted black for the top half of the building and white for the rest. An impressive, large brass gaslight hung over the sturdy oak door, and a wrought iron sign complete with the heads of a cock and a bull hung off the side of the building. While most of the streets in The Lanes were too narrow to allow a carriage through, luckily, the pub was at an intersection with a larger street they were able to navigate down.

Bear was waiting for them, leaning on the wall next to the door. It was not even three o'clock in the afternoon, so for the most part, the people out were merely locals going about their business. But if the occasional ne'er-do-well in the crowds had any thoughts about the toffs who had turned up, those thoughts were quickly dispelled when Wolf greeted the enormous and terrifying-looking Bear.

Leading the way into the Cock and Bull, Wolf was relieved to see that the public bar was mostly empty. One scruffy old man was nursing a pint of ale in a corner, but besides that, they had timed their visit well. Bear stood leaning on the bar, and behind it stood a woman polishing glasses. There could be no doubt this was Angie's sister Jeanie; the women looked so similar they could have been twins. She looked up as they entered, gave the same cheerful smile that always greeted Wolf when he visited Mickey D's house, and said, "Welcome. You must be the visitors Bear has told me about. Why don't you go through to the saloon bar where we won't be disturbed." As she said this, Jeanie pointed to a door off to the side and disappeared, presumably to meet them in the saloon.

"What is that smell?" the dowager asked in too loud a voice.

Replying at a much lower volume, Tabitha replied, "Ale and stale smoke, mostly. Trust me, this smells much better than the other public houses I've been in."

The dowager snorted in reply, then added, again too loudly, "I'm rather disappointed with the lack of people here. I'd hoped to mingle with the masses."

"We came now precisely because it would be quiet. Which I believe Wolf had already explained when you insisted on being in the party," Tabitha hissed, rather more vehemently than she intended.

By this time, they were following Wolf and Bear through the door to the saloon, but the dowager had time to hiss back, "I benevolently offered my services. You are the one who forced yourself into the outing." Tabitha chose to ignore this last statement, and anyway, there wasn't time to answer.

Jeanie was now behind the bar in the saloon and asked, "Can I get anyone anything to drink?"

Everyone declined except for the dowager, who asked, "What is the usual tipple in an establishment such as this?"

If Jeanie wondered at the condescension of the tone, she was polite enough to control her reaction and instead answered, "Ale or stout, mostly, for the men. Usually, a small beer for the ladies, sometimes cider."

"A small beer? What an intriguing name. I've never had any kind of beer. I will take a small beer then, madam."

Wolf, Tabitha, and Bear all exchanged glances. It seemed the dowager was determined to make as much of her afternoon's "adventure" as possible, even if the pub's emptiness didn't afford her the audience she had been hoping for. If Jeanie was pouring drinks anyway, then Wolf and Bear decided they might as well each have an ale. Tabitha declined.

"Tabitha, you really aren't an adventurous soul, are you?" the dowager said tauntingly. "You really should follow my lead and be more open to experiences outside of the cultured, intellectual ones offered by aristocratic society."

Tabitha glanced at Jeanie to see if she had heard this snobbish slight to her public house and social circle. But if the cheerful landlady had heard, she was wise enough to ignore the comment. Instead, she pulled a small glass of the lighter ale preferred by many of her female customers and two regular ales for Wolf and Bear. She then came around the bar and joined them at a small but mercifully clean and non-sticky table she'd indicated they should sit around.

The dowager sniffed at her drink, then took a small, hesitant sip. It was such a small sip that Tabitha wondered if she'd even drunk any. However, whatever little she may have tasted was clearly enough that the dowager was emboldened to take another, larger sip. And then another. Finally, lowering her glass, she pronounced, "This is delightful. I'm enjoying the somewhat bitter edge it has. Why on earth has this drink been limited to the working classes?"

Stifling a smirk, Wolf replied with a straight face, "I believe that provisions have been made recently so that select members of the middle class are also able to enjoy it."

The dowager narrowed her eyes, sure that she was being mocked but unsure how. Instead, she replied, "Jeremy, I believe I shall task you with working with Manning to ensure I have a regular supply of this small beer." She paused, considering her request. "There are various lunch dishes I believe would complement it beautifully. I'm thinking in particular of cook's cheese and onion pie. Of course, that isn't a refined enough dish to serve to guests, but I must confess to being rather partial to it when I dine alone," she said with a guilty giggle.

The vision of the Dowager Countess of Pembroke secretly indulging in the rather plebeian meal of cheese and onion pie accompanied by a glass of beer was so delicious that Tabitha made a mental note to tell Langley and Lily on their return. Though why on earth did the woman feel it appropriate to task the Earl of Pembroke with procuring her libations?

Jeanie nodded her head at the dowager's appreciation of her beverage and asked, "How can I help you all? Bear told me it has something to do with the death of that poor actress."

"Yes. We understand that the theatre company often drinks in your pub and, in fact, held their celebration here on the night of the murder. But beyond your impressions of them, we'd hoped, well…" Wolf paused. Was there an appropriate way to suggest to someone that you hoped they might have some of the same questionable contacts as their criminal relatives? Finally, realising there was no good way to sugarcoat the question, he said, "During my recent investigations, I've found that your brother-in-law can be a very useful source of information and connections in Whitechapel. I find myself without such a source in Brighton, and I wondered…" he stopped again.

Jeanie, taking pity on him, picked up his train of thought, "You wondered if Paddy and I could be the same source of information in Brighton as Mickey is in London?" Wolf nodded. Jeanie laughed, "Well, unlike Mickey, Paddy and I run a clean business here. However, you don't run a pub for more than twenty years without meeting a character or two and hearing a thing here and there. And Brighton isn't London; it's a much smaller pond. Most criminals have probably passed through here at some point for a pint of something."

The landlady smoothed the apron she was wearing and lowered her eyes for a moment, then raising them, she looked Wolf in the eye and said, "I heard what you did for Seamus. He's a good lad, for the most part. He's our nephew as well, you know." This was news to Wolf, and the surprised look on his face made this clear. Jeanie laughed, "I married Mickey's younger brother, Paddy. Seamus is the son of their sister, Maria. We help our own, so whatever you need, if it's in my power to help, I will. And so will Paddy."

As she said these words, a booming voice said from behind the bar, "Now, what are you promising on my behalf, lass?"

They all looked around to see a younger version of Mickey D, blue eyes twinkling, hair greyer than Mickey's, which was mostly white, beaming at them. If Jeanie looked like Angie's twin, Paddy had the same roguish but quite avuncular look as his brother. It was quite disconcerting to see this pair, a younger but otherwise uncannily similar version of the London gangster and his wife.

"Come in and sit down, Paddy. I was just telling his lordship here that we'll help him in any way we can in his investigation."

Paddy came into the saloon. He pulled a chair over to the table they were grouped around. Everyone introduced themselves with the dowager adding, "I hope you're even half the delight your brother is, Mr Doherty. I must admit that I can't remember the last time I was so charmed by someone. And, of course, the equally delightful Mrs Doherty."

"Aye, Mick had mentioned the dinner party with a bunch of swells. It seems he was just as taken with you, m'lady."

"Yes, in fact, your brother guaranteed me safe passage through the streets of Whitechapel at any time, even while wearing my diamonds. I wonder if you can make the same assurances in Brighton." At this statement, the dowager looked pointedly at Wolf. It was clear she hadn't forgotten or forgiven his demand that she remove her jewels.

Paddy chuckled, "I'm sorry, m'lady, but I don't have quite the power that Mick does. The best I can offer is that if your diamonds get stolen, I've a fair idea who in Brighton took them. But my best advice is, try to keep them out of the hands of the local coves."

The dowager looked to Wolf to interpret. "A cove is a thief," he explained, secretly happy that Paddy had reinforced his own earlier advice about the diamonds.

"Ah, yet another word to add to my growing criminal vocabulary," the dowager exclaimed eagerly.

Attempting to steer the conversation back to the matter at hand, Wolf explained the little they knew about Danielle's murder, Robert Charles' arrest, and their investigation so far into the theatre company. Paddy and Jeanie let him talk without interruption, but once he was done, Jeanie commented, "The victim, Miss Mapp, didn't come in here to drink with the others. I'd see her on the street sometimes, and of course, I recognised who she was because she stood out, you know. The large, dark-skinned fellow, Robert Charles, you said his name is. He came in with the rest of them occasionally. They've always called him Bobby."

"What were your impressions of him?" Tabitha asked.

Jeanie thought for a moment, then answered, "He always seemed like a very gentle man. Despite his size, he struck me as the type who wouldn't hurt a fly. He seemed a little slow, and the others would sometimes tease him for it. But it mostly seemed like good-natured ribbing. They didn't seem to hold his skin colour against him. Though, of course, many in here would mutter into their drinks. But he was large enough that no one was stupid enough to say anything to his face."

"What do you make of Mr Bailey?" Wolf asked. The man had seemed all joviality the two times they had met him, but was this the full picture?

Paddy and Jeanie both chuckled, "Yes, our Kit Bailey. Quite a character, isn't he?" Paddy answered. "He arrived in town more than twenty years ago. It was definitely before we owned this place. I was just working here then. But I remember him, right enough. He started as an itinerant actor, picking up a part here or there. Even back then, the company liked to drink here, and he would often join them."

"When did he come to own the theatre?" Wolf asked.

"Ha! He doesn't own it. He leases it. But he does run the company. He probably took that over about fifteen years ago. He'd been a permanent member of the company for some time by then. Along with his acting, he'd been responsible for staging some of the shows for quite a while. Who ran the company back then? Do you remember, Jeanie luv?"

"Yes, don't you remember, it was old Cameron Cook. He died of some kind of apoplexy, and the theatre owner offered the lease to Kit. It was quite a step up for him, but he pulled it off somehow. I heard some grumblings and rumours at the time. But he's done a fine job from what we can see. Now, it's hard to imagine the Royal under anyone else's command." Jeanie continued, "And to answer your question, as far as I've ever seen, Kit is all that he appears to be at first meeting: a loud, rowdy, cheerful man. I've heard the company griping on occasion. But no more than any workers do about the boss."

Tabitha was curious, "What do they gripe about?"

"The normal: the plays he chooses, the hours he expects them to rehearse, their pay, that kind of thing. But when he's in here drinking with them, they seem genuinely fond of the man, and I've never felt any particular tension."

This comment prompted Wolf to go back to one of their original reasons for coming, "We understand the theatre company or most of them were here the night of the murder. But we also understand that Miss Mapp, Mr Charles, and Mr Bailey were all absent." Wolf remembered that Kit had said he had popped in for a few minutes, but in Wolf's years of investigating, he'd found that it was sometimes helpful to say something that he knew wasn't true in order to gauge the reaction. Not that he thought that Paddy and Jeanie weren't telling the truth, but it was a technique that he'd discovered could spur some interesting reactions on occasion.

Jeanie thought for a moment, then said, "Are you sure he wasn't here? I could have sworn he came in. In fact, I remember him having some words with that Merryweather chappie. From the looks of it, things got a little heated there. Then Kit stormed out."

Now that was interesting, Wolf thought. That definitely wasn't Kit's version of the evening. And Merryweather Frost hadn't mentioned anything about a disagreement either. "Did you manage to catch anything of what they were talking about, by any chance?"

Jeanie blushed, "It's not that I was eavesdropping or anything," she said in an embarrassed tone. "But they were standing apart from the rest, leaning on the bar, and I couldn't help but hear. From what I can tell, they were arguing about money. It sounded like Kit owed Merryweather and was asking for more time to pay. Honestly, that was all I heard. I got called over to the other end of the bar, and the next thing I knew, Kit had stormed out."

"Did Merryweather leave as well?" Wolf asked.

"No, he went back to the group. When I looked over a few minutes later, he was all smiles again."

"What time did they all leave?"

"Oh, I couldn't say, but it was late. I remember that they were some of the last to leave. They were all joking that they could sleep late the next day. What time do you think that was, Paddy?"

"I remember throwing Joe Grant out past one in the morning, and they weren't here then. When did they start singing?"

"Singing?" Tabitha asked.

"Yes, it was a bit of a tradition with them. On the last night of a show, they'd come in here for drinks, and at some point, someone would yell for a tune, and they'd belt out some of the songs from whatever show had just closed," Paddy explained. "That young 'un, Jaqueline, I think she acted as Danielle's understudy. Well, she has a fine set of pipes on her, I can tell you that. I never had the pleasure of hearing Danielle sing, but it's hard to imagine she was better than Jackie. The crowd here always wanted her to sing."

At this, the dowager shot a pointed look at Wolf as if to say, "See, I told you it was the understudy!" He ignored her look.

Paddy continued, "I remember looking at the clock when she started singing, and it was about half past eleven by then. Normally, they'd sing a few songs, someone would buy them another round of drinks, and then they were done for the night. So, if they were gone before I threw Joe out, then maybe it was about half past twelve. Or thereabouts."

Paddy and Jeanie didn't have much more to tell. They promised to keep an ear to the ground and send word to Wolf if they thought of anything else. The dowager threatened to return for another small beer before she left Brighton.

CHAPTER 15

During the short carriage ride back to the hotel, despite her reluctance to get involved in the investigation, Tabitha couldn't help herself and asked, "I don't know anything of your interviews with the theatre company, but was anything that Paddy and Jeanie said useful?"

Wolf thought about the question. The only thing they had found out was that Kit hadn't been entirely honest, or at the very least, had made a sin of omission when he'd failed to mention his argument with Merryweather Frost. But he may have also considered it unrelated to the matter of Danielle's murder. They'd had a few things confirmed, but even knowing the time that the theatre company had left the pub didn't really help. He answered, "I'm not sure. We now know the time everyone was there until, or thereabouts, but we have no idea when Danielle was killed, so that doesn't really help us."

"Do you even know for sure she was killed that night?" Tabitha asked.

Wolf considered the question and realised that they'd been making an unfounded assumption about the murder. "No, we don't know that for sure. No one saw Danielle after the show ended, but that didn't seem unusual. It's clear she didn't socialise with the rest of the company outside of the theatre. But someone must have missed her, surely?" He paused, nervous about his next statement, "Arlene, Lady Archibald, didn't know much about Danielle's life. It seems their friendship was quite a circumscribed one in many ways."

Wolf looked up warily, unsure what Tabitha's reaction might

be at the mention of Arlene's name. Whether it was the dowager's presence in the carriage or regret at her earlier churlishness, Tabitha replied, "I believe you need to talk to Lady Archibald again. Does she even know that you have decided to investigate?"

Tabitha was right, he did need to talk to Arlene. Wolf was embarrassed to realise he had never told Arlene he was looking into Danielle's murder. To be fair, he doubted she had taken his uncertainty about doing so seriously. And he was sure that she'd taken for granted that she would get her way ultimately. Nevertheless, Wolf acknowledged to himself that his belief that he could investigate the murder yet have nothing more to do with Arlene was both naive and cowardly. Moreover, he could see how any reluctance to be in the same room as his first love would make Tabitha more suspicious, not less.

Considering Tabitha's words, he pondered that, while he might have to visit Arlene, he could provide himself with some measure of protection against her, "You are right. I believe I will visit her tomorrow. Lady Pembroke, would you care to accompany me?"

It wasn't often that the dowager was willingly invited into an interview rather than having to cajole and threaten, and the offer momentarily took her aback. She quickly recovered and replied, "Of course, Jeremy. It would be most inappropriate for you to visit a young widow alone." The dowager was clearly choosing to forget that Wolf had done just that the day before and continued, "And of course, I'd be delighted to see the charming Lady Archibald again. In fact, we must take Lily with us."

Wolf could see his plan to get information out of Arlene spiralling out of control, "While I'm sure that Lady Archibald would be more than happy to host you and Lady Lily for tea at some point, I believe our visit tomorrow should be just the two of us. I need to get information out of her, not discuss this season's fashions." The dowager snorted, but she didn't argue. Wolf glanced over at Tabitha. Would it be absurd to think she might agree to accompany them?

Tabitha caught the look Wolf gave her and knew what he was thinking. The truth was, she had been happier that afternoon than she had in days. She enjoyed being part of the investigative team again and had been wondering since they left the pub if she wanted to backtrack on her refusal to help with this case. Tabitha had not liked the person she had been since they first planned to travel to Brighton. She had been petty and childish. What kind of role model was she being for Melody and Rat? Melly might not realise that Tabitha wasn't investigating with Wolf, but Rat soon would, if he hadn't already.

However, Tabitha was also realistic about the dynamic that had sprung up between her and Lady Archibald. It had quickly become adversarial even without Wolf's presence. She knew that with Wolf in the room, the woman would become even more territorial, and that would be counterproductive to what they needed to achieve. Just as she had made a decision, the carriage arrived back at the hotel. Wolf helped the dowager out first and then held out his hand to Tabitha. On descending to the gravel drive, Tabitha kept hold of his hand for a moment and said quietly so the dowager, who luckily had ploughed ahead, couldn't hear, "I'm sorry, Wolf. I have behaved appallingly, and if you can forgive me, I would like to help with the investigation."

Wolf's heart leapt at Tabitha's words. He kissed her hand and looked deeply into her eyes, "Nothing would make me happier."

Tabitha smiled but added, "However, I do not think I should attend Lady Archibald with you tomorrow." Seeing Wolf's smile quickly fade, she hurried to say, "Not because I don't want to help, but because I believe my presence will be inexpedient to our goal. She believes I am a rival for your affection, and I do not doubt that she will spend more time trying to prove her pre-eminence in your regard than she will honestly answering your questions. And you will be distracted by concern for my feelings." Wolf, realising she was right, acknowledged the truth of her words.

Dinner that evening was a far jollier affair than it had been the previous one. Lily, thrilled at the reprieve from social calls that had unexpectedly come her way, had spent her afternoon curled up with a book and now was very cheerful. The dowager was eagerly anticipating her outing with Wolf the next day, and the tension between Wolf and Tabitha that had put everyone's nerves on edge for days had finally dissipated.

Over dessert, a delicious lemon mousse, the dowager said, "Now that Tabitha has stopped sulking and we are all officially investigating the murder, I suggest we pull the corkboard out of the luggage and set it up. In my room."

Tabitha, Wolf, and Langley all looked at each other. The dowager was staking her claim. She was ensuring there would be no repetition of events in Edinburgh when Tabitha and Wolf had conspired to keep her out of the command centre of their investigation and away from the corkboard covered with clues. Of course, then, their motivation had been mostly about keeping her in the dark as to the true nature of her granddaughter's relationship with the victim. But it was clear the dowager had learned her lesson and would never again give them the chance to marginalise her. Realising that her involvement in this investigation was inevitable at this point – Wolf had been the one to invite her to join him when he talked to Arlene – they all agreed with her plan, however reluctantly.

The dowager, emboldened by her win, suggested that there was no time like the present. She was sure it wouldn't be difficult for one of the servants to dig up the corkboard, and they could spend their time after dinner talking through what they had learned so far. Again, there wasn't the collective will to argue, and so, within the hour, they were assembled in her sitting room. Lily had excused herself, eager to get back to her book.

Tabitha had managed to collect a stack of plain note cards from the hall porter. Wolf and Langley had spent the time while they were waiting for the corkboard to be brought up, bringing Tabitha up to speed with their findings so far. As they spoke, she created notecards.

Tapping a pen against her lips as she tended to when deep

in thought, Tabitha considered the open questions. "I believe the biggest unknown so far is when the murder happened. We've been assuming it took place on the night of the final performance, but we don't know that."

Wolf agreed with her logic but pondered, "But why would Danielle have been in the theatre after that? The entire company had the next few days off, which is why the body wasn't found immediately. I think one question we need on the board is 'Who has keys to the theatre?' Because either she was killed that evening, or she or someone else opened up the theatre another day."

"I know you've said that you gleaned very little from your interviews of the theatre company, but was there nothing useful?" Tabitha pressed.

"I don't know how many times I need to mention the understudy, Julianne, or Jennifer, but she clearly has a motive," the dowager interjected stridently.

Glad to see that the dowager's sitting room had a couple of decanters, Wolf stood up and went to investigate what was on offer. From what he could tell, there was cognac and sherry. He enquired what the others wanted, and after pouring himself, Langley and Tabitha cognac, and the dowager sherry, he sat back down. "Why don't we put the understudy up on the board," he said in a conciliatory tone. Placated, for the time being, the dowager sipped on her sherry.

"What other questions do we need answers to?" Tabitha asked.

Bear, who hadn't eaten with them in the dining room but had been conscripted for the post-dinner war room session, said, "Well, there is the question of why Mr Bailey didn't mention the argument he had that night."

"Wolf and I discussed that, and it may be no more than it not seeming relevant to the murder," Tabitha explained. "He told us that he went and had a quick celebratory drink with the rest of the theatre company and then left after about twenty minutes, and Paddy and Jeanie confirmed that. But you're right; we've learned never to discount any piece of information too soon. So, I'll put it on a card for now." Tabitha paused and said, "Tell me again about Danielle's young admirer that Kit talked about."

Wolf thought back on their conversation, "Well, Kit said that Danielle had a lot of male admirers, which, of course, isn't uncommon in the theatre. But there was one who was particularly insistent. I believe he described him as a 'young, snot-nosed, arrogant ass.' He said he was a toff, but that could mean anything. Perhaps he was nothing more than a well-spoken law clerk."

The dowager rubbed her hands in glee at this information, "Why didn't you mention this earlier? A crime of passion! That's even better than the understudy as the murderer. We must begin the search for this miscreant as soon as possible. How do we track him down?"

"That's a good question," Wolf conceded. "Perhaps Arlene will know more about him."

The dowager was now like a child before Christmas and seemed barely able to contain her excitement, "I can just envision it now; the wastrel tries to force himself upon her, and she resists. Enraged at her resistance, he chokes her to death. Then, distraught at what he's done, he panics and stuffs the body in the nearest trunk."

Tabitha tried not to giggle at this melodramatic theorising; whether or not she was suited to investigating crimes, there seemed little doubt the dowager had missed her calling as a writer of penny dreadfuls. However, melodramatic rendition aside, the point was a valid one, and so Tabitha wrote on a notecard: Who was Danielle's ardent admirer? Wolf gathered the cards she'd written so far and started to pin them on the corkboard. They'd decided that when they weren't gathered to review it, the dowager would hide the board in her wardrobe where a maid wouldn't think of looking.

Standing in front of the board and reviewing what they knew so far, Wolf said, "There is one more thing we don't have the answer to: where was Robert Charles that evening? We know that he wasn't at the celebration, but if we could discover a credible alibi, perhaps we could persuade the inspector to release him, for now at least."

Turning back to the group, he said, "This is what I think we should all do tomorrow: Langley, you go to Danielle's residence tomorrow morning with Tabitha. Hopefully, you can swing around those earl credentials and can do some kind of search of her home."

"I'm happy to do that. Did she rent rooms or have her own establishment? And if it's the latter, would the servants still be there to let us in?"

"Langley," Wolf said with a slightly mocking air, "given your role in British Intelligence, I'm going to assume that you know how to pick a lock, at the very least." Cagily, Langley acknowledged he had those skills and that he and Tabitha would be able to adjust to whatever situation they came upon.

"Wonderful, then while you do that, I will take Lady Pembroke with me to visit the wardrobe mistress, Mrs Malloy," Wolf said, surprising the dowager that, yet again, she didn't have to force her way into inclusion. Seeing her evident surprise, Wolf explained, "It seems this Mrs Malloy is still quite affected from having found the body. This may be a situation that requires a more delicate touch than mine." Silently, Tabitha questioned whether the dowager's touch could ever be described as delicate, but she kept that doubt to herself.

"Then, in the afternoon," Wolf continued, "we will make our afternoon visit to see Lady Archibald. Lady Pembroke, perhaps you would be good enough to send your calling card tomorrow to alert her to our arrival." Their plans made, they adjourned for the night.

CHAPTER 16

The following morning, Tabitha and Langley set out for Danielle Mapp's house. Unfortunately, the hotel only had one carriage for use by guests, and there was no argument that the dowager would be the one using it. The hall porter assured Langley that he would be able to hail a hackney cab easily, and indeed, they had only a short wait before one pulled up outside the hotel.

Danielle lived near Preston Park, on Stanford Avenue. The hall porter estimated it would be a short trip and suggested they pay the driver to wait for them. As promised, the ride wasn't long, and before Tabitha knew it, they had pulled up on a quiet street just by the southernmost entrance to the park. With its decorative iron railings and tree-lined streets, Tabitha could see how this would be a charming place to live, enough outside of the centre of Brighton that Danielle might find some respite and peace.

The cab pulled up outside of an attractive-looking, yellow-bricked, semi-detached villa. It was three storeys with a large bay window on each level. The house and its neighbours on the street projected an air of solid, middle-class prosperity. The front door had a large, brass door knocker. Langley knocked on the door. Tabitha and Langley stood there for a few seconds, and then he rapped again.

After a couple more raps, it seemed clear no one was coming. There was a gate to the side of the house leading to its back garden. The gate was unlocked, and Langley led the way to the back of the house. The garden was simply laid out but well taken care of. They made their way to the back door and knocked again. Langley had no desire to scare a servant unnecessarily, and so he made a point of looking in the windows to see whether there was any evidence of habitation. Finally, he took out a set of lockpicks and easily opened the door to the kitchen.

The kitchen was the first and clearest indication that the house had been abandoned for some time. It was cold and lacking any of the smells that would normally hang around after baking or roasting. Everything was tidy, so it seemed as if the house hadn't been left in a hurry, but there was evidence of dust gathering on some of the surface, indicating it had been empty for more than a few days.

Leaving the kitchen and entering a hallway, the first room they came upon was a medium-sized dining room. Everything about the room matched their impressions of the house so far: solid, well-made, but not luxurious furnishings, nothing out of place, but dust starting to build up on the table and sideboard.

Increasingly sure there were no servants in residence, Langley stopped talking in whispered tones and said to Tabitha, "It seems to be abandoned. If you don't mind, why don't you go upstairs and see if you can find Miss Mapp's bedroom, and I'll see if there is a study of some kind."

Tabitha indicated her willingness to search the upper level alone, and they parted ways. There were two large bedrooms upstairs. The one in the front was prettily furnished but lacking any personal items. Tabitha assumed this was a guest room. By contrast, the room in the back clearly proclaimed itself a lady's sanctuary. The predominant colours were various shades of pink. The fabric choices spoke of the feel of luxury, but on a budget; the curtains were taffeta, the bedspread chenille. A heavy, somewhat cloying scent of perfume hung in the air, and Tabitha quickly traced this to a bottle on the dressing table.

The room wasn't untidy, but it was very busy. The bed had a multitude of decorative pillows on it, each in some shade of pink and decorated with lace. The dressing table was covered in bottles, brushes and hair ornaments. Something Tabitha was interested to see on the dressing table was a large, framed photographic cabinet card. It showed a young girl, she assumed Danielle, with a very dark-skinned, handsome man. The man was flashing a wide, bright smile that Tabitha was sure captivated audiences because she assumed this was Danielle's father, the famous actor Jonas Mapp.

Tabitha picked up the photo and studied the young Danielle. Based on her dress and loose hair, she guessed the actress must have been no more than eleven in the photo. It was clear even at that young age that the woman had been a beauty. She had almond-shaped eyes and a heart-shaped face. Her long dark hair hung in tight spiral curls over her shoulders. Unlike her father, she wasn't smiling, but she looked happy as she clung to Jonas' hand. Tabitha wondered why Danielle's Swedish mother wasn't also in the photo.

Despite feeling guilty at the intrusion, Tabitha made sure to search the room thoroughly. She went through every drawer, searched in the wardrobe, and even checked under the bed and mattress. But she found nothing. There were no love letters, no diary, nothing that might give any insight into Danielle's inner life. Tabitha hoped Langley was having more luck downstairs.

Leaving the master bedroom, Tabitha went up to the third floor. This seemed to be where the servants had lived. The emptiness of the rooms confirmed that the staff were long gone. Finally, convinced she would find nothing useful, Tabitha went back down to the ground floor in search of Langley. After discovering a comfortable parlour at the front of the house, Tabitha finally found him in what seemed to be the study. Unlike the other rooms, this one was a mess. Books had been pulled off the shelves, and papers were strewn over the desk.

"I'm assuming you didn't make this mess," Tabitha said.

Langley replied rather sardonically, "No, I did not. Clearly, someone was looking for something in here. The question is, did they find it?"

Tabitha abhorred a mess and couldn't stop herself from reshelving books and picking up papers from the floor. "Have you found anything interesting?"

"Well, certainly, we can add a bit more colour to our picture of Miss Mapp. She leased this home rather than owned it. It seems that it came mostly furnished. The lease has been paid through this month, which might explain why the house has been left untouched so far. She kept meticulous accounts, and the servants were due to be paid around the time she was murdered. I'm guessing that, with their mistress gone, they realised their pay was not going to be forthcoming, and all left."

Langley showed Tabitha an account book and pointed to some columns, "From what I can see, she lived within her means, but only just. She seems to have been careful with her household and her money, but it doesn't look as if there was much left at the end of the month to put away as savings. Did you find anything upstairs?"

"Nothing of note. There was nothing more personal than her perfume and hairbrush. If she had a lover, there was no evidence of him in her room," Tabitha answered as she continued to arrange papers and clear up the mess around her. "Should we assume that whoever made this mess found what they were looking for?"

"I have no idea. I would like to know if the police came here and made any kind of search of the house. It's certainly possible they made this mess. However, based on the conversation we had with Inspector Maguire, I seriously doubt that they considered it worth their time to do so. They fingered their suspect very quickly and seemed convinced they had the right man."

Langley considered his words, then continued, "We know that the body wasn't found for a few days, so there was definitely time for someone to come here and cover their tracks. Of course, until the body was found, there would be no reason for the servants to consider their jobs in jeopardy. Was the house broken into while they were still in residence? It would be helpful if we could track her household staff down."

Tabitha continued flicking back and forth through the

account book, "From what I can see, she employed a housekeeper cum cook, a Mrs Channing, and a maid called Daisy. There are records of a gardener, but from what I can see, he only came twice a week. When I hire servants for Chesterton House, I always check references. Why don't we see whether she has reference letters or any other information that may provide clues about where we might find these servants." She stopped flicking through the book and added, "We should also talk to some of her neighbours. I know that my housekeeper and cook are friendly with neighbouring servants.

An extensive search through the drawers failed to turn up any further information about the staff. Finally, convinced they would find nothing else of use in Danielle Mapp's house, Tabitha and Langley let themselves out of the back door. Walking back out to the front, Langley asked, "When we talk to these neighbours, who are we introducing ourselves as? It's not always helpful to come on too strong with the. "I'm an earl," line. On the other hand, given our clothes, we will have a hard time passing ourselves off as anything other than the aristocrats we are. What story will be both believable and helpful?"

Tabitha considered the question, "Well, we're going to have a hard time persuading anyone we're Danielle's relatives." Her eyes ran up and down Langley's fine-tailored clothes, "And no one is going to believe you're a solicitor in that suit. Perhaps telling the truth, or some version of it, is the best course of action. We will say that a friend of the deceased has asked us, well asked you, to look into her death, and we would like to track down her servants. I can't really come up with anything more credible."

Langley agreed, and they decided to start with the villa that was the other half of Danielle's building. The villa was the mirror image of the one they had just been in, but one loud rap on its brass knocker and the door was quickly opened by a pretty young woman.

"May I help you?" she asked pleasantly enough.

"We would like to speak to the lady of the house," Tabitha explained. "Would that be you?"

The young woman confirmed that she was indeed the mistress of the house. But once they briefly gave their agreed-upon story, the woman shook her head and said, "I wish I could help you, but my husband and I only moved in two weeks ago. We never had the opportunity to meet our neighbour, and all of our servants are also new to the house."

Langley and Tabitha apologised for the interruption, and the young woman was just about to close the front door when she paused and said, "I haven't met all our neighbours yet, but Mrs Murphy from across the street was the first person to come over the day we moved in. Every street has that one spinster or widowed older woman who seems to spend all day peering out through her net curtains and knows everybody's business. I get the sense that, on this street, that woman is Mrs Murphy at number ten. If I were you, I might start with her." They thanked her for this suggestion, and she closed the door.

Walking out to the street, Tabitha looked across the road. If there had been any doubt as to which house number ten was, a quick movement at the window as if a curtain was hastily being moved indicated that Mrs Murphy lived there and was on watch. Tabitha did think to wonder how long the woman had been watching and whether she'd seen them go around the back of Danielle's house. She pointed out the house to Langley, and they started to cross the street.

"Even Mayfair has its Mrs Murphys," Tabitha said knowingly. "At Chesterton House, we have Lady Davenport. The class may be different, but the twitching curtains as they spy on neighbours are remarkably similar. I suggest that we make full use of our titles for this call. I suspect that Mrs Murphy will greatly enjoy having an earl and a countess in for tea and telling the story of it for many months to come. However," she cautioned, "if Lady Davenport is anything to go by, we must be sure not to say anything that we're not comfortable with the entire neighbourhood knowing by dinnertime."

"Duly noted," Langley said.

It was evident that Mrs Murphy had watched them cross the

street and walk up to her front door because Langley had barely knocked, and it was immediately opened. Mrs Murphy, because they assumed that is who the woman standing in front of them was, must have been in her late sixties. Her flint-grey hair was pulled back in a rather austere chignon, and her beady little dark eyes peered out behind the door suspiciously. "Who are you, and what do you want?" she demanded.

Langley turned on all the charm he had at his disposal and said, "Might you be Mrs Murphy? I am Maxwell Sandworth, the Earl of Langley, and my companion is the Countess of Pembroke."

Mrs Murphy's initial reaction to this introduction was to snort in disbelief, "An earl and a countess come to call on me on a Thursday morning? What kind of fool do you take me for? Who are you really, and what do you want?"

It hadn't occurred to Tabitha that they might not be believed. Thinking quickly, she pulled out her mother-of-pearl card case from her reticule and took out one of her engraved calling cards. She handed it to Mrs Murphy, who looked impressed at the clearly expensive card but still said, "Anyone can get cards made."

Tabitha said, "Mrs Murphy, perhaps if we could come in and talk, we might assure you that we are indeed who we say we are."

"Let you in so you can slit my throat and rob me blind? I don't think so," Mrs Murphy said, crossing her arms defiantly.

Tabitha and Langley exchanged glances. This was a scenario they hadn't accounted for. Trying another tack, Tabitha asked, "Could we talk to you here then, perhaps? We have been told that if anyone knows what is happening on this street, it's you."

If Tabitha had hoped this statement would flatter the older woman into cooperation, she was mistaken. The beady little eyes flashed with irritation, and the woman demanded, "Who has been calling me nosy? Is it that Mrs Smith at number fifteen? She thinks she is so much better than me because her grandfather used to make soap for the old King George when he was Prince Regent and first built the Pavilion. Or so she says."

It was clear this conversation was getting off-track quickly. Finally, trying the last trick in their arsenal, Tabitha said, "We are investigating the murder of your neighbour, Miss Mapp and need your help." This got Mrs Murphy's attention, and the door opened a little wider. The truth was that the newspapers had been quite light on the details of the murder, and Mrs Murphy was eager for new titbits. Particularly ones that no one else on the street knew yet. The chance for such valuable nuggets of gossip was too good to ignore, and with a quick look up and down at Langley, Mrs Murphy decided her chances of being murdered by him were slim enough and stepped back to let them enter her house.

Despite her reluctance to welcome potential murderers into her home, once Tabitha and Lord Langley were settled onto the overly flowery, rather lumpy sofa, Mrs Murphy forgot all about her suspicions. In fact, she decided rather quickly that they likely were the aristocrats they claimed to be. She liked to think she was a good judge of character, and certainly she knew she was an excellent judge of breeding. Her visitors' perfect manners and fine clothes smacked of gentry at the very least. Mrs Murphy quickly realised that she'd almost let a golden opportunity pass her by and given up the bragging rights to hosting some toffs for tea and being at the forefront of the murder investigation. She could never have forgiven herself.

On seeing her guests settled, however uncomfortably, on her sofa, Mrs Murphy bustled off to make tea. She had a maid of all work, but she only came in mornings, and so Mrs Murphy, who rarely entertained visitors, had to search through the kitchen to find some shortbread biscuits and quickly give the good china a rinse.

While she was in the kitchen, Langley whispered conspiratorially to Tabitha, "How do we politely ask a busybody what she knows without calling her a busybody?"

Tabitha smiled and replied, "Take your lead from me. Having spent quite a few afternoons with Lady Davenport, I believe I have the measure of Mrs Murphy."

The lady herself came back into the room bearing a tea tray a couple of minutes later. She poured the tea and offered around the shortbread. Finally, she settled in her favourite armchair and, while dunking her shortbread in her tea, asked, "So, you said you're investigating the murder. But you don't look like any policemen I've ever seen." She said this, looking pointedly at Tabitha and then chuckled, finding her own joke very amusing.

Langley answered, slipping easily into the languid, indolent earl persona that served him well when necessary, "Heaven forbid, my dear Mrs Murphy. I am the fifth Earl of Langley, not a Bobby. However, the countess and I have a personal interest in Miss Mapp's murder." Mrs Murphy leaned forward, but if she thought Langley would be confiding his closest kept secrets to her, she was to be disappointed, and he said no more about why they were investigating.

Tabitha picked up the questioning. She took a sip of tea, and then, looking over the teacup at the expectant gossip, she asked casually, "How long has Miss Mapp been your neighbour, Mrs Murphy?"

"Oh, now, let me see. It must have been at least five years ago because Mr Murphy, God bless his soul, was still alive. And I remember that because I recall saying to him that I'd heard that they have cannibals in Africa. But you know, it turns out she wasn't from Africa at all. Can you credit that? It turns out she was an American. Though, I don't know for sure that they don't have cannibals there as well. Anyway, Mr Murphy died four years ago last spring, so maybe five years, give or take."

Mrs Murphy took a breath, then continued, "And of course, I wasn't sure about her to begin with, and then when I heard she was an actress, well, you can imagine. What was I saying? Oh yes, well, in the end, she was a perfectly well-behaved neighbour. Kept to herself. There were no gentleman callers because that's always a worry with actresses, isn't it? And all in all, it was quite a shock when I heard what happened. Because you don't expect it with someone you know, do you now?"

As this monologue continued, Tabitha gave Langley a

knowing glance; she'd never had any doubt that it would be a matter of a simple question or two to wind Mrs Murphy up and then she'd tell them everything they wanted to know and more. So much more. But that was the price they had to pay.

Finally, Mrs Murphy took a long enough pause for breath that Tabitha was able to ask innocently, "Are Miss Mapp's servants still living in the house? We knocked on the door and even went around the back, but no one seemed to be around."

"Like rats deserting a sinking ship, that's how quickly they were out of here as soon as we got news of her death. I wouldn't have thought that of Sylvia Channing. My maid, Rachel, sometimes used to pop over there to borrow a cup of sugar or the like, and she was as surprised as anyone the way they just upped and left. Rachel did tell me that Mrs Channing, as she liked to call herself, had been planning to leave anyway. Apparently, she's been saving to open a bed and breakfast on the seafront. So, she was going to give her notice anyway. But even so. And I would have expected more from Daisy Jenkins. I've known her since she was a young 'un. Her mother is the housekeeper at the big house on the corner. There's no loyalty these days." Mrs Murphy sighed at the perfidy of the servant classes.

Langley exchanged a look with Tabitha. They had got the information they'd hoped for. How much longer until they could escape? Correctly interpreting his look, Tabitha put her teacup down. If she had learned nothing else from her mother, it was how to exit a social call gracefully. "Thank you so much for your hospitality, Mrs Murphy. I fear we have overstayed our welcome. She stood, and Langley followed her lead. Before Mrs Murphy knew what was happening, Tabitha had crossed the room, shaken her hand, and headed for the door.

Mrs Murphy watched them leave. It wasn't until she heard the front door slam behind them that she realised they hadn't told her anything about the murder that she didn't already know. Never one to dwell on the negatives of a situation, Mrs Murphy took another shortbread biscuit, dunked it into her tea, and consoled herself with the thought that she'd had an earl and countess over for tea, and wouldn't that make Mrs Smith green with envy.

CHAPTER 17

The visit to Mrs Malloy's daughter's house had been disappointingly unfruitful. The daughter, distracted by a screaming baby and a demanding toddler, had told Wolf and the dowager that her mother had needed more peace and quiet than she found staying with her grandchildren and so had upped and left a couple of days before to stay with her cousin out on the South Downs in a place called Saddlescombe. The daughter, Maddy, managed to disentangle herself from her toddler long enough to say that her mother had been thinking about retiring for a while and helping her cousin with her teashop. Finding a dead body had been the final straw that had made up her mind. Wolf considered the state of decomposition the body was likely to have been in by then and was very sympathetic to Mrs Malloy's anguish.

Wolf and the dowager were back in the carriage within fifteen minutes. "I have never been in a proletariat residence before," the dowager mused. "It was very noisy, wasn't it? I don't remember any of my children making those sounds." Wolf didn't point out that he was sure all of the dowager countess' children had cried and screamed just as much as Maddy's. However, the dowager had nursery maids, nannies, and governesses to deal with such things.

"Will we travel out to this Saddlescombe in search of Mrs Malloy?" the dowager continued.

Wolf thought about this question, "I'm not sure at this point. I'm assuming Inspector Maguire interviewed her when the body was found. It may be more expedient to have Langley pull a few strings and get a look at those case notes. Let's see how the rest of today's inquiries go and then see if it's worth having him call in a favour. Depending on what we read, we can decide if the trip is worthwhile."

"Does Maxwell really have that kind of power?" the dowager asked with genuine admiration. "And to think, I remember him as a knock-kneed brat in short trousers. I really should consider how I might best use my access to such power. There are definitely more than a few members of society I am sure have some deep, dark secrets that even I have not been able to ferret out." Wolf was as certain that Lord Langley would not be sharing any of those secrets with the dowager as he was certain there was little to be gained in pointing that out to her. So, he let the woman muse on the topic for the rest of the journey back to The Grand.

The two expeditionary arms of the investigation met back at the hotel for a working luncheon. Bear and a bored and irritated Lily joined them. The young woman had planned to use her grandmother's absence that morning to steal out and visit the Royal Pavilion Gardens. However, the short and fruitless visit to Mrs Malloy's daughter had returned the dowager to the hotel far sooner than her granddaughter had counted on, and the trip had been postponed.

Over poached sole with hollandaise sauce, the two groups took their turn relaying what their reconnaissance had uncovered. Wolf and the dowager went first because they had the least to report. When they were done, Wolf put forward his suggestion that Langley use his influence to get them access to the police case files.

"I have the authority to do that. But just be warned, we won't make any friends if I throw my weight around in this way. We should consider whether that is the best use of such firepower."

The dowager, who had battleground intuitions to rival the greatest generals, considered his warning and said, "Jeremy, I believe Maxwell's concern is one we should give serious weight to. Mrs Malloy found the body. What more can there be to her story? You are always the first person to counsel that the simplest explanation is usually the correct one. Let us assume, for now, that this woman likely has no more to tell and that we have more compelling avenues of examination. Not the least of which is identifying and locating this young scoundrel who is almost certainly our killer."

Wolf had no good reason to argue against this reasoning, and so the conversation turned to Tabitha and Langley's findings. They took turns recounting their observations from their exploration of Danielle Mapp's home. They then briefly described their conversation with Mrs Murphy. Both of them were building to the climax of their story: their hunt for the maid, Daisy Jenkins.

On leaving Mrs Murphy's house, Tabitha and Langley had walked to the large house on the corner, and when a plump, friendly-looking woman with a large ring of keys at her waist answered the door, they enquired if she was Mrs Jenkins. Unlike Mrs Murphy, Mrs Jenkins had taken one look at their clothes and deportment and did not doubt that Tabitha and Langley were the aristocracy they claimed to be. The family of the house was away for the week, but Mrs Jenkins had invited the couple on the doorstep into the house and had been happy to serve them tea in the drawing room and answer some questions.

Mrs Jenkins confirmed that her daughter, Daisy, had been Danielle's maid for approximately six months. She relayed that her daughter was very happy in the position and that Danielle had been a kind and undemanding mistress. She said that after the murder was discovered, Daisy had left Danielle's house and had stayed with her mother for a week before finding a new position in Bournemouth.

Wolf interrupted the narrative to ask, "Did Mrs Jenkins mention what Daisy and the housekeeper had thought when their mistress didn't come home for three days?"

Tabitha answered, "Apparently, it wasn't unheard of for Danielle to stay away for a night or two. While she usually gave her staff warning, neither the housekeeper, Mrs Channing, nor

Daisy felt they were owed such an explanation and so were not unduly worried."

"Did they have any idea where she spent the nights she was away?" Wolf asked.

"They did not. Mrs Jenkins confessed that there had been speculation of a lover, but they had no evidence of such."

The dowager, seizing on this comment, interjected, "Perhaps this young ne'er-do-well who murdered her had already taken her virtue on a previous occasion and, the night of the murder, was importuning Miss Mapp to continue favouring him. She grew weary of sullying herself and had refused to share his bed that night. And so, he strangled her." Suddenly, realising that Lily was at the table, the dowager blushed slightly and said, "Lily, dear. Surely, you've eaten enough. Why don't you go and fetch your hat and have Mary accompany you and the children to those gardens you've been begging to be allowed to visit."

Lily was astute enough to seize an opportunity when it presented itself and didn't even take the time to argue that she was old enough to listen to such conversations. Instead, she leapt up and was away from the table almost before the dowager had finished her sentence. With the young woman no longer at risk of being corrupted by her salacious musings, the dowager continued, "We all know how actresses can get caught up in such scandalous relations. You may not remember, Tabitha, but the rest of us need only reflect on Miss Langtry's interludes with Bertie, amongst others, to see that the theatre is a career that breeds licentiousness."

No one else at the table felt inclined to speculate as to what Danielle had been doing with her evenings and with whom. Certainly, there was little to no evidence that she had been spending them with the young "toff". Instead, Wolf tried to move the conversation back to the actual story Langley and Tabitha had been telling and asked, "So, it wasn't until the murder was discovered that the servants left the house?"

Langley answered, "Yes, exactly. The body had been found on a Tuesday afternoon, and the police had gone around to

Danielle's house before the evening was out. They questioned the housekeeper and maid, found they knew very little and left. The two women, realising that their imminent pay day would not be happening, packed their things and left the house. They had no idea who, if anyone, would inherit whatever effects their mistress owned and knew the house was only leased."

Wolf took a sip of wine and considered the story Tabitha and Langley had told so far. The part that intrigued him the most was the ransacking of the study. He said, "I'm assuming that if the house had been broken into while the servants were there, they would have mentioned it to the police."

"And cleared up the mess," Tabitha pointed out. "It had to have happened once they'd left. Was someone watching the house? I think we need to talk to the housekeeper, Mrs Channing. If she is running a bed and breakfast on the seafront, perhaps the hall porter or even Paddy and Jeanie will have some idea where we can find her."

Everyone agreed that was a valid line of inquiry. Bear volunteered to try to track Mrs Channing down.

"Do we have any reason to assume that the ransacking of the study is connected definitively to the murder?" the dowager asked. Tabitha was just silently commending the woman for turning to a more sensible line of inquiry than her previous melodramatic flights of fancy when the dowager continued, "Though perhaps the murdering young lover had sent her letters or the like and broke in to retrieve the evidence."

Tabitha sighed but did acknowledge that at least the first part of the dowager's sentence was valid, "When we're done here, I will go and write up notecards for everything we've discovered. Whether the search of the study and the murder are necessarily linked has to be put down as an open question. On the face of it, one would assume the answer is yes. But, they may be unrelated." Again, everyone agreed, and the lunchtime meeting soon wrapped up. Tabitha had notecards to write up, Langley had plans to work with Rat on his lessons when he returned from the gardens, and Wolf and the dowager had to prepare for their afternoon visit with Lady Archibald.

Because the dowager had the corkboard and spare notecards in her suite, Tabitha followed her upstairs to retrieve them for the afternoon. Entering the suite, the dowager called for her lady's maid to pull the corkboard out of the wardrobe and indicated that Tabitha should sit. Tabitha had not anticipated a social visit, but curiosity got the better of her. She took a seat on the sofa as the dowager took the armchair, which, of course, was the higher seat.

The dowager steepled her fingers and observed Tabitha for a few moments before speaking, "It seems you've decided to stop sulking and join in the investigation."

It wasn't clear if there was an implied question hidden in that statement. Tabitha chose to take the dowager's words at face value while ignoring the judgement rendered and merely said, "I told Lord Pembroke yesterday that I'm happy to help in any way I can."

The dowager snorted at this statement, "Did you now? Let me offer you some unsolicited advice, Tabitha. Don't play games for too long. Even the most ardent admirer will eventually lose patience and look elsewhere."

Tabitha flushed at the personal nature of the advice, though nothing but a slight flare in her nostrils indicated her irritation. She had no wish to expose her innermost thoughts to her mother-in-law and so tried to compose herself before answering, "I'm sure I have no idea what you mean. I am not playing any games and have no admirers." Even as she said these words, Tabitha realised how disingenuous they were; she knew exactly which admirer the dowager was talking about. But she believed that admiration was all it was. Tabitha was quite sure of one thing: she had no desire to have this conversation with the dowager countess.

"I'm an old woman and don't have the time to dance around a topic. Let me speak plainly; it is quite clear that you removed yourself from this investigation in a fit of pique at an old love reappearing in Jeremy's life. Yet, from what I have seen, you do not give him any indication that an overture of romance would be well-received. I know you are young and that, perhaps, my son was not the best person with whom to practice directing Cupid's bow, but even you must realise that any man needs a little encouragement. One might even say some subtle direction and sometimes redirection."

By this time, Tabitha was extremely uncomfortable. She had no desire to discuss her romantic life, or lack thereof, with the dowager, and she certainly had no intention of being coached in the art of seduction by the woman. "Mama, I can assure you that any feelings between Wolf and me are nothing more than those of friendship."

The dowager snorted again, "Ha! I have a great many friends, and none have ever looked at me as he looks at you. And as you look at him, I might add."

There was one nagging question that Tabitha couldn't help but ask, "Are you encouraging a romance with Wolf? Honestly, I would have assumed that was the last thing you desire."

"And yet again, you presume to know what I think and feel," the dowager said with a sniff. "Jeremy is a young, vital, wealthy man. He will marry at some point. I've noticed the vultures circling already; those mamas who view him as the perfect catch for their insipid daughters. The only thing keeping them at bay is your unconventional living situation, which leaves the women of society unsure of how available for marriage he really is. But mark my words, if there is no engagement forthcoming, particularly once the season is in full swing, they will throw caution to the wind. To be even more blunt, if you don't marry him, someone else will."

These words so entirely mirrored Tabitha's thoughts that she felt some hot tears begin to prick at her eyes. Resolute in her intention to mask her emotions in front of the dowager, she tried to control her breathing and will the tears away. It took Tabitha a few moments, but she eventually got her emotions under control. Once she had, she looked directly at the woman who had always acted as if she loathed her, and certainly had made it very clear to Tabitha and to society that she blamed her daughter-in-law for her son's death. Unable to think of a better way to phrase her thoughts, she pressed on with the question she had asked, "And you wish for me to be the person Wolf marries?"

The dowager's answer was short and to the point, "You are a known quantity."

So that was it. At least this answer made perfect sense and righted the topsy-turvy world into which Tabitha had momentarily found herself thrust. Whatever her feelings about Tabitha, the other Lady Pembroke had already experienced what it was like to be the dowager countess with Tabitha married to the earl. But if Wolf married another woman, how might that impact the dowager's power and influence? While Tabitha's mother, Lady Jameson, was certainly no wilting wallflower, she had three other daughters and a son to manage. She had neither the time nor interest in battling for control of her youngest daughter. But another mama, with less to occupy her time and energy, might take it upon herself to attempt to knock a woman who wasn't even the current earl's mother off her perch. That was to be avoided at all costs!

Now that they were having this conversation, there was a question Tabitha had long wondered about, "Mama, why did you never remarry? You were certainly young enough when Jonathan's father died."

Again, the answer was brief and to the point, "Because, unlike you, I never met a man who was worthy of me."

Of course, the situation had been very different for the dowager countess; she was mother to the inheritor of the title. And while he was an awful husband, Jonathan had been a slightly better son. If not loving, he had been dutiful and respectful. But Tabitha had not been able to provide Jonathan with an heir. If Wolf were to marry, Tabitha was sure she would be shunted off to the side by the new countess.

Tabitha had no desire to prolong this conversation, and seeing the maid enter the room with the corkboard, Tabitha took it and left. The dowager watched her go, chuckled, and said, "Foolish girl. It seems the dance will continue for a while longer."

CHAPTER 18

Riding to Kemptown in the carriage with the dowager, Wolf couldn't make up his mind about what, if anything, he should disclose about his prior relationship with Arlene. He realised that the dowager likely already guessed the outlines of their history. Was it necessary to say more in anticipation of what Arlene might reveal? His state of mind must have shown on his face because the dowager said, "Jeremy, you needn't look as if you are going to the gallows. Lady Archibald seems delightful. I might add that it is a matter of pride for a woman to believe that a man never forgets her or moves on. But that doesn't mean she has any serious interest in reigniting old embers."

Wolf wasn't so certain. And he did wonder if the dowager's words were wishful thinking; it was one thing for her to find the dusky Lady Archibald amusing company. It was another to contemplate her as the next Countess of Pembroke and the mother of the next earl. However, as far as Wolf was concerned, that was never going to happen, and all he had to worry about was getting through this afternoon's tea unscathed.

The ride wasn't long enough, and before Wolf knew it, they had pulled up outside of Arlene's house. "What a delightful area," the dowager said, looking towards the private gardens at the centre of Sussex Square. "Why, if one squinted, it could almost be Mayfair.

Arlene's butler had the door open before they even finished descending from the carriage, and the woman herself stood waiting to greet them. She welcomed the dowager as if she were a dear friend of old, and gave Wolf her hand to kiss with a sly look. "Lady Pembroke did not mention that you were to accompany her," Arlene said silkily. "What a delightful surprise to find that you cannot stay away."

Wolf didn't bother to contradict her and merely followed into the drawing room. The tea tray was already set out this time, and as soon as the dowager was settled on the pink silk sofa, Arlene made sure she was well supplied with tea and finger sandwiches.

The dowager looked around, "What a delightful room. It feels au courant but not garishly so. The colours are so soothing."

Arlene blushed prettily, "It means so much to hear you say that, Lady Pembroke. I actually chose the colours and most of the pieces myself."

"Did you now? I must say, I don't usually approve of members of our class lowering themselves to do the work of tradesmen. Lady Chistlethwaite likes to call herself a landscape artist, but as far as I can tell, she is merely a gardener in a silk dress. However, when the results are as charming as these, one can be persuaded to overlook any lapse in judgement."

To her credit, even Arlene's well-practised mask of dispassionate hauteur was momentarily knocked askew by the dowager's patented compliment wrapped in a subtle insult. However, she quickly recovered, trilled a carefree laugh, and said, "Oh, Lady Pembroke, what an original you are."

Wolf had neither the patience nor the inclination to sit through any more of this verbal badminton and so launched right in, "Arlene, we have come to ask you some questions about Danielle."

Arlene arched one eyebrow, and Wolf answered the unspoken question, "Yes, I will take on the investigation. It is far from obvious to me that the police haven't arrested the right man. However, it is obvious that even if Robert Charles turns out to be guilty, he was arrested on the flimsiest wisp of evidence."

"Thank you, Wolf," Arlene said with apparent sincerity. It means a lot to me to know that Danielle will get some justice. What do you need to know?"

"From what we've heard so far from the theatre company, Danielle seems to have kept to herself outside of rehearsal and show hours. She certainly didn't accompany everyone to the celebration after the last show of the run. Was that usual?"

Arlene sighed, "Wolf, it is not easy having my skin colour in England. And Danielle was far darker skinned than I am. Even the most liberal and accepting people still see us as other in many ways." Anticipating the words about to spring to his lips, she said, "Even you, Wolf. This isn't a criticism. But it is exhausting to be reminded of this fact in large and small ways all day, every day. There is barely an interaction I have outside of this house where I don't have to steel myself for a comment, a slight, or a look. Truly, I believed, naively now I realise, that becoming a baroness would insulate me. But it didn't. If anything, it brought me into a social circle even less inclined to accept me."

Now, the dowager was the one about to interject. But Arlene put up a hand to stop her and said, "I have lived this my entire life. My grandfather tried to shield me and, to some extent, by hiding me away in the country, succeeded. During my marriage, I again thought that a retreat from society would bring me some peace and that lifestyle suited my husband's inclinations anyway. I don't know why I thought I could enter Brighton society any better as a widow than I had on the baron's arm. But it has been hard."

Arlene turned away for a moment, and Wolf could have sworn she was holding back tears. "Danielle was one of the few people who understood what it was like for me. Her talent opened doors for her, but it rarely opened hearts. At the end of a work day, she was not inclined to socialise with people she knew muttered about her behind her back and visit public houses where she ran the risk of being turned away at the door or worse."

These were the most sincere, heartfelt words Wolf had ever heard Arlene utter, and suddenly, he was second-guessing every harsh thought or judgement he had made about her over the years. He had told himself that he understood why she married Lord Archibald, but had he really? He had thought he understood what she would have been exposing herself to if she had married Wolf, giving up the protection that her grandfather's name and wealth had provided. But hearing her words now, he realised how selfish he had been as a callow youth to have had such expectations of her.

Regretting her moment of vulnerability, Arlene took a moment to compose herself and said, "But enough of that. The simple answer is yes; Danielle preferred to be at home when she was not at the theatre. It would have gone unremarked upon that she had not gone out with the others."

"Her body wasn't found for three days. Why wouldn't her servants have reported her missing?"

"I'm sure they would have eventually. But I don't think most servants would take it upon themselves to question the comings and goings of their mistress. And who would they have reported it to? The police? I suspect she would have needed to be missing for more than a couple of days for the Brighton Borough Police to rouse themselves to do much. She was a dark-skinned actress. I'm sure they would have made certain conjectures about her behaviour and sent the servants on their way."

Although Arlene's words were laced with bitterness, Wolf couldn't argue with her logic. He said, "We spoke to the mother of Danielle's maid. She said that her daughter and the housekeeper speculated that Danielle had a lover, which was why she was sometimes away for a night or two. Did she, and if so, do you know who he was?"

"If she had a lover, she never spoke of him. Sometimes, when she came here for dinner, she would stay the night. Perhaps those were the times that caused the servants to gossip."

Changing tack slightly, Wolf asked, "Mr Bailey, who runs the theatre company, told us that Danielle had a particularly persistent admirer. He referred to him as a "young, snot-nosed, arrogant ass."

The dowager jumped in, eager to deliver her verdict, "I believe this young man is our murderer. I feel it in my bones. Your friend spurned him. Enraged, he strangled her." Yet again, the dowager was quite caught up in her bloodthirsty replaying of the crime.

"Well, Danielle had many admirers," Arlene acknowledged. "Of course, this is hardly uncommon among actresses. Many of these admirers did nothing more than send flowers and gifts backstage. But others were a little more insistent. From what Danielle told me, this Viscount Tobias Williams definitely didn't take no for an answer."

The dowager had been gleefully leaning forward as Arlene had started to answer, but suddenly, her entire demeanour changed; she sat up, her face suddenly a picture of concern and confusion. "Viscount Tobias Williams, you say? Surely you are mistaken in the name."

"I am sure that is who the young man is," Arlene countered. "In fact, Danielle showed me various letters and notes he had written her. Each one was increasingly demanding and, one might even say, aggressive."

"Did you ever meet this young man?" the dowager asked. Wolf couldn't place her tone of voice. But if he'd had to put a name to it, he would have said she was fearful. Did she know this young man?

"Actually, I did, but only once, and briefly. Let me see now. He was of medium height and build, with dark brown hair that was unfashionably long and hung over one eye. And his face seemed to set in a sullen sneer as if everything and everyone in view displeased him. He was young, probably not even twenty years old, with enough arrogance for a man of great achievements, twice his age. I know that Danielle had tried to deal with him quite kindly. Apart from anything else, she was far too old for him. And she was not one of those actresses looking for a titled man to keep her as his mistress. But this Viscount Tobias would not be put off."

While Arlene had described the young man, the dowager had visibly blanched. She now stood and said, quite abruptly, "Do excuse me, dear Lady Archibald. But I find I suddenly have a terrible headache coming on, and I believe I must return to the hotel and lie down."

Whether Arlene had noticed the change in the dowager while she had been talking, she was polite enough not to comment. Before Wolf knew it, they were back in their outerwear and in the carriage. Wolf glanced at his pocket watch and saw that barely fifteen minutes had elapsed since they'd entered the house. The dowager was uncharacteristically quiet for the entire carriage ride home. Normally, Wolf wouldn't have minded the peace and quiet, but he was genuinely concerned that the dowager might be ill.

Finally, as they were about to pull up at The Grand, he said very gently, "Lady Pembroke, I must ask, how bad is your headache? Can I call a doctor for you?"

For the entire carriage ride, the normally imperturbable dowager countess had been staring out of the window, lost in thought. Now, she turned to face Wolf and answered, "Viscount Tobias Williams is my godson. His grandmother, Lady Charlotte Williams, is my one true friend in this world. I knew the boy had developed a bit of a wild streak, but I can't for the world believe him capable of murder."

Whatever Wolf believed had been the cause of the dowager's sudden turn, he hadn't been expecting her to say this. "Did you know he was in Brighton?" he asked.

The dowager shook her head sadly, "The last letter I received from Charlotte, Lady Williams, she wrote that her son Clarence, the earl, was at his wits' end with what to do with the boy. Tobias had been at Cambridge but had been sent down for a multitude of infractions. You know better than I how much bad behaviour is usually tolerated at Oxford and Cambridge from the sons of the nobility. I can only imagine how appalling his behaviour must have been to cross that line."

Wolf nodded in agreement. While he had neither the money nor the inclination during his Cambridge days, he had certainly known many wild sons of the aristocracy who had done their utmost to bring shame on their family names and had still managed to remain at the university. The dowager continued,

"Charlotte wrote that Tobias had come to her asking for money to clear some gambling debts. It seemed he was afraid to ask his father."

"Did she give him the money?"

"She did. But against her better judgement. But he is her only grandson, and she has always doted on the boy. Perhaps too much, if you ask me. The last I heard from her was probably eight weeks ago. I've been so caught up with Manning's arrest and then with going to Scotland that I had neglected to reply to her letter. Now, I have no idea what I will say." She turned to Wolf with genuine despair on her face, "Wolf, you must drop this investigation immediately. I cannot be the cause of Charlotte's grandson going to the gallows."

Wolf was unsure how to answer her. It went against everything he believed in to wilfully overlook a crime merely because of a personal connection to its perpetrator. But they didn't even know that this Viscount Tobias had been the person who attacked Danielle. And that is how he answered her, "Lady Pembroke, let us not get ahead of ourselves. Would you have me not investigate even if it turns out that Lord Tobias had nothing to do with the murder?"

The dowager shook her head but answered, "But I know you, Jeremy. If you investigate and then find out that he did kill that woman, you will feel compelled to act. The only way to save Tobias is to stop investigating while we're sure of nothing."

"And let a potentially innocent man hang for the crime?" Wolf asked. Because that was what sat at the crux of this matter. If there had been no suspect arrested, perhaps, only perhaps, he might have entertained the dowager's request. But he could not see an innocent man go to the gallows, knowing that he might have done something to prevent it. Pressing his point, Wolf continued, "If we hadn't intervened, Manning would have hung for a crime he didn't commit. You were the person who insisted I do everything in my power to prevent that from happening. Does Robert Charles deserve any less?"

The look in the dowager's eyes suggested that, yes, in fact, she believed he did deserve less. Whether it was because of the colour of his skin or for no other reason than that he wasn't someone she depended on to make her life run smoothly, it was clear the dowager did not believe the two situations to have equal merit. But she could also see that she would not win this argument with Wolf. Instead, she said, "Promise me you won't rush to judgement if it seems he might have been involved."

Wolf answered as honestly as he felt able, "Lady Pembroke, I promise I will do everything in my power to make sure that justice is served as fairly and honestly as possible." While the dowager was astute enough to realise this was not the answer she had been hoping for, she was sure enough of her powers of manipulation that she accepted Wolf's words for now in the certainty that she could manage whatever situation they later found themselves in. He continued, "We do need to find your godson and talk with him. Do you have any idea where he might be staying?"

The dowager shook her head, "I can send his grandmother a telegram. But based on what I've heard of the boy recently, our best bet is to find the most disreputable gaming house in Brighton and look for him there." The dowager's voice had been heavy with sarcasm as she said this, but as it happened, Wolf thought it was a good idea. He intended to find Bear and send him out to talk to Paddy and Jeanie and ask where they might expect such a dissolute youth to be losing his money.

The dowager was so discombobulated by what they had heard from Arlene that she barely noticed Tabitha as she passed her in the hotel lobby and merely muttered something about having to lie down. Tabitha looked at Wolf for an explanation. In reply, he took her arm and steered her towards the hotel library that he hoped would be unoccupied at that time of the day. Luckily, the only person making use of the library at that point in the season was Lady Lily, and she was still happily making the most of her opportunity to visit the Royal Pavilion Gardens.

Tabitha sat in one of the library's large leather armchairs, and Wolf took its twin opposite to her. "What on earth has happened? Mama looked as if she had seen a ghost, and you've dragged me in here to talk. Why, you were not even gone an hour, and that included the drive there and back."

"Arlene knew who the young, arrogant, snot-nosed toff is." Tabitha waited, and he continued, "Viscount Tobias Williams."

Tabitha's face was still blank. "I have no idea who that is," she confessed.

"He is Lady Pembroke's godson and the grandson of her dearest friend."

Tabitha couldn't help herself and replied, "She has a dearest friend?"

"Apparently. She begged me to drop the investigation now before we discover too much and cannot turn back."

Tabitha's initial reaction to this was incredulity. But then she considered that in the three years she had known the dowager countess, the woman had usually behaved as if she believed that there was a different set of rules for the wealthy and titled than for everyone else. How much more so when she believed a deviant was someone close to her?

"I assume you refused her?" Tabitha asked, not seriously concerned that Wolf would have indulged such entitlement.

"Of course. I gave her some vague platitudes, but she is too sharp not to realise that she wouldn't get her way. I believe she is genuinely fearful that her godson could be the murderer," Wolf acknowledged.

Tabitha couldn't help herself. She knew it was petty, but she had to add, "Rather ironic, given the glee with which she was spinning increasingly lurid theories about Danielle's admirer earlier. It seems that was only fun when he might have been someone else's godson."

"Indeed. Anyway, our top priority now is to find this young man. Even if he didn't kill Danielle, he may be able to provide us with information."

"Wouldn't he have come forward if he had?" Tabitha asked.

"Not necessarily. I doubt that the murder of a dark-skinned actress in a regional theatre would have made news in London.

And it's unlikely that someone like the viscount would take a local rag, particularly if he is just visiting. We haven't looked at it."

Tabitha acknowledged this statement, "So you think he doesn't know she's dead? How could that be? If he was that infatuated with her, wouldn't he have noticed he hadn't seen her in more than three weeks?"

"You'd think so. But this is all mere speculation until we are able to talk with him, which is why I need to find Bear and have him ask Paddy and Jeanie about any gambling houses in Brighton. This isn't London; how many can there be?"

There wasn't much more to say, so Wolf left to find Bear, and Tabitha continued to sit in the library pondering the latest developments in the investigation.

CHAPTER 19

The dowager did not join the others for dinner in the hotel restaurant that night. Nevertheless, the talk was lively, and by the time the meal was almost over, plans were forming for that evening and the following day. Bear had managed to track down an address for the bed and breakfast that Mrs Channing had recently opened on the seafront, and Bear planned to visit it in the morning. He had also managed to get a list of gaming houses from Paddy.

"Mind you, he said that some of these are not much more than some dog fights. He's marked the ones that might more appeal to a young aristocrat and that are known for baccarat and piquet," Bear explained.

It crossed Tabitha's mind that this might not be the most appropriate conversation to be having in front of Lily. But then she considered that Lily was only a few years younger than she was. Tabitha's brief but unpleasant marriage might have matured, perhaps even hardened, her beyond her years. Still, she acknowledged that Lily was a modern young woman, and there was no need to wrap her in swaddling clothes.

Bear continued, "Brighton isn't London; there is a limited circle of people sufficiently well-heeled or at least with more time on their hands than good sense. Paddy recommended which places we should start with."

Even with her exposure to some of the uglier elements of London life over the prior few months, Tabitha's knowledge of the dark underbelly of polite society was still extremely limited. She asked with genuine curiosity, "Can anyone just gain entry to one of these clubs?"

It was a fair question, and Lord Langley answered, "In London, it does vary from place to place. Much of the gambling the aristocracy indulges in takes place in private clubs such as Whites. However, when an establishment is purely for the purpose of gaming, they are usually happy to admit anyone who seems flush enough to play."

Wolf considered Bear's information. "Langley, Bear, there is no time like the present. I suggest we begin this evening with the most likely places on Paddy's list and work our way down."

Tabitha felt she had to point out the fatal flaw in the plan, "None of you know what the young man looks like. Medium height and build with dark hair is hardly a uniquely identifying description."

Wolf realised that Tabitha was right, of course. "Then what do you suggest we do?"

"I believe we should repeat our success in Edinburgh and have Bear draw a portrait based on the dowager countess' description." This had been a tactic they had employed very successfully during their previous investigation. Bear was a surprisingly good artist. Tabitha had no idea how he managed to wield a charcoal or brush so deftly with his huge paws, but somehow, he did. For that investigation, he had sketched while Lily described her missing friend Peter. She had then suggested improvements until the drawing was a good enough representation of the missing man that they could use it to get a positive identification from a witness.

Given the dowager's absence from dinner, it was unclear if she was in either a physical or mental state to receive visitors. Tabitha suggested that she check on the older woman and make the request. If the dowager felt up to the task, Tabitha would then fetch Wolf and Bear. "The worst that will happen is that you will have to postpone this outing until tomorrow evening. I realise this isn't ideal, but we have no choice at this point," she argued persuasively.

The dinner party adjourned, and it was decided that Bear,

Langley, and Wolf would have some brandy in the library while Tabitha went to call on the dowager. Making her way to the woman's suite, Tabitha wasn't sure what to expect. This behaviour was so out of character that she wondered if, in fact, there was a physical component. While it was tempting to imagine the dowager countess as having unflagging vitality, the truth was that, contrary to what she might like people to believe, she did not have superhuman powers and was not immortal.

Tabitha knocked softly at the door. It was answered by the dowager's lady's maid, Withers. "I'm just checking on her ladyship," Tabitha said quietly. "When she didn't join us for dinner, we were all worried."

"Tabitha, is that you?" the dowager's voice rang out from the sitting room. "Withers, it is all right. You can let her ladyship in."

The dowager was in the armchair with her feet on a footstool. On the table in front of her, there was a tray with the scant remains of a meal on it. Tabitha was relieved to see the woman still had an appetite.

"Come and sit, Tabitha. I'm not dying, at least not yet. It was merely a headache."

Tabitha sat on the sofa as Withers picked up the tray and left the suite, presumably to return it to the kitchen. "We were all worried, Mama."

"Ha!" the dowager said, managing to imbue that one syllable with a surprising amount of cynicism. "Is that what you all were, worried?"

"Indeed." Tabitha paused, unsure what she should admit to knowing. She certainly didn't want to be the cause of the headache reappearing. "Wolf told me about your godson. I can see why that was such a terrible shock."

In the three years that Tabitha had spent in the dowager's orbit, she had never seen the woman be anything less than in total control of her emotions. Even at her son Jonathan's funeral, she was the personification of a British stiff upper lip. But that evening, the dowager seemed vulnerable. That was not a word that Tabitha would have ever thought to use in relation to the dowager countess, but it was the word that sprung to mind as she looked at the woman, who suddenly seemed quite old and frail.

As if she had seen her vulnerability reflected in Tabitha's eyes, the dowager sat a little taller and snapped her countenance back to its usual dispassionate stoicism. "One never likes to imagine the worst of one's friends and family," she said.

The irony was that the dowager often gleefully imagined the worst of them, Tabitha thought. Instead, she said, "We need your help, Mama."

"And what might that help entail?"

"Bear has a list of the gaming houses in town, and Wolf and Langley intend to accompany him to some of them tonight in the hope of discovering your godson. But, of course, they have no idea what he looks like. So, we need you to describe him while Bear attempts to sketch the viscount's likeness."

This was the first the dowager had heard of Bear's artistic talents, and she raised her eyebrows sceptically. However, she didn't mention her thoughts on his likely abilities but instead said, "They do not need a drawing because I will be accompanying them."

So many thoughts ran through Tabitha's head on hearing this that she was lost for words momentarily. The idea of the elderly Dowager Countess of Pembroke, who just a few minutes ago seemed to be ailing, visiting the gaming houses of Brighton was absurd. While Tabitha herself was usually not shy in insisting she be included in all aspects of an investigation, even she hadn't expected to be taken along for that evening's outing.

Realising that this was not her battle to fight, Tabitha merely said, "Lord Langley and Wolf are in the library. Why don't I go and get them, and you can discuss your suggestion."

The dowager narrowed her eyes but didn't argue. Tabitha rose, quickly exited the room and made her way back down to the library. Bear, Wolf, and Langley were sipping their brandies and discussing nothing in particular. They looked up when she entered, and Wolf asked, "Is her ladyship willing to describe her godson to Bear?"

In a very uncharacteristic gesture, Tabitha walked over to where Wolf sat, picked up the brandy snifter sitting on the side table by his chair, and took a long sip. Wolf looked up at her in surprise, "What's wrong? Did she refuse to cooperate?"

"Worse. She insists on joining you for the evening."

Langley shot up, "She cannot be serious? Women are rarely in attendance at such places, and when they are, they are usually..." he paused, embarrassed and lost for a better word than the one he was about to use.

Wolf finished his sentence for him, "They are not women of quality."

"You don't have to persuade me. You notice I did not insist on joining you," Tabitha protested.

"How did you answer her?" Wolf asked.

"I didn't. I told her I would bring you up to discuss it with her." If Tabitha felt any guilt, she didn't show it.

Wolf didn't blame her; Tabitha was the person least likely to persuade or dissuade the dowager at the best of times. Instead, he said, "Then let us go forth, into the lion's den."

"Perhaps, like Samson, we will discover something sweet instead," Langley quipped.

Wolf looked at him and said drily, "Well, if you are so confident of that, you can be the one to argue her out of joining us."

The three men rose, and Tabitha led the way back up to the dowager's suite. Withers had beaten Tabitha back upstairs and again opened the door. This time, she stepped back immediately to let them enter.

Tabitha noted that, in the few minutes she had been gone, the footstool had been removed, and any trace of vulnerability clinging to the dowager had disappeared. "Ah, Maxwell, Jeremy, and even Mr Bear, do come in and take a seat." While Tabitha took the armchair opposite the dowager, the three men sat in a row, squashed onto the rather small sofa, perching on its edge as if they were back in school, waiting to be caned.

If they were expecting her to speak first, then they were to be disappointed. The woman knew the value of strategic silence too well; let them squirm. Finally, realising that if he didn't speak up, they might be sitting there all night, Wolf cleared his throat and said, "Lady Pembroke. Dear Lady Pembroke." The dowager raised her eyebrows at his blatant attempt to pander but still said nothing. He continued, "You must realise how impossible it would be for you to accompany us this evening. Gaming halls are no place for a dowager countess."

The dowager didn't answer immediately, instead inspecting her nails as if expecting to find them anything other than perfectly groomed. Finally, when the silence had become quite unbearable, she replied, "And tell me, Jeremy, what ill consequences do you think might befall me if I should ignore your advice?" This was a good question and one Wolf hadn't thought to have an answer ready for. He had assumed that given the dowager was usually one of the first people to pass judgement on the societal transgressions of others, those ill consequences would be self-evident and not need to be enumerated.

Langley, displaying a remarkable lack of insight for one who assessed people and situations professionally, blundered in, saying, "What will people think?"

The dowager's head shot up, and she stared at him with such icy contempt that the normally unflappable Lord Langley shrunk in on himself and looked, and probably felt, for all the world like a naughty seven-year-old boy. "What will people think? Maxwell, they will think what I tell them to think. I do not follow society; I lead it! If I choose to attend gaming rooms, then by next week, to do so will be considered à la mode."

If anyone in the room questioned the veracity of that statement, they were wise enough to keep silent. The dowager then continued with her final charge, "And Tabitha will join me."

Tabitha looked up in shock at this statement. She'd had no expectations that she would be one of that evening's party, no matter what the dowager might demand for herself.

Wolf, looking even more shocked, declared, "Lady Pembroke, I must most respectfully tell you that will not be happening. I refuse to allow it."

Up until that point, Tabitha had found the scene unfolding before her to be amusing. But at Wolf's words, she whipped her head around to glare at him and said, "Excuse me, but you can refuse nothing when it comes to my person or actions." She then turned back to the dowager and said, "Mama, I believe I will be joining you this evening. I will go and change. Shall we meet in the lobby in thirty minutes?"

Ignoring the stunned look on Wolf's face, Tabitha rose and left the room. As the door closed behind her, the dowager clapped her hands and said, "Withers, let us retire to my bedchamber. We will need to review my evening dresses. We had not packed with an evening in the gaming rooms in mind. Perhaps the deep purple velvet will do." She then stood, looked at the three men still sitting uncomfortably on the sofa, and said, "Gentlemen, I will meet you downstairs in thirty minutes."

CHAPTER 20

Wolf made sure to be down in the hotel lobby well before the thirty minutes. He intended to have a discreet chat with the hall porter on duty before anyone else was down. Taking the man aside, he showed him Paddy's list and asked in a low voice, "Which of these are the least disreputable?" He knew that Paddy had indicated which ones he believed might appeal to Viscount Tobias. But that didn't necessarily correlate with reputability.

The porter examined the list for a minute or so, then took a pencil from behind his ear and made some notations next to a few of the names. Showing Wolf the list, he said, "So, I've made a few marks. The ones with an asterisk by them won't be open off-season. They depend too heavily on tourists. The ones with an X by them should be avoided at all costs. The ones with a checkmark, well, they're probably not up to London standards, but you won't have your pocket picked at least."

There were only two such places marked. Wolf had to hope that they would find Viscount Tobias at one of them that evening. The porter continued, "When you get to the door, tell them Marty Malcom sent you. Guests occasionally ask me to recommend such places, and I always send them to one of these two. They'll make sure you're taken care of."

Wolf thanked the man and then asked if they might have the carriage for the evening. Bear would have to sit up next to the driver, but he'd prefer that anyway. There had been no debate about having Bear accompany them that evening. His size would dissuade all but the most foolish from bothering their group.

Tabitha hadn't been sure what to wear for their evening adventure. She could have stayed in the evening gown she'd worn to dinner. But it was quite simple, and she felt that if she was going to shock society by accompanying the men to a gaming room, she might as well do it in the grandest style. After consulting with Ginny, she'd decided to wear the beautiful, chic, wine-coloured silk dress she'd worn to a soiree thrown in their honour in Scotland. Just as then, she paired it with a beautiful but simple red garnet necklace. Ginny took down Tabitha's glorious chestnut hair, then restyled it with a few loose ringlets left to frame her face.

"You look lovely, m'lady," Ginny said with pride. "Are you excited?"

"Well, to be honest, I agreed to this outing to show Lord Pembroke that he may not dictate my actions. But now, I find myself quite nervous. I have no idea what the right gown for such an establishment might be. Let us hope that we don't make ourselves too conspicuous."

Tabitha took one final look in the mirror, accepted the luxurious black silk cape that Ginny held out for her, and made her way downstairs.

Wolf found that Tabitha's beauty and poise frequently took his breath away, but when he saw her exit the hotel lift into the lobby, he thought she had never looked more beautiful. While he had seen her in that evening dress before and thought how well it suited her then, there was something about her that night, maybe her hair, maybe the brightness of her eyes, that was particularly becoming. He approached her and took her hand, bringing it to his lips. Looking into her eyes, still holding her hand, he said, "You look beautiful, Tabitha. Truly stunning."

Tabitha blushed and thanked him for the compliment. They moved to the front of the hotel lobby, where there were groups of chairs scattered about. They had barely been seated a minute when Bear joined them. He had walked down the stairs and so had missed Langley, who joined them not long after. Finally, at exactly thirty minutes after they had parted, the dowager entered the lobby. She had indeed worn the deep purple velvet dress, and it suited her well. Tabitha noted that she had brought her silver-topped cane with her. The dowager didn't always use a cane, and Tabitha wondered if this was an indication that the famously stubborn woman was still not feeling well but refused to back out of the evening.

As they made their way to the carriage, Wolf briefly relayed the conversation he'd had with Mr Malcom, the porter. It was a short trip to the first gaming house on the list, Markers. For all anyone could see from the outside, it was an unexceptional, unassuming townhouse. There was no signage announcing the activities within, and the only indication that they had the right place was a very large, unpleasant-looking fellow standing by the door. Wolf approached him and dropped Marty's name. It wasn't necessary, though. Jim Brown, or Knuckles as his friends and enemies called him, knew the drill; anyone who looked rich enough was welcome to enter the establishment. And enough jewels had passed through Knuckles' hands when he was a young man that he knew that the necklaces that the women wore weren't glass.

If Knuckles had any thoughts about why such high and mighty-looking women might be gracing an establishment like Markers, no one would have known from his face, though Knuckles' face had taken so many beatings over the years that it wasn't the best display case for his emotional state. With a nose that had been broken three or four times, a cabbage ear, and a few broken and missing teeth, Knuckles looked intimidating even when he was positively joyful. However, Knuckles did take his time to eye up Bear warily. Either these toffs were planning to cause some trouble, or they were smart enough to know how to avoid it.

If the exterior of Markers was inconspicuous, the interior made up for that. From the moment the group, led by Wolf, walked into the townhouse, they were surrounded by opulence. It seemed that no expense had been spared to ensure that guests enjoyed all the luxury that plush carpets, crystal chandeliers, and copious amounts of marble could confer.

They handed their outwear to a serious-looking butler who wouldn't have been out of place in a duke's mansion in Mayfair. The butler then led them through to a room on their right. "We have some of the lower-stake games, such as euchre, in this room. While the higher-stakes games of baccarat and piquet are in the back room," the butler intoned. Tabitha wondered what the upstairs rooms were used for, but the butler didn't seem inclined to stay and chitchat and quickly left them in the front room.

A footman was circling with glasses of champagne, and everyone took a glass. Luckily, the room wasn't too busy, and it didn't take the dowager long to scan the room and announce, "He's not here. Let us move to the back room."

The group moved towards the back of the townhouse, into a large room, perhaps made up of what had originally been two rooms. This room was as opulent as the rest of the house, and the crystal chandeliers cast a soft glow on the green baize of the gaming tables. The low hum of conversation was interspersed with the occasional laugh and clink of the cut-glass crystal whisky tumblers and champagne flutes. All the men were elegantly dressed in evening wear, but they were as absorbed and serious in the gambling chips before them as a surgeon preparing for his first incision.

The room housed various tables around which men were gathered. Because, yes, Tabitha and the dowager were the only women in the gaming house. This room was busier than the front one, and some of the gamblers were so absorbed in their games that they didn't notice the newcomers. However, a couple of patrons looked up as they entered the room with a mix of curiosity and irritation - women were an unnecessary distraction to the business of gambling.

The dowager elbowed Wolf and, pointing to the furthermost table where a very intense game of baccarat was taking place, whispered, "Over there, the young man sitting next to the man with the monocle. That's Tobias." The dowager pointed to a young man of perhaps eighteen or nineteen. As he had been described, his most notable features were an overly long fringe of dark hair that kept falling over one eye and a sullen snarl on his face, as if he were angry at everything and anything.

Wolf realised that they hadn't discussed how to approach the young man and glanced over at Langley, who had been thinking the same thing and shook his head. Luckily, with the dowager in tow, there was no need for Wolf or Langley to improvise. Before Wolf knew it, she had handed him her champagne flute and was striding over to the table, causing enough of a commotion that now everyone looked up. The young man she was headed towards raised his head and visibly blanched. Tabitha could see his Adam's apple bobbing as he swallowed a few times.

The dowager went up to the baccarat table and just stood there, saying nothing. She stood there, and she glared at her godson. Moments passed, and the dowager just stood there. Tobias was now so flustered that, when the round ended, he placed his cards down, scooped up the meagre pile of chips in front of him, and said in a highly aggrieved tone, "Gentlemen, it seems Lady Luck has not been with me tonight, so I bid you adieu."

Seeing Tobias stand, the dowager cocked her head in the direction of the hallway and turned with the absolute expectation that the young man would follow her. As she passed by the rest of her group, she said quietly, "Follow me."

With the nervous-looking young man trailing them, the group made its way back to the relative quiet and privacy of the hallway. Moving as far from the gaming rooms as possible, Viscount Tobias stood in front of his godmother with his hands in his pocket and a very sullen look on his face, "What on earth are you doing here, Aunt Julia?" he said in a voice thick with a mixture of irritation and guilt.

"What am I doing here? What are you doing here, young man? The last I heard from your grandmother, you had pleaded with her to settle your gambling debts, and yet here you are, clearly busy racking up more." The dowager paused, then said with the sagacity of one who had known many dissolute men in her time, "You know, Tobias. It is one thing to be an inveterate gambler and quite another to be an incompetent one. At least Lord Edwards normally makes more than he loses, no matter the shame he manages to bring on his family in the process."

"I'm not an incompetent gambler. The cards are just against me tonight," the young man said, pouting. If the conversation were not about the very adult pastime of gambling, Tabitha might have thought the young man was being admonished for his lack of skill at a nursery game of hide and seek, such was the petulance in his voice.

"I will not bother to debate your adeptness or lack thereof, Tobias. There are far more important things I wish to speak to you about."

At these words, it occurred to the young viscount that his godmother's shocking appearance in front of him at the baccarat table may not have been a horrifying coincidence. As this realisation hit him, he looked even more worried and stammered, "Whatever you wish to say to me, this is neither the time nor the place. I will wait on you tomorrow."

"Ha! What do you take me for, young man? Your mother may be soft-hearted and soft-headed enough to fall for your nonsense, but I certainly won't. You will return to our hotel with us now, and we will talk there."

The young rake's face showed his unwillingness to accompany them, but it also showed his resignation at his fate. Watching this interaction, Wolf realised that he had no idea how he and Langley would have commanded compliance with their demands without the dowager's help. For young Tobias clearly had a healthy terror of the petite old woman with the steel grey eyes that were currently shooting daggers at him. While she had no way to compel his obedience physically, it had never occurred to the dowager that this would be any kind of impediment to achieving her aims. And it wasn't.

CHAPTER 21

Bear and Langley offered to walk the short distance back to the hotel. Under other circumstances, Wolf might have felt the need for Bear to remain in order to be sure that Tobias didn't try to escape. But it was obvious that the dowager's hold over her godson was a far tighter noose than any physical threat.

Once in the carriage, Tobias sat silently in the corner, sulkily looking out of the window. The dowager chatted away as if he wasn't present, "You know, Tobias was a delightful little boy once. Highly intelligent and very mature. He had a very refined palate for a child, and I would delight in exposing him to new and increasingly exotic foodstuffs when he would visit. I encouraged his interest in new scientific breakthroughs and took him to lectures at the Royal Academy on occasion. I really have no idea what happened to make him the young man we have here now."

If Tabitha had felt some sympathy for the young man as his godmother started reminiscing, this only increased as the dowager got into her stride, "You know, his mother wanted to make some religious aunt of hers his godmother, but her mother-in-law, Charlotte, interceded. She made clear that it was not his immortal soul they should be worried about but the trouble his corporeal appetites might cause. Clarence had been a bit of a rake in his youth, and Charlotte realised there might be a familial predisposition to such youthful indulgence." If this news about his father surprised Tobias in any way, there was nothing in his countenance that revealed it.

The dowager continued with a certain ruefulness in her voice, "I believed that I had done my part to ensure that Tobias was set on an appropriate path of gentile industriousness. One doesn't want to encourage an aristocratic young man to go into trade. However, his interest in science, particularly engineering, seemed wholly appropriate. I know lots of titled gentlemen who like to tinker with so-called inventions. Indeed, until he went to Cambridge, there seemed no reason for concern. From what I could gather from Charlotte, it seems he fell in with a bad crowd who encouraged his worst impulses towards drinking and gambling and who knows what else. His parents were quite beside themselves with worry."

Finally, Tobias was roused to comment, "Perhaps they should stay out of my business, and then they would not worry."

The dowager replied sharply, "Stay out of your business? Is that what you think your parents and grandmother should do? You certainly sang to a different tune when you wanted their money to bail you out. You should be ashamed of yourself, Tobias." Tabitha observed the young man. If he did feel any shame, it wasn't indicated by the look on his face or his behaviour.

Before the conversation could get any more heated, the carriage pulled up outside of the hotel. By the look on Tobias' face, it seemed as if it occurred to him that if he were to bolt, this would be the most opportune time. The dowager, also interpreting his facial expressions, took hold of the young man's jacket sleeve. While the woman would have been no match for the young man if he had chosen to pull out of her grasp and escape, either good breeding or some modicum of sense prevented him from making that rash decision.

The dowager led Wolf, Tabitha and Tobias up to her suite, instructing the hall porter to send Langley and Bear up once they arrived back at the hotel. As the lift doors opened up onto the corridor where both the dowager's suite and her own were located, Tabitha realised that the corkboard and blank notecards were still in her room, so she detoured to retrieve them.

By the time Tabitha was admitted into the dowager's suite by Withers, Tobias was seated on the sofa, and the dowager was in her higher armchair, glowering down at him. Wolf had pulled up a chair from next to the little desk in the corner of the room. Tabitha balanced the corkboard back on the sideboard and then took the other armchair. Any question as to whether to wait for the others was made unnecessary by a sharp rap at the door. Withers went to answer it, and Langley entered the room. It seemed Bear had decided his particular talents were not needed for this part of the evening's activities and had repaired to the suite he shared with Wolf.

Langley settled himself at the other end of the sofa from Tobias. The tension in the room was so thick Tabitha felt it was almost corporeal. Deciding that nothing was to be gained by having nerves stretched so thin, Wolf suggested they make use of the libations the room had to offer. Tobias jumped at the offer of some liquid courage.

"I think you have had quite enough to drink tonight, young man," the dowager proclaimed. "Though, Wolf, a little sherry would be lovely, thank you."

"I am not a child, Aunt Julia." Tobias' words were belied by a pout and whine that would have done a sulky seven-year-old proud.

Wolf knew better than to debate this with the dowager and poured brandy and sherry for everyone except Tobias. When they were all seated with drinks in hand, the dowager sent in the advance scouts, "So, Tobias, what brings you to Brighton?" This was said in a deceptively gentle tone as if she truly were nothing more than a devoted godmother enquiring about a beloved godson.

Unfortunately for Tobias, he was not battle-hardened enough to recognise this question for what it was and visibly relaxed. Perhaps it was just a horrible coincidence that had brought him face to face with Aunt Julia that evening, and the tongue lashing he was about to receive would be nothing more than of a kind with the ones he regularly received from his parents and grandmother.

"Oh, you know, this and that?" Tobias said in the offhand, relaxed tones of one who believed he knew the extent of the pain ahead of him and was unworried by it. He continued, "I have a chum from Cambridge whose parents have an old pile just outside of Brighton. Draughty old place, but it'll do while I, well, while things…" realising he was leading the conversation back into dangerous territory, Tobias fumbled for how best to phrase his current situation.

He needn't have bothered; the dowager was more than happy to finish his sentence for him, "While your irate father cools down?" she asked sweetly.

The dowager's question was said so kindly and with such evident sympathy in its tone that Tobias looked up with hope in his eyes and answered, "Well, yes. Pater was mad as hops the last time I saw him. I actually thought I was going to get a batty-fang, and so I skipped out of town for a while."

The dowager narrowed her eyes and said in a far less sympathetic tone, "Young man, I have no idea what you are talking about. Is there a reason you can't speak English?"

Tobias stared at her, unsure what was unclear about his statement. Wolf decided that, for the sake of expediency, he would translate, "Lady Pembroke, what I believe Viscount Tobias is trying to articulate is that his father was extremely angry. So angry that the viscount feared a beating, and so left London."

"Then why didn't he just say that?" she demanded. "So you slunk out of town with your tail between your legs and are imposing upon the ill-judged generosity of the family of one of your ne'er-do-well friends?"

While that wasn't how Tobias would have phrased it, his godmother's words captured the essence of the situation, and so the young man merely nodded his agreement.

"I see. And, rather than using this sojourn to reflect on your disreputable behaviour, you instead decided to transplant your malfeasance to a new geography?" Tobias had drunk a lot of champagne that evening, and it had definitely dulled his wits.

But even so, he was beginning to realise that the worst of this tongue-lashing might be ahead.

Not quite ready to go in for the kill yet, the dowager reverted to her more gentle tone and asked, "And how do you like Brighton? I hear it has its charms, though, for the most part, they are lost on me."

Happy to be back on safer ground, Tobias sat back, more relaxed, and answered, "Oh, you know, it's not so bad. There are some pleasant enough diversions if one is creative in seeking them out."

Tabitha almost gasped out loud at the young man's naivety in leading the conversation onto such treacherous ground. He really was arrogant enough to believe himself at least somewhat in control of this conversation. Foolish boy, Tabitha thought as she watched the dowager gather her forces and deliver the decisive blow, her coup de grâce.

"Pleasant enough diversions? Is that what you were able to find, you say? Was the actress, Miss Mapp, one such diversion?" Of all the things Tobias thought his godmother might berate him for, it was clear that this had not been on his list.

Tobias froze, his eyes wide, "I know no such person," he lied unconvincingly.

"Is that so?" the dowager asked, slowly articulating every word, her voice dripping with incredulity.

Still unsure precisely what his godmother actually knew, Tobias shifted tack a little and blustered, "Well, maybe I've seen someone of that name perform once or twice. I'm not really sure; all these actresses blur into one, don't you know?"

"Do they? I would have thought that your many visits to her backstage and accompanying flowers and piteous, pleading notes might have been reminder enough."

At this, Tobias sat up ramrod straight and protested, "Who told you they were piteous and pleading? That isn't at all true!" As he said these last words, it dawned on him what he had admitted to.

The dowager smiled with bloodthirsty appreciation of the

fatal wound she had inflicted, "Let us skip over your tall tales for now, Tobias," she said as if they had been debating whether he had stolen biscuits from the kitchen or not. "And instead, move forward to the part where Miss Mapp is murdered most brutally, and you are a prime suspect."

It was hard to imagine that Tobias could have faked his shock at these words. But what was so horrifying? That he was a suspect or that his godmother knew enough to believe him one? It turned out it was neither of these, or at least they were not the most shocking part of the dowager's pronouncement. "Danielle is dead?" he asked in horror. "When? how?"

Normally disinclined to interrupt the dowager when she was in full battle charge mode, Tabitha couldn't help exclaiming, "How could you not know about this? She was murdered over three weeks ago. It was on the front news of the local paper multiple times."

"I don't read the London rags, let alone the Brighton ones," the young man explained. "It's all too damn depressing. The last time I saw Danielle was on the final night of the last show. She was very blunt, rather cruelly, I have to say. She made it clear she would be leaving word at the stage door that I was no longer to be admitted. Under any circumstances. She said some very hurtful things as it happened." Tobias said this last sentence in an aggrieved tone that, given the woman's death, showed a shocking self-absorption.

Tobias continued, "Anyway, she demanded I leave her dressing room, and so I did. I left the theatre and went and drowned my sorrows."

"And she was still alive when you left?" Wolf demanded.

"Of course she was still alive. What do you take me for? And who are you? None of you introduced yourselves, you know. Damned impolite, if you ask me."

Wolf inclined his head towards the dowager, unsure how she wanted to play this situation. "Not that you are in any position to make demands, but this is the new Earl of Pembroke, and next to you on the sofa is the Earl of Langley. I'm assuming you recognise my son, Jonathan's widow from the funeral. Now that the niceties have been taken care of, hopefully to your satisfaction," the dowager added sarcastically, "may we proceed?"

Tobias didn't reply, and so she stormed onwards, "Why should we take your word that she was alive when you left?"

"Well, that fellow, that hulking, dark-skinned chappie who was always hanging around her, escorted me out at her command. Highly inappropriate, as far as I'm concerned. He walked me out the door and up the street as if I couldn't be trusted. Anyway, I don't know why he bothered; that door automatically locked, so it's not like I could have re-entered."

Tabitha held up a hand to stop Tobias' story, "Wait, so you left Danielle alive and exited the building with Robert Charles through a door that automatically locked?"

"Isn't that just what I said? Is that his name? I suppose it must be. Danielle called him Bobby. So that was likely who he was."

Tabitha and Wolf looked at each other. "We have to take this information to the police," Tabitha exclaimed. Tobias is Robert Charles' alibi."

"Alibi for what?" Tobias asked in genuine confusion.

"Robert Charles, Bobby, was arrested for Danielle's murder. Your failure to come forward with this information has kept an innocent man in the police cells for weeks and might have led him to the gallows," Langley explained. If Tobias felt any guilt at this, it was, again, hard to tell.

It was decided that they would accompany Tobias to the police station the following day to give Robert Charles his alibi. The young man indicated his preference to return to his friend's home for the night, but no one trusted him to reappear the next day, so it was determined they would have the hotel send up a trundle bed, and he would sleep in Wolf's room, under lock and key. There was some protestation, but from what Tabitha could tell, it seemed as if the dowager had pummelled any real fight the young man had in him. Finally, accepting his fate, he let himself be led off by Wolf to his bed for the night.

Langley and Tabitha were left with the dowager, who took another sip of her sherry and asked, "Do you believe him?"

Tabitha thought for a moment before replying, then answered, "I do. His shock on hearing about the murder was very convincing. What do you think, Lord Langley?" Langley agreed. He'd interrogated enough people over the years that he had a good, professional sense for when he was being lied to.

"Well, then, let us hope and pray that this Inspector Maguire also believes him," Tabitha observed. "Then, regardless of whether we can solve this murder, we can at least ensure an innocent man doesn't hang for it."

CHAPTER 22

The following morning, over breakfast, which Viscount Tobias, dressed in some of Wolf's clothes, sulked his way through, the rest of the group decided on a division of labour for that morning. Tabitha and Wolf would visit Kit Bailey and find out who might have keys to the theatre. Meanwhile, Lord Langley and the dowager would accompany Viscount Tobias to the police station to provide a witness statement and an alibi for Robert Charles. Because there were worries about both Tobias' willingness to cooperate and Inspector Maguire's to accept the alibi and free his prisoner, it was agreed that the dowager would be part of that group. It was an unspoken but accepted fact that no mere police inspector could withstand her withering glare, let alone her rapier-sharp tongue.

Realising that she was, yet again, free to do as she pleased, Lily almost skipped away from breakfast, eager to be out of sight before her grandmother changed her mind and decided to stay back and torture her.

It was a dreary, overcast day, and Tabitha was worried about how Mary would occupy the children if they couldn't walk on the beach, ride donkeys, or make yet another visit to see the Punch and Judy show. Tabitha excused herself from the breakfast table and went to speak with the always helpful hall porter, Mr Champion, about any games the hotel might have for use by guests.

She found Mr Champion directing a bellboy as to where to take a guest's luggage and explained her dilemma. "Well, you've come to the right man, that you have, m'lady. We have a nice selection in the library, and I'll be happy to send whatever you want up to Lord Langley's suite. We have Checkers and Ludo and a few others that I think the nippers will enjoy. And I'll make sure the kitchen sends up a plate of treats for them as well. Nasty weather like this is going to last all day. At least that's what Mrs Champion's rheumatism predicted."

Tabitha thanked Mr Champion and felt less guilty about leaving Melody and Rat. She returned to the breakfast table, only to hear the tail-end of a scolding being administered by the dowager to Viscount Tobias, "You will stay here, under my watchful eye until this matter is sorted out to my satisfaction. At which point, you will be dispatched home to be dealt with by your long-suffering parents."

"I am an adult," Tobias said petulantly, sounding anything but that, "not a child to be ordered around as his elders and so-called betters see fit."

Tabitha sat down to have one last cup of coffee and watch this exchange that was certain to end badly for the young man. Really, it was quite unbelievable that he didn't yet realise the gravity of the situation he had found himself in. And by the situation, Tabitha didn't even mean the murder enquiry. Rather, she meant that Tobias didn't appreciate that his godmother was sighting in on her prey, his bad behaviour, with an inescapable determination.

The dowager had been sipping her tea as Tobias made this desperate yet foolish statement. Eyeing her godson over her teacup, she then replaced it in its saucer, dabbed around her mouth with her serviette, and asked, "Is that how you see things?"

Foolishly continuing to stumble into enemy territory unarmed, Tobias said with a misplaced bravado, "Yes, that is how things are, in fact, Aunt Julia."

"Let me be very clear about one thing, dear Toby," his godmother's use of his childhood nickname should have warned him if her tone didn't. "I had no problem boxing your ears when you were a boy, and I would have no problem boxing them now. You think because you're now taller than I am, you are safe from me? Most people are taller than I am, but I have never let that deter me. And it won't in this case."

The young man went red with embarrassment but, amazingly, seemed to take her words seriously. Tabitha reflected that it was a mark of how formidable the dowager's personality was that, despite her diminutive size, Viscount Tobias clearly believed her more than willing and able to follow through on her threat.

Sensing a twitch of Langley's mouth at her words, the dowager turned to him and said, "And I'm not sure what you're smirking at, Maxwell. I boxed your ears more than once as well and would similarly have no qualms about doing so again." The Peer of the Realm and member of British Intelligence immediately corrected his facial expressions and averted his eyes.

Wolf realised that, although this scene had some entertainment value, it was getting them nowhere. Robert Charles was still languishing in that police cell, and they had a duty to ensure the innocent man was released immediately. He stood and said, "Shall we agree to meet down here, ready to leave in twenty minutes?" Everyone but Tobias nodded their agreement.

By the time they returned to the lobby, the rain had started to fall. Mr Champion suggested that they all take the carriage and drop Tabitha and Wolf at the theatre before carrying on to the police station with the dowager, Langley, and Tobias. It would be rather a squeeze. But it was such a short distance, and the rain was now coming down so heavily that everyone agreed it was the best plan. The ever-helpful hall porter also provided umbrellas.

Arriving at the theatre, Tabitha was glad to see that the stage door was propped open. Relieved not to have to wait out in the street in the rain, she followed Wolf in. The backstage area was quiet, and no one seemed to be about. Hoping he could remember his way through the labyrinth of corridors, Wolf continued to what he hoped was Kit Bailey's office. Despite a couple of false turns, they eventually found the right door, and Wolf knocked.

Having not accompanied Wolf there previously, Tabitha was intrigued by what the backstage operations of a theatre were like. She eagerly anticipated meeting this Christopher "Kit" Bailey she had heard so much about. Wolf had given her a very amusing recitation of the dowager's interaction with the theatre company impresario. Few people were able to stand their ground against the Dowager Countess of Pembroke. Tabitha could hardly wait to take the measure of the man, who, by Wolf's telling, was singularly unaffected by the older woman's patented disdain. In fact, seemed to have found it entertaining.

A booming "Enter!" followed Wolf's knock, and he opened the door to find Kit at his desk, which was covered in papers. "Ah, dear boy, how nice to see you again." Just then, Kit noticed Tabitha standing behind Wolf. Kit had been quite the Don Juan in his day, and he still lived under the illusion that the years had done nothing to diminish his charms. It was not uncommon for him to spot a young woman and ask his companions, "Do you think she is too young for me?" only to be greeted by guffaws.

The room was as headache-inducing and cramped as Wolf remembered. Kit stood and indicated that Wolf should enter his small, messy office while simultaneously making eyes at Tabitha. At least, he believed he was making eyes; she wondered why this old man was leering at her. "Lord Pembroke, how nice to see you again. And who is your charming companion?" Kit said with a lasciviousness that he didn't even try to hide.

Wolf appreciated the man's help so far and certainly didn't want to antagonise him. But he wouldn't allow Tabitha, or indeed any woman, to be talked to in that tone. He entered the office, pulled one of the chairs out for Tabitha to sit, and then said very pointedly, "You are in the company of the Countess of Pembroke, my cousin's widow and a key member of my investigative team."

It was impossible to say if Kit heard the intended rebuke; the man was not known for his sensitivity. However, even he knew that one did not continue to ogle a titled lady openly, so he kept his eyes trained on Wolf as he said, "Welcome to you both. How can I help you on this dreary morn?"

"Yes, it is a rather miserable day," Tabitha agreed.

"The rain, it raineth every day," Kit remarked. Seeing his guests' blank stares, he continued. "The Bard. *King Lear*. One of my favourites. Did you know that Shakespeare…"

"We'd like to ask you a few more questions," Wolf interrupted, not wanting to get sidetracked by Kit's exposition.

Kit was too goodhearted to be offended at Wolf's interruption and cheerfully replied, "Ask away, milord!"

Deciding to begin with a less challenging question, Wolf asked, "How many people have keys to the theatre?"

Kit stroked his white beard as he thought, "Well, let's see. I do, of course. And Mildred at the box office. Then Mrs Malloy has a set. The prop master, Danny, has a set. Honestly, I'm not sure who else. Once the box office takings are safe every night, there's not much here worth stealing. So, I've never been too worried about who wants to have keys."

There was one question that Wolf needed an answer to before they revealed any more, "Did Robert Charles have a set of keys?"

"Bobby? Good heavens, no," Kit said immediately.

Wolf looked over at Tabitha, unsure where to go next with his questioning. Deciding they had nothing to lose by showing at least some of their hand at this point, Tabitha took over and said somewhat cagily, "There is a possible witness who may be able to provide Robert Charles with an alibi for the night of the murder."

Kit's eyes opened wide with surprise. But his words conveyed more equanimity than his face, "Well, isn't that wonderful? Great news indeed."

Tabitha thought she sensed a little unease in the man's voice despite his proclaimed gladsomeness. She decided to wait and see what Kit's reaction was before she revealed that Langley was on his way to the police station with Tobias at that moment. Kit continued with what seemed like disingenuous casual curiosity, "And who is this witness?"

"An admirer of Danielle's, Viscount Tobias Williams," Tabitha watched Kit's reaction carefully.

Wolf added, "I believe that you described him as a 'Young, snot-nosed, arrogant ass'."

Apart from a slight twitch of his cheek, Kit's reaction was unremarkable as he replied, "Ah yes, that love-sick puppy. I've had to throw him out of here myself on occasion. Why will young men never realise that 'Love sought is good, but given unsought better'?" Kit added, *"Twelfth Night."*

Wolf wondered if the man had a Shakespeare quote for every occasion. "It seems that Miss Mapp had made very clear to Viscount Tobias that he was no longer welcome to visit her dressing room and had asked Bobby to escort him out. They left the theatre together, and the door locked behind them. If Bobby didn't have a key, as you've just said, then it would have been impossible for him to have re-entered the theatre and killed Danielle."

"Isn't this just the best news I could have received today," Kit claimed over-enthusiastically.

Wolf had one more question to ask, "Previously, you had said that you had no idea who the supposed witness was to Danielle's rebuffing of Mr Charles. Now you've had a bit of time to consider further, might you have any thoughts? Because in interviewing your theatre company, no one admitted to being this person. Which leads me to believe that either someone was lying to us or the police."

Kit said nothing to indicate which of these two scenarios he considered the most likely. However, a slight tightening around the man's mouth led Wolf to believe they wouldn't get much more help from him, and so he felt there was little to be lost by asking, "One last question, Mr Bailey, Kit. A witness informed us that on the night of the murder, when you stopped by the celebrations at the pub, you had an altercation with Mr Frost, Merryweather. Can you tell us what that was about?"

The tightening around Kit's mouth now caused his jaw muscles to clench, and he answered in a dry, cool tone, "I'm not sure how that is relevant to Danielle's murder."

"Mr Bailey, it has been our experience that it is impossible to know what will or won't be relevant to an investigation. Therefore, we must gather all the information we can, even if it appears to be innocuous," Tabitha explained sweetly.

Finally, unable to keep his evident tenseness from seeping into his voice, Kit snapped, "That has been your experience, has it, Lady Pembroke?" His tone was so dismissive and sneering that even Kit seemed taken aback and quickly said, "I must apologise, milady. But this is a very distressing personal matter, and I would rather not talk about it."

Playing his trump card, Wolf said, "We were told that you owed Mr Frost money and were asking for more time to repay it."

These words were met with a stony silence. Waiting a few more moments, Wolf rose and said, "In that case, I bid you a good day, Mr Bailey." Tabitha then stood as well, and the two of them left the office and found their way out of the theatre. Relieved to see that the rain had subsided somewhat to a slight drizzle, Wolf put up the borrowed umbrella and held it over Tabitha's head as they walked back to the hotel. Even so, the walk was cold and miserable enough that they agreed not to discuss the interview until they were back in the warmth of the hotel.

Arriving back at The Grand, Wolf gave the wet umbrella back to Mr Champion and asked if it was possible to get some tea served. They agreed to deposit their outerwear and meet back in the library.

Wolf was the first back downstairs and wasn't surprised to find that the library's only inhabitant was Lily, who was sitting in a leather armchair in front of the roaring fire, happily reading. She looked up as he entered and asked, "How was your expedition, Cousin Jeremy?"

"Interesting, to say the least. I am waiting for your Aunt Tabitha to join me so we can discuss our observations." Seeing the young woman close her book and stand, he added, "You are welcome to join us. Please don't feel the need to leave on our behalf."

Lily shook her head and said, "Please don't take this the wrong way, but I find all this talk of investigations boring in the extreme. It was one thing when it involved someone I knew. But now, while I appreciate the importance of proving this man's innocence, I would rather not listen to any more of it than I already have to during meals. I will retire to my room and read there." She thought for a moment, then added, "After all, if you are back, it will not be long before Grandmama returns, and I'd rather be out of sight when that occurs.

Wolf acknowledged the wisdom of her decision and watched her leave. Lily must have crossed paths with Tabitha because only a few moments later, his investigative partner entered the room, gently closing the door behind her.

No sooner had Tabitha sat than there was a knock on the door, and a maid entered with a tray laden with a teapot and cups, a plate of sliced cake and another with what looked like cucumber finger sandwiches. The maid put the tray down, then excused herself, closing the door behind her.

Tabitha poured a cup of tea for them both, put a slice of cake and a couple of sandwiches on a plate for Wolf, but took nothing for herself and then sat in the chair recently occupied by Lily.

"So, what did you make of our conversation with Kit Bailey?" Wolf asked.

"Well, he's definitely hiding something. The question is, what?"

CHAPTER 23

The hotel's carriage had pulled up in front of the impressive Brighton Town Hall. The dowager said, "Well, I have to admit, I'm pleasantly surprised that this is the police station." Realising how quickly the dowager's good impressions were going to be changed by their descent into the subterranean police lair, Langley held his tongue and helped her out of the carriage. They made their way into the building, the dowager on Langley's arm, and Tobias following sullenly behind.

As Langley turned towards the staircase that would lead them into the basement, he said, "The building is the town hall. The police station is located down here. As they reached the bottom of the stairs and made their way into the low-ceilinged, windowless room that served as a waiting area, the dowager sniffed an indication of the reversal of her admiration.

Luckily, the constable behind the desk was the same one they had dealt with before. He looked up and recognised Langley as the toff who had been flashing his credentials around previously. "How can I help you today, m'lord?" he asked with just enough civility.

Langley explained that they needed to talk to the inspector again. The constable may have sighed, but he didn't argue and once more led them down the dank corridor. As they followed the policeman, the dowager tugged slightly on Langley's arm. He bent down, and she said in not nearly a quiet enough voice, "Are we heading to the inspector's office, or is this the prison?" Luckily, Langley was saved from having to answer by their arrival at the door to Inspector Maguire's office.

The constable knocked, and again, a bark of, "Enter," came from within. The constable opened the door. The office was as unappealing as Langley remembered, and the expression of irritation in Inspector Maguire's blue eyes was equal to the last visit. However, that irritation was quickly replaced by curiosity as the inspector took in the dowager and Tobias lurking at the rear.

"Lord Langley, back again, I see. And with company. How can I help you?" as he said this, he waved his hand to dismiss the constable.

Langley let the dowager enter before him and take a seat, and then he took the other chair. Viscount Tobias entered the room and said, "So, I'll just stand here, shall I?" No one paid any attention to the petulant young man who stood in front of the inspector's desk as if he had been called to his headmaster's office for a tongue-lashing.

Inspector Maguire took in Langley's companions: the tiny, old woman with those steel-grey eyes that looked as if they didn't miss a thing and the sulky young toff who seemed very unhappy to be there. What on earth did these people want now?

"I will get to the point," Langley said. "This is the Dowager Countess of Pembroke, and this young man," he indicated to Tobias, "is her godson, Viscount Tobias Williams."

"That is a lot of titles to squeeze in such a small, simple police inspector's office," Maguire noted sardonically. "It is a pleasure to meet you, milady and milord."

"That remains to be seen," the dowager answered in a tone so cold that Maguire almost felt his fingers chill. The woman's voice had an imperiousness to it that Inspector Maguire was all too familiar with, and he wasn't looking forward to where this conversation might be leading.

Langley wanted to save the dowager's firepower as a last resort and tried to inject some respect into his voice as he said, "Lord Pembroke and I felt it was our civic duty to bring Viscount Tobias to talk to you as soon as we realised that he was one of the last people to see the murder victim, Miss Mapp, alive."

Now, this was far more interesting than Maguire had anticipated. "Was he now?" he asked. "Milord," he said, addressing Tobias, "if that is the case, why did you not come forward before now?"

While this was precisely the question they had asked the previous evening, the dowager, always on the alert for officiousness in others, answered for her godson, "Viscount Tobias was not aware that a murder had taken place. If he had been, he would, of course, have immediately come forward. Indeed, as soon as we alerted him to the fact last night, he demanded that we come here first thing this morning so he could make a statement." That this was not what Tobias had demanded was immediately evident from his scowl as the dowager spoke. By Maguire's professional assessment, there was nothing about the glowering young man who stood before him, hair flopping over one eye, shoulders hunched, and arms folded in front of him in surly defensiveness that spoke to an eagerness to perform his civic duty.

The inspector directed his next question at Tobias, "And do you have anything else to report, milord?"

The dowager poked her godson, who brushed his hair out of his face only to have it immediately fall back over his eye. "What, Aunt Julia? Why can't you tell it?"

"Were you not complaining about being treated like a child just this morning?" the dowager scolded. "Well, this is your chance to behave as an adult." When her words did nothing more than make Tobias pout even more, the dowager rolled her eyes, sighed, and then relayed his description of being walked out of the theatre by Robert Charles the night that Danielle was murdered. She then added the information about the self-locking stage door.

When the dowager was done, she paused and added, "So, it seems there has been a gross miscarriage of justice. It is lucky for this Mr Charles that I was on hand to bring this key piece of evidence to your attention."

Again, Inspector Maguire directed his question to Tobias, "Is this correct, milord?" He received a grunt in response. Malcolm Maguire was a very ambitious man and was the youngest policeman to make inspector in the history of the Brighton police force. He carefully weighed what he'd been told and by whom he had been told it. There was no doubt that the chief inspector would be very unhappy to have what he thought was a done-and-dusted case unravel again. But he also knew that this Lord Langley had important connections in Whitehall. But more than any of that, as he looked at the woman in front of him, he weighed how much he wanted to get on her bad side.

Finally, Inspector Maguire stood and went to the door, leaning out into the corridor. He yelled, "Jenkins", and then went back to his desk. A moment or two later, a short, plump policeman barrelled into the room and then stopped short when he saw the clearly important visitors in his boss' office. "Jenkins, let Robert Charles go," Maguire ordered.

"Go, sir? But isn't he due to go to trial next week?" the policeman mumbled.

"Let him go," then the inspector smirked just a little, "into these people's custody."

"What do you mean into our custody?" the dowager demanded. However she had imagined this visit proceeding, it was never that it ended with them leaving with responsibility for the accused man.

"The only way I can release him is into your custody. You have presented a witness with what seems like a credible alibi. However, we have no other suspects, and so while the trial will be suspended, I cannot exonerate Mr Charles yet. Therefore, someone has to take responsibility for ensuring he doesn't skip town."

"Inspector, do I look like a prison warden to you?" the dowager demanded. Maguire thought, did she really want him to answer that question?

Luckily, he was saved from having to answer by Langley, who interjected, "I would be happy to take responsibility for the young man, inspector." The dowager looked at Langley and raised her eyebrows. But she didn't say anything. She assumed it was clear to everyone involved that she had not agreed to this plan.

The inspector nodded, and Constable Jenkins left. While they waited for the constable to return, Langley asked nonchalantly, "By the way, you mentioned a witness to Mr Charles having a heated conversation with the deceased. Who might that happen to be?"

Maguire narrowed his eyes; despite the seeming insouciance of the question, the inspector was well aware he was being pumped for confidential witness statements. On the other hand, if Robert Charles wasn't the murderer, did it really matter what someone said they heard? Taking another look at the rather terrifying little old woman, Maguire decided to err on the side of self-preservation and answered, "Actually, it was Mr Christopher Bailey, the theatre company owner."

Whatever answer Langley had expected, it wasn't that. However, if he had any follow-up questions, they were pre-empted by Constable Jenkins's return with a terrified-looking Robert Charles in tow. The constable pushed the man into the office.

"Release him from the handcuffs", Maguire ordered.

Bobby Charles looked at the people in the office in evident confusion. Who were they, and why was he here?

"Mr Charles. Mr Charles," the inspector repeated when the prisoner was unresponsive. The sleep-deprived, hungry, and despondent young man lifted his head to look at Maguire. But he still didn't say anything. The inspector had dealt with the same behaviour when they first arrested Robert Charles and had tried to interrogate him. As soon as they had mentioned the actress' death, the man had turned his face to the wall and said nothing.

Deciding that the sooner he got all of these people out of his office, the better, Inspector Maguire decided to proceed regardless of Bobby's unresponsiveness. "Robert, Bobby, these people have brought evidence that you may not have killed

Danielle." At her name, Bobby looked pained but still said nothing. "Based on what they have told me, I am willing to release you into their custody. Do you know what that means?" Bobby shook his head. Maguire sighed and explained, "It means you have to stay in Brighton and do whatever they say. If you try to leave, I will have no choice but to have you arrested again. Do you understand that?"

Finally, Bobby spoke, saying, "Yes, sir." If he wondered who these well-dressed people were he was to go with, he didn't say it.

As they left the police station with Robert Charles in tow, it occurred to Langley how inappropriate it would be in every way to have the grimy, foul-smelling young man share a carriage with the dowager. Or, at the least, how inappropriate she would find it. "Lady Pembroke, I will walk back to the hotel with Mr Charles while you take the carriage with Viscount Tobias."

Tobias looked up at that. Was it genuine concern for how the middle-aged Langley could handle the large man in his custody if he chose to flee, or more likely, an unwillingness to spend time alone with his godmother? Whatever the reason, he said, "I will walk with you." He added vaguely, "To help." Langley had harboured some of the same concerns Tobias might have had and so wasn't inclined to refuse the company.

Despite his fears, Bobby Charles was nothing but docile and compliant for the walk back. He said nothing, but he gave no indication that he was planning to escape. When they arrived at the hotel, a new concern struck Langley. They couldn't just parade the man through the hotel lobby in his current state. He assumed the hotel had a service entrance and led the way back up the street from the direction they had come in until he found a gate that led to a courtyard at the rear of the hotel.

A couple of maids were in the courtyard hanging out laundry. They started at the intruders into their space, their eyes bulging both at the grandeur of two of the interlopers in their domain and at the huge, dirty man in ragged clothes in their company.

Langley was unsure how to explain their presence, and so

merely lifted his hat and said, "Good morning, ladies. We're sorry to interrupt your work." With that, he led the way through the back door, which he hoped wouldn't lead to a kitchen full of more servants. Luckily, it led into a dark hallway that had a door that did lead to the kitchen, but also a narrow, uncarpeted staircase. Assuming that if they walked up three flights, they'd eventually come to a corridor from which they could make their way to his suite, Langley led the way, with Tobias bringing up the rear and Bobby between them.

Making his way from the back staircase to his rooms was not the end of Langley's travails. As he arrived at the door to his hotel suite, he paused. From within, he could hear chattering, giggles and barks; Melody was in the room with her puppy, Dodo. Unsure where else to take Bobby, Langley indicated that Tobias should stay outside with the other man while he went into the room. Once inside, Langley told Mary that she should take Melody and Dodo into the bedroom and entertain them until he told them to come out. Servants didn't ask questions, and Mary obediently took her charges into the other room.

Rat, who had been reading a book by the fire, stood up and asked, "Is everything all right, m'lord?"

In answer, Langley opened the door and beckoned for Tobias and Bobby to enter. Rat had spent enough time on the streets of Whitechapel that there wasn't much that fazed him. While he cocked an eyebrow at Bobby's appearance, he said nothing. Tobias, however, stared at the young boy and asked in an arrogant voice, "Who is this? You should send the child away, Langley. This is no place for him."

Lord Langley coolly replied, "This is Rat, and I suspect he has more gained life experience and wisdom in his eight years than you have in twice that." Tobias sneered but said nothing more.

Langley turned to Rat, "Can you search the hotel and see if you can find Lord Pembroke? He and Lady Pembroke went out separately to us, so they may not have returned yet." Rat was an intelligent and resourceful young man. Langley had no doubt he would track Tabitha and Wolf down.

As Rat left the room, Ashby, Lord Langley's valet, emerged from the second bedroom. "I thought I heard you m'lord." Ashby glanced at Bobby, "Is there anything I can help you with?"

Ashby was a large man, taller and broader than his master. Looking at him gave Langley an idea, "Ashby, this is Bobby Charles. Can you please help him clean up and then provide him with some fresh clothes? He seems as if he's about your size." Ashby had served as Lord Langley's valet for more than twenty years. In that time, he had fulfilled some unusual requests. At this latest order, he merely nodded his head and indicated for Bobby to follow him out of the suite towards the servants' rooms. He certainly wouldn't be using his lordship's bath to wash all the dirt off the mysterious stranger.

CHAPTER 24

It hadn't taken Rat long to find Tabitha and Wolf in the library, still discussing their conversation with Kit. The boy didn't relay much except that Lord Langley required them in his suite. Consumed with curiosity, they followed Rat upstairs and into Langley's room. There, they found nothing more mysterious than the man himself and Tobias, minus the dowager.

"Good work, Rat," Langley said, patting the boy on the shoulder. "Why don't you go and get Mary and Melody? Your lunch should be arriving any minute." Turning back to Wolf and Tabitha, he said, "Her ladyship should have preceded us. Why don't we all make our way to her suite? Do you think the hotel can be prevailed upon to send us up some lunch? I don't believe our conversation is suitable for a public restaurant."

Tabitha offered to go and talk to Mr Champion and see what could be done while the rest went down the hall to the dowager's rooms. The ever-present Withers answered the door, then stood back to let them in.

The group settled themselves around the room and waited for Tabitha to return. They didn't have to wait long. She had found Bear while she was in the lobby and brought him up with her. Bear had gone to visit the bed and breakfast they had been told Mrs Channing was now running with her sister.

As Tabitha and Bear entered the room, a still-sullen Tobias asked, "Is there a reason I need to be here? I've done what you asked of me and went to visit that unpleasant policeman. There is no longer any need to keep me prisoner here."

"You are going nowhere, young man, until this case is solved. You were the last person to see the victim, and who knows what else you might have just forgotten to mention." The dowager was brusque, but no one disagreed with her. It seemed that Tobias had a selective memory for anything that didn't interest him, and no one was convinced he had divulged every possible detail.

The dowager continued, "Moreover, I do not trust you to be out of my sight. You will stay here and only speak if you have something worthwhile to contribute." The young man went to a chair in the far corner of the suite and sat down, determined to sulk his way through however long this boring gathering lasted.

Everyone else did their best to squeeze into the room, with Bear offering to stand when it became clear they had run out of chairs. Withers suggested bringing a chair from the dressing table in the bedroom, and with that accomplished, they all sat and began to discuss their findings from their respective expeditions that morning.

Langley and the dowager told the relieved group that Bobby Charles was now free. However happy everyone was to hear this news, they were also more than a little surprised to find that they now had custody of the man.

"Where is he to stay, and what is he to do?" Tabitha asked. While she was sure the hotel had rooms available, she did wonder how willing they would be to accommodate Bobby. Moreover, how comfortable would he be there?

The group discussed all possibilities for a few minutes until Tabitha turned to Wolf and said softly, "I think the answer to this particular problem is obvious." He looked at her quizzically; what was obvious about this? Tabitha continued, "You must ask Lady Archibald if we might impose upon her and have Bobby join her household, at least for the time being."

As soon as she said these words, Wolf knew Tabitha was right. Of course. Bobby would be safe, well cared for, and comfortable in Lady Archibald's Kemptown house. And Arlene did need to be told that at least one of her objectives had been met; Bobby

Charles was free, at least for now. Nevertheless, Wolf's face mirrored the panic and confusion he felt at the suggestion. Over the past few days, it had felt as if things were back to normal between Tabitha and him. He had tried to forget Arlene's origination of the investigation and pretended to himself that he could avoid her company. But he knew that was yet more cowardice on his part. His brief visit the day before with the dowager hadn't relieved him of any of his fears.

Correctly interpreting the source of Wolf's obvious angst, Tabitha took pity on him and said, "I suggest that you write to Lady Archibald as soon as we are done here. Give her an update on Mr Charles' release and ask her if she can accommodate him, at least until he is formally exonerated. Assuming she agrees, you and Bear, or Langley, can accompany him over there later." This was a sensible suggestion, and Wolf nodded his agreement.

Just as Tabitha and Wolf had resolved one issue before them, there was a knock at the door. Withers went to open it and found a maid on the other side. Tabitha had suggested to Mr Champion that the group would be perfectly happy with a light, easy-to-eat meal of some sandwiches and the like. The man had taken her at her word, and now the maid rolled in a trolley laden with a variety of sandwiches, mini sausage rolls, and other finger food. There was also a pot of tea and some slices of cake. The group filled up plates and then returned to their seats. Tabitha also took the opportunity to have Withers retrieve the corkboard and notecards.

For a few minutes, no one spoke as they munched on food and drank tea. Tobias had initially boycotted the meal in protest at his "imprisonment". But when it became clear that he would miss out on sausage rolls if he didn't hurry, he put his high dudgeon aside temporarily and filled up a plate with food.

Finally, their hunger somewhat satiated, Wolf said, "Bear, why don't you go first? Did you find Mrs Channing, and if so, what did she have to say?"

The large man put the dainty china plate on the side table nearest him and cleared his throat. "Well, I found her easily enough. Paddy was right about which bed and breakfast it was. It seems that she had been in discussion to purchase it for a while now, and her employer's death just freed her from the necessity of giving her notice, which she was about to do anyway."

"Did you learn anything more than that she is a disloyal, ungrateful servant?" the dowager demanded, taking great exception to the idea that a servant might seek to better her life.

"Yes, milady. It seems that Miss Mapp had accepted an offer from another theatre company. Apparently, there's a new theatre opening soon called The Hippodrome. It was originally used as a circus or something like that. So, it's quite extravagant inside. Anyway, the intention is not to host plays as such, but a mixture of operettas, vaudeville acts, music hall kind of stuff. Well, it seems that the owner had approached Miss Mapp a few weeks ago and asked her to headline the new company.

"According to Mrs Channing, Danielle didn't enjoy the kinds of performances they put on at the Theatre Royal. She preferred singing to acting, and The Hippodrome was offering her the chance to focus on that. They were also going to pay her more. And here was the interesting thing: Miss Mapp was worried about the financial security of the Theatre Royal. Apparently, Kit Bailey is pretty heavily in debt. It seems he has something of a gambling problem."

At this, Tobias swallowed his sausage roll and interjected nonchalantly, "I should say he does. I've seen that old duffer at the track. He has a real thing for the gee-gees. From what I've seen, he loses more than he wins."

All heads snapped around to stare at the young man. "Why exactly was it that you didn't think to share this information before?" the dowager demanded, echoing all of their thoughts.

"Aren't you investigating a murder? How is it relevant if some old fool cares to throw his money away on the nags?" Tobias asked in genuine bemusement.

Thinking to try to spare the young man from his godmother's wrath, Tabitha said far more gently than the boy deserved, "Tobias, all information is important. We never discount any evidence until it can be disproved. This may turn out to be very relevant."

Tobias didn't look as chastened as one might have expected and instead said, "Well, you know it now, don't you?" He then folded his arms and continued his sulk.

Realising that they had more important things to talk about than Tobias' communication failures, the group instead considered the import of his information. Tabitha had been writing up notecards. Now she stood and walked to the corkboard and pinned them. "So, we know that Kit is having financial problems and that Danielle accepted a position with another theatre company. The question is, did Kit know about this?" She turned and faced Bear as she asked this.

He shook his head, "Mrs Channing didn't say. It seems that Miss Mapp shared limited information with her staff. The only reason that Mrs Channing even knew about the new position was because she happened to see a contract in Miss Mapp's study. She swears that she didn't mean to read it, but it fell on the floor when she was dusting, and when she picked it up, she realised what she was holding."

"Let's add nosy to this woman's deficits as a servant," the dowager proclaimed.

Ignoring her, Tabitha asked, "Did she have anything else to say?"

"Not really. As I say, Miss Mapp was quite tight-lipped around her servants."

"Well, at any rate, I believe we now know why the study in Miss Mapp's house was ransacked," Langley pointed out. "We didn't find such a contract there, so it seems that was what had been taken. Given this, I believe that we may now have a motive for her murder."

Wolf agreed, "Indeed. Not only was Danielle leaving Kit's theatre company, but she was going to a new competitor. For a man already struggling financially, that must have been a hard pill to swallow."

Tabitha considered his words, then asked, "Are we saying that we believe Kit Bailey murdered Danielle?"

"Well, he certainly had motive, it seems. And he was definitely quite evasive this afternoon," Wolf added. Tabitha and Wolf then relayed the details of their earlier conversation with Kit Bailey.

When they reached the part where they had asked again if Kit knew who the supposed witness was, only to be met with silence, Langley interrupted, "I believe we can help with that. I asked Inspector Maguire that question, and it seems that the person who claimed to have heard Danielle and Bobby having a heated conversation was none other than Mr Bailey himself."

By the time this was confirmed, most in the room had been expecting such an outcome.

"This really is looking grimmer and grimmer for our rapscallion thespian," the dowager said in a tone that was just a shade too gleeful. While the dowager still harboured a secret suspicion that the murderer would turn out to be Danielle's understudy, there was a lot more pleasure to be derived from the thought of that rude man in those garish clothes getting his comeuppance.

Tabitha started to pace the room, thinking out loud, "So, Danielle receives an offer to move to another theatre, and on the last night of the show, she tells Kit. Perhaps she flaunts the fact that she has a contract in his face. Furious at the thought of how he will suffer financially with her gone and determined that his new competition won't have this advantage over him, he strangles her and stuffs her body in the trunk. He then heads out to meet the rest of the company at Paddy and Jeanie's. But when he arrives, he gets accosted by Merryweather Frost, to whom he owes money."

Tabitha looked around to see if anyone disagreed with her timeline so far. When it was clear there was no dissent, she continued, "At some point, he remembers the contract, breaks into Danielle's house and ransacks her study to find it so there is no evidence that she was planning to leave the Royal. Then, when the body is discovered, Mr Bailey tells the police that he knew Bobby was infatuated with Danielle, and claimed to have overheard her spurning his advances. This information supported a presumption the police were already inclined to make about Bobby's guilt, and so the statement was just accepted at face value."

As they all contemplated Tabitha's words and looked at the notecards on the board, everyone was led to the inescapable conclusion that she was correct. Everyone, besides the dowager, found that conclusion rather sad. While it had been obvious that Christopher "Kit" Bailey was something of a rogue, he had seemed to err more on the loveable side. Yes, the man clearly had a rakish side to him, but he'd also struck most of them as a larger-than-life character who was basically goodhearted. To think that he might have not only murdered a woman but then framed another man for that murder was profoundly depressing.

Aside from the dowager, Tabitha's experience of Kit had been the most negative of the little group's, and even she felt disturbed by her deductions. The last murderer they had caught had been an unpleasant man she had disliked immediately. The first murderer had been a wholly sympathetic woman who had killed for good reason. This murder was different. But then, she reflected, if she wanted to be involved with investigations going forward, she could hardly expect every case to fall neatly into either the "evil villain" or "justifiable action" category.

Looking around the room at the rather glum faces, Tabitha asked, "So, what do we do now? Hand this evidence to the police?"

Wolf thought about this question; no police inspector liked to be told that a suspect had made a fool of him. Having already told Inspector Maguire that he had arrested the wrong man, adding to that by telling him he had done so because Kit Bailey had played him would be unlikely to go down well. At the moment, they had nothing but circumstantial evidence.

While everything pointed to their conclusion being the correct one, the only out-and-out lie they had caught Kit telling was when he'd said that he'd had no idea about any altercation between Danielle and Bobby. Though, on reflection, they had asked him if he knew who the witness was, and he had deftly answered a slightly different question. Perhaps, he might argue now that it hadn't been an argument he'd heard, per se. There was little doubt in Wolf's mind that the intent of his question to Kit had been clear. However, on neither of the two occasions when the question of the witness had been raised had he actually stated, "I have no idea who that might be," but, instead, had managed to elude answering the question directly. Was this sufficient evidence of a canny criminal, though?

Voicing these concerns out loud, Wolf added, "Of course, it is possible he did overhear some kind of conversation between Danielle and Bobby and is also the murderer."

"Why does that distinction matter?" the dowager asked.

"Well, because Inspector Maguire may argue that, just because it seems Bobby didn't murder Danielle, doesn't mean they didn't have words. Kit could have overheard something and just been unwilling to admit to us that he was that witness. That is hardly proof he is a killer," Wolf explained.

Seeing that the dowager, unwilling to accept that her most recent nemesis could be anything other than a cold-blooded murderer, was about to argue, Wolf added, "Please, don't get me wrong. I am sure we have identified our killer. Tabitha and I both came away from our last conversation with the man sure he was hiding something. And his professed delight in Tobias' alibi for Bobby seemed wholly disingenuous. However, knowing it and proving it are very different things."

In the dowager's eyes, the badly dressed Bohemian who had refused to be cowed by her already had his death warrant signed and sealed and was on his way to the gallows. She would accept nothing less at this point. Untrusting of whether Wolf or Langley was up to the task of persuading that wet-behind-the-ears police inspector, the dowager said, "I believe I must be the one to direct the authorities to do their duty and arrest that man!"

No one wanted to be the person to tell the self-important

dowager that not even she had the force of personality to demand that a police inspector arrest someone where there was purely circumstantial evidence. Desperately searching around for something to distract the old woman, Wolf said, "I have an idea. Lady Pembroke, Langley, remember when we discussed our interviews with the theatre company? Both Kit and Merryweather had mentioned a planned company outing tomorrow to a place called Devil's Dyke."

Wolf then proceeded to explain to the rest of the group about the particular theatrical superstition that the Theatre Royal indulged in. He ended with, "I suggest that we attend this outing."

The dowager, still enthralled with her plan of storming the Brighton Police Station demanding justice, asked petulantly, "What is such an outing likely to produce, Jeremy?"

Wolf had to admit he was unsure. However, he pointed out, "Given the conversation that Tabitha and I had with Kit this morning, I think it very unlikely he will allow us back in the theatre to question him or anyone else. However, he can't stop us from coincidentally gathering in the same public place. Perhaps in a more casual assembly than a formal interview, Kit, or someone else, may let something slip." Wolf paused, then added, "If we are certain that Kit is our killer, then the evidence is out there somewhere. There is no such thing as a perfect crime."

The dowager snorted, "And if there were, it wouldn't have been masterminded by that buffoon!"

CHAPTER 25

The makeshift lunch was brief, and the group prepared to disperse to their various afternoon tasks. Wolf needed to pen a note to Arlene, and Tabitha intended to get Melody and Dodo to go for a walk on the seafront. Langley wanted to spend time with Rat, working on his lessons. The dowager, realising how she had been neglecting her granddaughter's education, planned to find a soon-to-be unhappy Lily in order to continue preparing her for her coming out season.

Before they went their separate ways, there was the open question as to who was to keep watch over Tobias. The group looked at each other, no one wanting to volunteer to take the sullen young man with them. Finally, the dowager sighed and said, "I will take Tobias with me. As it happens, I need to assess just how much work will need to be done on Lily's ballroom skills – I suspect I will be hiring a dancing master. Tobias can dance with her so I can make my assessment."

However self-involved he was, even Tobias realised that the group wasn't far from drawing straws to see who was unlucky enough to be stuck with him. Sticking out his lower lip, he said irritably, "I'm not a child, you know. I can be left alone for five minutes." The group ignored him. He added, "And I'm not a trained dancing monkey." When he saw that no one was paying any attention to his complaints, Tobias realised he had no choice but to go along with the dowager's plans for his afternoon. But he was determined that, while he might have no choice but to dance, no one could prevent him from wallowing in his misery.

Wolf returned to his suite with Bear to write the note to Arlene. He sat at the table at the window, staring out at the seafront, unable to summon the right words. Ten minutes had passed, and not a word had been written beyond "Lady Archibald, I am writing…"

Bear watched his friend struggle and finally said, "This isn't a love letter or a confession you're writing, it's just a brief note. What's the problem?"

Wolf sighed and put down his pen. What was the problem? He chewed his lip as he looked at the still, mostly blank page in front of him.

"Do you want me to write it?" Bear offered.

"Thank you, but I can do this. I just need to think about how to start. It feels as if every interaction with Arlene has been fraught with intense emotion and unspoken words. While I won't comment on whether your judgement of Arlene ten years ago as being manipulative has merit, certainly the Arlene of today is playing games. I'm just not sure what the goal or the rules of those games are. Am I putting myself under an obligation by asking her this favour? Will she view it as such?" The words tumbled out of Wolf. His dear friend listened sympathetically. He was the person who remembered Wolf's romance with Arlene and how broken Wolf was in its aftermath.

Bear didn't like Arlene and never had. But, as he formulated his answer, he tried to put those feelings aside, "You are the one who did her the favour; she asked you to prove Robert Charles' innocence. Now that you have, you are putting him into her custody. I don't believe that puts you under obligation at all. If I were you, I would state the situation in a very matter-of-fact manner using the rationale I just laid out. Then say that, if it is acceptable to her, you and I will deliver Mr Charles into her care this afternoon."

Wolf considered his friend's words of wisdom, then set to writing the note. It only took a few minutes, and when he was done and Bear had looked it over, he sealed it up to send with one of the hotel's page boys for delivery.

When Wolf was done, Bear took the envelope to deliver down to Mr Champion. "I'll ask to have the page boy wait for a reply," he said.

Left alone, Wolf went back to staring out of the window. He wanted to be done with this case and with Brighton. He hoped that within a day or two, he could pack up his motley collection of companions, and they could make their way back to London.

Wolf had been thinking about Tabitha's suggestion that he continue taking on cases. What would that even look like? Did it just mean that he would not resist when investigations came his way? Would he actively seek them out? He thought back to how he and Bear had got almost all of their work as thief-takers in their Whitechapel days: word of mouth. When he had first met Bear, he had a certain reputation in London, mostly as a reliable, honest giant of a man who could terrify most people into compliance. Wolf's intellect and polished manners had been the perfect complement to those skills, and work had just seemed to flow their way.

Perhaps he shouldn't overthink this and instead embrace an openness to investigating and see what transpired. Of course, continuing to investigate would undoubtedly mean continuing to do so with the dowager's "help"; the woman wouldn't be shaken off easily. On the other hand, Wolf had to admit that she could be quite useful. Sometimes.

As he continued to look out at the seafront, he caught sight of Tabitha walking with Mary, Melody and Dodo on the promenade. Deciding he needed a distraction, he jumped up and went down to the hotel lobby. He asked Mr Champion to send the page boy out to find him as soon as he returned with a reply. He then left the hotel and crossed the King's Road, walking in the direction he had seen Tabitha walk in.

It was a cold but mostly sunny day. Fluffy white clouds moved gently over the sparkling English Channel, but darker clouds out at sea promised the possibility of rain later. Following the sound of Dodo's bark, Wolf realised the little group was making its way to the bandstand that jutted out over the pebbled beach and was connected to the promenade by a short bridge.

The bandstand was a delightful, wrought-iron confection. Wherever intricate details and ornamentation could be squeezed in, they had been. The bandstand itself was comprised of a series of ornately designed columns holding up a highly decorative wrought-iron canopy under which the performing bands could gather. A white, equally decorative, wrought-iron railing ran around the outside edge.

As he approached the bandstand, Wolf could see that Tabitha and her charges were already over the bridge, and Melody and Dodo were running wildly around the bandstand while Tabitha was leaning on the railings, looking out at the sea. Wolf was still too far away to be able to see her expression, but standing there alone, staring out at the water, she seemed melancholy. Was she concerned about his proposed visit to see Arlene? And if so, why? Wolf shook his head; he would never understand women, and he would certainly never fully understand this woman. Perhaps, he thought, that enigmatic quality was part of her charm.

By the time he reached the bandstand, Melody was running up and down the little bridge, holding Dodo's lead. The puppy was even more excited than the little girl, and its tail was wagging furiously. When Melody saw Wolf at the end of the bridge, she careened towards him, and Dodo's barking reached a fever pitch of excitement. Wolf squatted down and opened up his arms. The little girl ran into them and hugged him. He hugged her back with one arm and patted the puppy's head with the other.

Dodo was a Cavalier King Charles Spaniel. Her coat was a rich chestnut colour and was medium-length, silky, and beautifully feathered. She had deep brown, soulful eyes. The dog had been a gift to Melody from Langley during her "holiday" at his home. Initially, Tabitha had been very reluctant to have a dog at Chesterton House. But the puppy seemed to have grown on her. For his part, Wolf had been raised around dogs and was delighted at the new addition to the household.

What was perhaps more surprising, at least to Wolf, was

not his spontaneous show of affection for the dog but rather towards the little girl holding the lead. Initially, Wolf had accepted Melody into the household with very grave reservations. Some of those concerns for her future had been mitigated by Langley's adoption of Rat as a mentee. Still, his concerns had gone beyond the asymmetry of the life she would be raised to compared to her brother. However, Wolf realised that he had grown genuinely attached to the little girl in her own right. As Wolf stood up, he saw that his arrival had interrupted Tabitha's reverie and that she had turned to watch his interactions with Melody and Dodo. Even from this distance, Wolf could see that she was smiling at the sight.

When the little girl had first arrived, Tabitha had made it very clear that if Melody wasn't welcome at Chesterton House, then she would establish her own household elsewhere. A few months ago, this was a sufficient threat to make Wolf put aside his concerns. Now, Wolf couldn't imagine his home without Melody, Dodo, and, most of all, without Tabitha. He stood where he was on the bridge and watched her. The sea breeze was making a mess of her hair, and he was sure it had brought a ruddiness to her complexion. But to Wolf, nothing could detract from her beauty. In fact, this only enhanced it.

Tabitha and Wolf started walking towards each other, meeting up under the canopy of the bandstand. Now that he was close to her, Wolf could see what an enigmatic smile Tabitha was wearing. He cocked his head questioningly. She replied in a gently mocking tone, "What would you know, milord?"

"Your thoughts. You seemed many miles away as you looked out to sea. But as you walked here, it seemed as if your thoughts were of a more mysterious nature."

Tabitha shook her head and answered, "There was nothing mysterious about my thoughts. I was merely observing how natural you looked with Melody, as if you had been parenting her since birth."

Tabitha's words somewhat took him aback. Was this what he was doing? Parenting? His thoughts must have shown on his face, and Tabitha rushed to add, "I mean nothing more by that than that Melody's comfort with you and yours with her are heartwarming."

Despite Mary standing off to the side, showing perfect servant discretion, and Melody and Dodo continuing to race up and down the bridge, the moment suddenly felt very intimate. Wolf wasn't aware of the crash of the waves or the dog's excited yelps as he crossed the rest of the space before them and took Tabitha's hand in his. Staring into her kind, intelligent hazel eyes, he said, "If seeing me so with Melody makes you happy, then I have all I want and need."

His words were said so softly, but with such intensity, that Tabitha had to break the lock of their eyes and look away. She stared down the beach for a moment, then looked back at the wonderful man standing in front of her with such clear affection lighting up his face. Feeling a sudden moment of clarity, Tabitha answered equally softly, "When we return to London, let us speak more."

Wolf might have asked what they would speak about, but he knew. What he wasn't sure of was where that conversation might lead. Tabitha gently removed her hand from his, and Wolf nodded in acknowledgement of her words.

They spent the next twenty minutes playing on the beach with Dodo. The puppy seemed to have gotten over her fear of the water and was proving to be a good swimmer. Watching her chase stones thrown by Tabitha and Melody, Wolf hoped the little dog didn't get into distress; she might not mind swimming in the frigid seawater, but he was less enthusiastic about a possible rescue mission.

They were so absorbed in their game that no one noticed one of the hotel page boys, in his distinctive red uniform with gold trim, approach them. It seemed that Arlene had replied immediately to his note. Wolf took it from the boy and quickly scanned it.

"What does she answer?" Tabitha asked with genuine curiosity. Her first impression of Lady Archibald had not been a positive one, but she had to believe that anyone worthy of Wolf's love had redeeming qualities. Would the woman open up her home to Robert Charles despite any potential scandal that might attach to her for doing so?

"She says that she is more than happy to provide Bobby with somewhere to stay and employment for the time being. She asks that Bear and I call in an hour." As he said the words out loud, Wolf realised what mixed feelings he had about Arlene's answer. On the one hand, it solved a very immediate problem: what to do about Robert Charles. On the other, it required him not only to spend more time with Arlene but to show the appropriate gratitude for her help. He could only imagine how much she would enjoy that scene.

CHAPTER 26

Wolf left the others on the beach and returned to the hotel. He found Bear back in their suite, again by the window sketching. "It doesn't matter how many times I draw this vista, I find something new," he observed. "If we stay here much longer, I will go back to the shop I found and buy some new watercolour paints. I want to try to capture the motion of the water if I can. Even though I'm no Turner." Looking at the man's sketches, Wolf reflected, not for the first time, that Bear was unnecessarily self-deprecating and had more talent than he gave himself credit for.

Seeing the note from Arlene in Wolf's hand, Bear put down his charcoal and asked, "Did she agree?"

"She did. Can you go and find Ashby and make sure that Bobby is ready to leave?"

Bear left the room and returned a few minutes later with Wolf's valet, Thompson, rather than Ashby. They had Bobby in tow. Washed and dressed in some of Ashby's clothes and satiated from the large lunch the hotel had provided, Bobby Charles seemed less disengaged and sustained eye contact while Wolf explained the proposal to him.

Aware that, regardless of Inspector Maguire's constraints, Bobby was an innocent man, Wolf wanted to ensure he willingly assented to their plan. "Mr Charles, if you do not wish to stay, at least temporarily, with Lady Archibald, you do not have to. Do you understand that?" Despite his improved focus, Bobby was still uncommunicative. "Can you indicate your preference?" Wolf tried again.

Thompson, who had been hanging back, now moved forward and laid a gentle hand on the large man's shoulder, "It's okay, Bobby. You can answer his lordship. Is this something you would like?"

Rather than answering Wolf, Bobby turned towards Thompson and said, "Yes, Jimmy. I'd like that. Lady Archibald was Miss Danny's friend."

Realising that his valet had somehow made a connection with Bobby, Wolf suggested that he join them in their visit to Kemptown. He was no longer worried that Bobby would try to escape, but he still wasn't convinced that the man might not erupt violently in some way. If Thompson was able to communicate with Bobby, it made sense to have him accompany them. The valet was holding a small carpetbag in one hand. Wolf looked at it enquiringly.

"Ashby had a few shirts and other items of clothing that he thought might see Bobby through for now," the valet responded to the unasked question.

The group descended to the lobby, only to be informed that the carriage was not available. Mr Champion offered to hail a hackney cab, but Wolf decided that he was sure enough of Bobby's acquiescence that it wasn't necessary to contain him in a vehicle. Bobby didn't say anything during the walk, but he willingly followed the little group, staying close to Thompson. Wolf did wonder what Thompson had done to win over the previously uncooperative man. It made Wolf wonder if Thompson had hidden talents that might be of use in any future investigations.

When they arrived at Arlene's Kemptown house, Wolf realised he had a new social conundrum; under normal circumstances, any accompanying servant would enter through the back of the house. But these weren't normal circumstances, so when the butler opened the door, it was to find the unusual group led by Wolf, requesting an audience with his mistress.

The butler relieved them of their outerwear and then showed the group into the sunny, well-appointed drawing room. Arlene was sitting at a little desk, writing and, on their entry, rose and came forward to greet them. "Wolf, thank you for everything you have done to exonerate Bobby." Wolf was quick to make clear that the young man wasn't exonerated yet but had merely been released into Langley's custody. "Nevertheless, he is out of prison, and that must be progress," Arlene said.

As she spoke, Arlene turned to Bear, who was standing a little behind Wolf, "Bear, it is good to see you again after all these years."

Whatever Bear's private feelings about the woman, he was too well-mannered to do anything but bow over the proffered hand and say, "Lady Archibald. I hope you are well."

If Arlene thought anything about the man's curt, formal statement, the graceful bow of her head in return indicated nothing amiss in his greeting. She then turned to Bobby and went and took one of his large, rough hands between her two elegant, soft ones and said with genuine happiness, "Bobby, I am so happy to see you set free. I am so sorry for what you have been put through. I know that you loved Miss Danny and would never have hurt her." Bobby didn't reply, but slow tears started running down his cheeks at the reminder of the deceased woman who had meant so much to him.

It was clear from Thompson's attire that he was a servant, so Arlene merely nodded her head at him and then welcomed the group into the drawing room. The social protocol was unclear for such a situation, and Thompson decided to err on the side of caution and choose to stand by the wall, with Bobby beside him, while Wolf, Bear and Arlene sat.

"Do you have any idea how long Bobby will be on this probation?" she asked.

Wolf shook his head, "While we have a witness who has provided a clear alibi for Bobby, Inspector Maguire refuses to exonerate him while there are no other suspects."

"Do you have anyone you suspect?" Arlene asked.

Wolf looked at Bear and said, "Could you take Thompson and Bobby and see if you can find the butler and have him show

Bobby where he will be sleeping?" Despite his reservations about being alone with Arlene, he wanted to be able to speak freely with her.

Once they were alone, Arlene asked, "Can I assume that you do have a suspect?"

"Indeed. Christopher Bailey."

Whatever Arlene had expected him to say, it clearly wasn't that. She laughed as she said, "Surely you can't be serious? That old dandy? Why on earth would he have killed Danielle? She was his biggest star. I don't know the man personally, but he is a well-known and well-liked Brighton fixture and quite the popinjay by all accounts."

"Exactly, she was his biggest star," Wolf answered. "Did you know that Danielle was planning to leave the Theatre Royal and had accepted an offer to be the marquee star for the new Hippodrome?"

Given Arlene's previous obvious lack of awareness of the details of her murdered friend's life, Wolf was unsurprised when she said, "Leave the Royal? I had no idea. I mean, I knew that she had her issues there and would like to have focused less on acting and more on singing, but she never said a word about the Hippodrome. From what I've heard of the place, I can see how that would be a far more appealing situation for her." She paused and thought for a moment, "I can see how knowledge of that might give Mr Bailey motive, but even so, I cannot imagine him resorting to murder."

"It seems that Mr Bailey has a rather unsuccessful gambling habit and could ill afford the already faltering theatre to lose its biggest headliner." Despite these words, Wolf could see that Arlene was still unconvinced. Her scepticism made him even more sure that the police would not have acted on their purely circumstantial evidence. It seemed that Kit Bailey's jovial persona might hold the man in good stead in the face of anything but concrete proof.

"I will assume that you have good reason for suspecting Mr Bailey, but how do you intend to prove that he killed Danielle?"

That was the question, wasn't it? Wolf thought. He answered honestly, "I am not sure. The last time Tabitha and I spoke with him, we raised his hackles enough that I doubt we're welcome back in his theatre to ask more questions. We do know that the entire theatre company is planning a trip to a place called Devil's Dyke tomorrow afternoon."

"At this time of the year? Why on earth would they do that? I doubt even the funicular railway is running. You know it's the highest point on the South Downs. Even on a nice day, it'll be windy and cold up there." Arlene shook her head in bemusement at the thought of the outing.

"My understanding is that there is some superstition about visiting there before a new show starts," Wolf explained.

"Ah, that would explain it then. Danielle would sometimes talk about the many, often ludicrous, superstitions that theatrical folks believe in. Did you know that you can't say 'Macbeth' in a theatre? What happens when the play is *Macbeth*? But these things are taken very seriously, so I can see why they would make the trek up there, regardless of the weather, if they've somehow convinced themselves that doing so brings luck to a production."

Arlene paused and then asked, "Regardless, I'm not sure how such an outing helps your investigation."

"We are planning on visiting at the same time," Wolf explained.

Arlene quirked an eyebrow. Wolf sighed; the flimsiness of the plan was not lost on him. Sighing again, he said in a rather dejected voice, "I am hoping that by the time I return to the hotel, Tabitha will have come up with more of a plan." Realising what he had said, Wolf added, "And Lord Langley, of course."

At that moment, there was a light knock on the door, and the maid entered with a tray of tea and biscuits. Arlene indicated that she should pour for them both and then leave. Once the maid was safely out of hearing, Arlene replaced the cup she had just been sipping from in its saucer and asked Wolf surprisingly gently, "Do you love her?"

Wolf could have pretended not to know of whom she was speaking. But they had known each other far too long for that kind of disingenuousness. Instead, he answered, "I believe I do."

"And have you told her so?"

"Not in so many words," Wolf admitted.

"Then in what words?" Arlene asked in a mocking tone. "No, don't answer that. Wolf, you are hardly a young boy with wisps of hair on his chin playing at being an adult. If you love the woman, tell her in no uncertain terms. What on earth is holding you back?"

Wolf may not have been a young, green boy, but in that moment, he felt like one. When challenged like this by Arlene, all the reasons he'd been telling himself seemed inconsequential. Finally, he landed on, "Well, because of our unusual living situation, for one thing. If she does not return my feelings and rejects my suit, then what? We keep living in the same house anyway?"

Arlene cocked her head to the side, considering his words. "Do you have any reason to believe she doesn't return your feelings?" Before he could answer, she said in a firm voice, "Because I can assure you that she does."

Wolf wasn't sure what he was more surprised by, that Arlene believed that or that she was sharing her belief with him. Seeing the look of surprise on his face, she laughed lightly, "You wonder how I can be so sure? A woman knows these things, Wolf. I certainly know when I face a rival, and there is no doubt in my mind that when we met the other day, that is how she viewed me."

Wolf had heard enough about that tea party to feel compelled to offer an opposing narrative, "Is it not possible that she was merely reacting to what I'm sure was provocative behaviour and words on your part?"

Now, Arlene laughed a full, deep-throated laugh. Wolf had always loved her laugh; there was nothing demure about it. "Oh, Wolf, you do know me well, don't you?" Arlene said, still chuckling. "Yes, it's true. I may have goaded her somewhat.

Nevertheless, her willingness to engage in battle spoke as clearly as any declaration; she was fighting for you."

Honestly, Wolf thought this was absurd, but he knew that Arlene would not be deterred now she had her mind set. Instead, he looked away and said in a quiet voice, "It isn't only about her feelings for me. My cousin, Jonathan, her deceased husband, was a brute of a husband in every way."

"Yes, I had heard that when I asked around."

Wolf whipped his head back around to face her, "You were asking around about Tabitha?"

"Well, about you mostly. I get the London papers and had read of your cousin's death and then your ascendency to the earldom. I was still in mourning then for Archibald, of course. But when my year was over, I intended to write to you."

Arlene didn't need to make clear why she had planned to make contact again; he was now an earl, and she was a rich widow. In her mind, there was no good reason why they couldn't pick up where they'd left off a decade before.

"Of course, I had no idea what your marital state was, and so I made some enquiries. People were very eager to tell me the scandalous news that your cousin's widow was still in residence at the ancestral home. But quite a few of them also made mention of how she was likely better off without your cousin." Arlene said this all in a very matter-of-fact tone, as if her investigations into his potential eligibility as her second husband were the most reasonable thing in the world.

Wolf was tempted to address her behaviour but realised there were more important things to discuss. Instead, he said, "Indeed, Jonathan hurt Tabitha in ways that went beyond the bruises he so often inflicted. I get the sense that she may be unwilling ever to trust a man again."

"So, she has been living with you for months and has investigated multiple cases with you, and yet you believe she doesn't trust you?" Arlene scoffed.

"Well, of course, she trusts me in that sense. But that is very different from being my wife and under my total control."

Arlene took another sip of her tea and considered her next words carefully, "Wolf, I suspect that the problem is not that she doesn't trust you, but that she doesn't trust herself not to make the same mistake again. But she was a young, naive girl when she married your cousin, and I'm sure she was rushed into it by her parents. Isn't that always the way in the aristocracy? But this is a different situation; she does know you in a way I'm very sure she didn't know Jonathan before marriage. Tabitha must trust that she is able to make a more mature, informed decision this time around."

Arlene's words were surprisingly insightful, but Wolf had to ask one more question, "Why are you encouraging me to declare myself to Tabitha if you have, well had, well, if you were thinking…?" he wasn't sure how to phrase this.

Luckily, Arlene saved him from floundering any further and said, "I have seen too much of life and think too well of myself to fight for a man whose heart is elsewhere."

The conversation had veered off-topic, and determined to shift from the maudlin tone of the past few minutes, Arlene put down her teacup and said, "But let us return to the conundrum of your investigation. In lieu of any better idea from Lady Pembroke, I agree that we might as well meet the theatre company at Devil's Dyke and see if we can shake something loose."

"We? Surely, you're not planning to join us?" Wolf asked in amazement.

"Why not? You don't know where you're going, and I do. And anyway, it will make a good excuse for why we happen to be up there; we shall say that I insisted on showing my dear, old friend one of the great views of the region." It was no worse an idea than anything else he had, and so, with some reservations about the potential personality clashes of such an outing, Wolf agreed.

CHAPTER 27

Wolf and Bear walked back to the hotel in their usual companionable silence. Thompson had stayed behind to help Bobby get settled. Bear, a taciturn man at the best of times, walked next to his friend, unsure whether to ask about Wolf's conversation with Arlene or not. He felt that Wolf's normally stellar intuitions about people were off when it came to his former love, muddied by his confused feelings. Bear valued their friendship too much to continue to push his own narrative about Arlene when Wolf had made clear he disagreed.

Finally, when they were almost back at the hotel, Wolf slowed down and said, "Can we stop for a moment?"

There was a lowish wall not far up, and Bear pointed to it and said, "Let's sit."

Even then, Wolf didn't immediately open up. This might have been a very uncomfortable silence between two other people. But Bear merely sat looking out at the sea, the grey clouds now closer than they were and definitely a harbinger of rain to come later that day. Seagulls screeched overhead, and on the beach in front of them, they could see Melody's favourite, the donkey rides. Finally, Wolf said, "Arlene encouraged me to tell Tabitha plainly about my feelings for her."

Whatever else Bear had thought Lady Archibald and Wolf had talked about, it wasn't that. He turned his face towards Wolf in surprise, "She did?"

Wolf cared too much for his friend's honest, sage advice to be petty in vindication. Instead, he said, "I believe she may be right.

Indeed, even Tabitha said that we should talk when we return to London. Perhaps I lay all my cards on the table and then deal with whatever ramifications there are from that. That was certainly Arlene's advice."

"Arlene told you to do that?" Bear said, now unable to keep the cynicism from his voice.

"She admitted to initially hoping to reignite the flame between us – and yes, she acknowledged that my new rank was part of that. Arlene is a complicated woman. However, it seems she is too proud to pursue a man whose heart is elsewhere." Bear was satisfied with this explanation. It bolstered his belief that Arlene would have no interest in Wolf if he were not now a rich earl but also assured him that his friend was safe from any more of the woman's machinations.

Wolf then added, "And she intends to join us tomorrow." Before Bear could comment, Wolf continued, "Perhaps it isn't such a bad idea. If we are not to immediately put the theatre company on alert about our suspicions, we need to appear to be holidaymakers taking in a local favourite pleasure spot. How much more credible is that when we have a local friend who has suggested bringing us there?"

"On the same afternoon that the company happens to be there? You don't think that will raise any alarm bells?" Bear asked.

Wolf thought about the question. "The only person we are really concerned about alarming is Kit, and he wasn't the person who told us about their outing. If it comes up, I will merely say that Arlene had mentioned what a magnificent view there was from the spot, and I had alluded to having heard as much elsewhere. While it may not forestall all suspicions, it at least gives us a plausible back story for our visit."

Bear wasn't convinced, but he had no better idea. But he did have to ask, "Even if you are right, how does this help us advance the case in any way?"

Wolf shook his head; therein lay the rub. He had no idea.

Back at the hotel, he found the dowager, Langley, and Tabitha taking tea in the charming little nook off the hotel lobby. Bear indicated his preference to return to their room, but Wolf joined the group. Noticing the absence of both Lady Lily and Viscount Tobias, Wolf asked where they both were. He was particularly worried about where the young man might be.

"It seems that an afternoon of dancing may have created a friendship of sorts between my granddaughter and my godson. I might have actually seen the boy smile once or twice. In fact, I am certain there was one time when something akin to a laugh was heard. Afterwards, Lily volunteered to take him to the Royal Pavilion Gardens and show him some of her favourite plants. I'm not sure how one has favourite plants, but it seemed like a harmless enough activity and Tobias showed surprising interest, so I gave my blessing. I sent Withers as a chaperone. I'm not sure that young maid of Lily's is up to the task."

Wolf stole a glance at Tabitha. Their eyes met, her eyebrows raised just slightly, and he saw confirmation that she also believed Tobias' interest might be less in the plants and more in the tour guide. If any such thoughts had crossed the dowager's mind, she gave no indication. Certainly, Tobias' gambling habit and sullenness aside, Lady Lily could do worse than a viscount who was to inherit an earldom.

Everyone was happy to hear that Bobby had been welcomed into the Archibald household and pleasantly surprised to hear that Thompson had formed a trusted connection with the young man so quickly. "While we remain in Brighton, I will ask Thompson to keep an eye on Mr Charles," Wolf remarked. He was as relieved as everyone else at this one seemingly resolved issue. He then casually remarked that Lady Archibald planned to join their outing the following day. Tabitha raised her eyebrows again but said nothing. He then pointed out that, even if that helped give them a credible reason for being at Devil's Dyke, "It doesn't help us advance the investigation. Does anyone have any ideas?"

"I have been thinking about this," Tabitha admitted. "I believe we need to provoke our villain into acting. We must force him to show his hand."

"Even if I agreed with you," Wolf said, "how do you suggest we do that?"

"We had mentioned a possible alibi for Bobby when we spoke with Kit. But let us take Tobias with us, which I'm assuming we would have done anyway, and make much of what a sterling witness he was. We can take some license with the truth and not mention that Inspector Maguire does not consider Bobby exonerated yet. Instead, we can indicate that the police are now actively looking at other suspects and believe that it must have been someone who was already in the theatre that night."

"Is this true, though?" Wolf asked. "It is possible that Danielle let someone in."

"It is," Tabitha conceded. "But all we need to do is to spook Kit. There is a limited universe of people such a description could apply to, and he's definitely at the top of that list. If our plan is to provoke him to some kind of action that reveals his guilt, then we needn't be too worried about logic.

It was a decent plan. Well, it was their only plan so far. Wolf poured himself a cup of tea, adding milk and sugar while he contemplated it. Finally, putting down the spoon he had used to stir his tea, Wolf said, "Let me just replay this out loud: we assume that Kit lied about hearing harsh words between Danielle and Bobby on the night of the murder in order to bolster the police's unfounded accusations against the man. With Bobby under lock and key and Inspector Maguire disinclined or discouraged from considering any other suspects, Kit believes he is safe from suspicion."

Everyone nodded along with this narrative. Wolf continued, "We asked some questions the last time we spoke with him that clearly got under Kit's skin. Once he hears that Bobby is definitely no longer a suspect, will he worry about where our questioning might lead? And even if he does, what do we expect him to do?"

"That is what I don't know. And he is unlikely to act while there are so many witnesses, but perhaps it will spur him to do something," Tabitha suggested.

"I hate to throw cold water on this idea," Langley said, "but it doesn't sound very safe. Intentionally prodding a known killer to act in desperation hardly sounds like a sensible plan."

"Pish posh, Maxwell," the dowager exclaimed. "I never realised how lily-livered you can be." She added in an only slightly quieter voice, "Does our government realise how fainthearted you are?"

Langley wisely chose to ignore the insult. Wolf, however, did acknowledge the wisdom of the man's words, "Langley has a point. I'm assuming we were planning to bring everyone with us tomorrow in order to make the outing more credible. Do we really want to stir the hornet's nest with the children and Lily around?"

"No one is more concerned about the children's safety than I am," Tabitha said, somewhat offended that anyone would suggest otherwise. "I thought we might bring both Bear and Ashby with us. They are both very large men, and we could ensure they keep close to Kit at all times. Mr Bailey doesn't strike me as a man with enough bravado to attempt anything rash if there is a chance of injury to himself." This was a good point, and no one had anything to counter it with.

Seeing that there was some semblance of consensus around what amounted to the best plan they had, Wolf excused himself to speak to Mr Champion about the logistics of their trip. Arlene had said she would bring her carriage and meet them at the hotel at one o'clock the following afternoon. While they didn't know the exact time the theatre company was planning to visit, it seemed wise to go earlier in the afternoon rather than later. If Wolf, Bear and Ashby walked to the station, they could all squeeze into Arlene's plus the hotel's carriage.

As always. Mr Champion, the hall porter, was a font of useful information. The train was part of the Brighton to Portsmouth line that branched off to Devil's Dyke. Mr Champion went behind the desk and came back with a train schedule. "Let me look here. I know it goes less frequently after the summer months. Let's see. Right, here it is. There's one that goes at thirty minutes past one and then not another one for two hours." Wolf thought this would give them ample time if Arlene was arriving at one.

"What do we do when we get off the train?" Wolf asked. "Someone had mentioned a funicular but questioned if it would be open this time of year."

"Oh, it'll be running. It only opened in July this year. I haven't been on it myself, but Mrs Champion took the nippers one Sunday in August and said it gave her quite the fright, it did. Mind you, it doesn't take much to scare Mrs Champion, if truth be told. But my Charlie and Mimmy loved it. They would have kept going up and down on it if Mrs Champion had been inclined to spend the money on such nonsense. However, the funicular only goes up and down to Poynings on the other side. You'll have to take one of the waiting charabancs from the station. Don't worry, they'll be waiting for the train."

Mr Champion rubbed his chin in thought, "It's going to be mighty windy up there this time of the year. You best wrap up warm, particularly that little Miss Melody. We can pack you some refreshments, or there's The Devil's Dyke Hotel, where they serve coffee and pastries. The place didn't used to be much, but since Mr Hubbard bought the estate and expanded the hotel from what was there, it's become quite the fancy spot."

Satisfied that they at least had the logistics of their outing planned, even if the details of how it was to help the investigation were still looser than he would have preferred, Wolf returned to report to the group.

The rest of the afternoon and evening were quite uneventful. Tobias and Lily seemed to have enjoyed their excursion and chatted happily about it over dinner. Well, Lily chatted happily about the plants they had seen, and Tobias seemed unpersuaded of the delights of foliage but was generally quite talkative and even cheerful, for once. Everyone noticed the change in the young man, but not one wanted to remark on the change for fear he might ricochet back into his normal grumpiness.

Lily and Tobias were informed of the group's plans for the

following afternoon, though they were not apprised of the real reason for the outing. Again, the absence of sullen complaining from Tobias was noteworthy. Tabitha watched the two young people chatting as they ate. She couldn't tell if Tobias' evident admiration was reciprocated. Lily was always happy when talking about anything botanical, and it may have been that her flushed cheeks were nothing more than excitement at the apparently rather rare shrub she seemed to have come across. It was hard to imagine that the very intellectual and serious Lily could be taken with Tobias. Of course, Tabitha reflected, the young man might have hidden depths she had yet to experience.

Tabitha then looked over at Wolf, who was sitting across from her and talking to Langley at his right. He seemed more at peace than he had of recent. Did something happen at Lady Archibald's? Certainly, this change seemed to have happened sometime between when they had spoken at the bandstand and dinner. She had believed the moment they had shared earlier had been meaningful; it had felt that way to her, at least.

Tabitha had carried the burden of so many conflicting emotions over the last months. And those feelings seemed to have built to a crescendo over the last few days. Tabitha was self-aware enough to realise that Lady Archibald had been the catalyst for this sudden escalation. It was one thing to know on an intellectual level that one day, Wolf would fall in love with someone else and marry. It was quite another to find herself face-to-face with a flesh and blood willing candidate.

Somehow, in that one brief moment on the bandstand, she felt as if so many of her questions and worries had melted away. And she had believed that Wolf felt the significance of that moment as well. But had he? Maybe she had misread the situation, and it was instead his conversation with Lady Archibald that had brought him such serenity.

CHAPTER 28

The following morning, everyone went about their separate activities. They had agreed to a very early lunch so as to be ready to leave at one o'clock. When informed by Mr Champion that the restaurant would not be serving lunch until noon, the group opted for another lunch of sandwiches and the like in the dowager's suite. This had the added benefit of allowing them privacy to review their plan for the afternoon.

Everyone gathered at thirty past eleven and, again, did their best to find seats. Lily had opted to eat lunch in Langley's suite with Rat and Melody, and Tobias had shown a sudden keenness to get to know the children. At least this left fewer bodies to accommodate.

Well supplied with sausage rolls, wedges of game pie, and sandwiches, the group settled down to talk. They had brought out the corkboard for reference in case there was anything they had missed or forgotten. Nibbling on a truly excellent sausage roll, Tabitha looked over at the notecards. She was even more certain than she'd been the other day that Kit Bailey was their culprit.

Finishing her sausage roll and wiping any crumbs from her mouth with her serviette, Tabitha said, "How do we casually introduce the topic of Bobby's supposed exoneration? Particularly if Kit is unwilling to engage with us anymore?"

This was a good question. The dowager chimed up, "What about if we bring Mr Charles with us? That will certainly make the point."

It was a decent suggestion and would certainly neatly solve this problem. However, Tabitha was the first to counter, "If we were talking about anyone other than Bobby Charles, I might agree, Mama. But I think that both temperamentally and given what he has been through recently, this is an unfair position to put the man in unless we have no other choice."

Wolf concurred, "He is just settling into Lady Archibald's household. To rip him out and make him interact with a bunch of people he might rather not ever see again and then expose him to their reactions to his freedom just doesn't seem like something that Bobby would react well to."

The dowager never enjoyed being disagreed with, but this time, she had no good rejoinder. Instead, she said, "Leave this to me then. I am more than capable of ensuring that coxcomb hears the news."

Everyone else exchanged nervous glances. The dowager was not known for her subtlety. However, Wolf reflected, perhaps it was precisely her heavy-handedness that would work well in this situation. Even in Kit's brief interaction with the woman, it must have been obvious to him that she felt free to say whatever was on her mind whenever she wanted to say it. The announcement of Bobby's freedom, coming from the dowager, could be seen as yet another ill-considered statement. The rest of them might even protest at her inappropriate timing. Wolf didn't quite phrase his agreement in these terms, but he did agree that the dowager might be just the person to let slip the news.

There wasn't much else to decide; it was agreed that Bear and Ashby would not let Kit out of their sights during the afternoon, and beyond that, the group would take the opportunity to socialise with the rest of the company in the hope that someone might say something in casual conversation that they had omitted to mention when formally interviewed.

The group broke up twenty minutes before Arlene's anticipated arrival. Everyone went to gather their outerwear – with another reminder from Wolf that it would be windy up on the Downs. The rain that had poured down the previous night had been replaced by a reasonably sunny but rather chilly day. Langley agreed to send Lily and Tobias to gather their things, after which he would round up Melody, Rat, and Dodo and bring them downstairs. Mary was to have a well-deserved afternoon off.

Tabitha was one of the first to gather in the hotel lobby. The only other person there was Wolf. She approached him hesitantly. Superficially, nothing had changed between them since their recent detente. But it felt as if something had changed; she just wasn't sure what. Wolf, for his part, was oblivious to the consternation he was causing. As far as he was concerned, Tabitha had said they would talk when they returned to London, and after his conversation with Arlene, Wolf was now surer about what he would say when they did.

Wolf smiled as Tabitha approached and said, "Bear has gone to alert Ashby, and once they're here, I'll walk with them to the station." He paused, "Unless you would prefer me to accompany you?" He didn't have to say that he meant in case of any more outrageous behaviour by Lady Archibald. While Wolf was satisfied that Arlene had no immediate expectations of a romance with him, it didn't mean that the woman was about to fly a white flag and become Tabitha's best friend.

Tabitha touched his arm, "I'll be fine. I'm more than capable of handling Lady Archibald."

No sooner had she said that than the woman herself swept into the lobby. Wolf wondered why she hadn't remained in the carriage and sent a servant or porter in to announce her arrival. But Tabitha didn't have to wonder. The naturally alluring Lady Archibald had clearly gone to great efforts to ensure she was even more captivating than usual. Her walking dress was made of richly textured emerald velvet. The shade of emerald perfectly complemented her mesmerising green eyes. She wore a matching coat over it with a burnt orange fur trim at the collar, around the hem and at the cuffs. To complement the outfit, she had a fur muff and a green velvet hat that was set at a jaunty angle with two orange feathers in it. The woman looked ravishing, and she knew it.

Tabitha didn't know the details of Arlene's conversation with Wolf the day before, but if she had, she might have been hard-pressed to reconcile the woman's proclaimed acceptance of Wolf's feelings for Tabitha with her obvious peacocking. As it was, Tabitha merely saw Arlene's ostentatious sashay into the lobby and was immediately on her guard. Tabitha's own outfit was hardly shabby, but she had dressed for warmth and comfort above all things and now felt positively dowdy in comparison.

If there had been any doubt that Lady Archibald was pleased with the juxtaposition of their two outfits, that was dispelled by the sly smile that slipped across her lips as she glanced in Tabitha's direction. Of course, all of this was lost on Wolf. For the most part, even Arlene's spectacular outfit was wasted on him. He would have thought Tabitha beautiful if she were in sackcloth and ashes.

However, Lady Archibald's outfit was not wasted on the dowager, who was walking towards the lobby just as Arlene was approaching Tabitha and Wolf. "Lady Archibald, what a spectacular outfit," the dowager exclaimed. She looked pointedly at Tabitha, then back at Arlene and said, "The rest of us are positively put to shame." Tabitha ignored the veiled barb. She was sure that at least some of the dowager's enthusiasm for Lady Archibald was feigned and said more about the old woman's delight in tweaking Tabitha's nose than anything else. Given that, it hardly made sense to allow the dowager the pleasure of believing she'd scored a hit.

The rest of the party quickly gathered, and whether by foot or by carriage, they made their way to the station. The train was quite short, comprising two first-class carriages, a saloon, four third-class carriages and a guard's van. Their group was so large that they bought up all the first-class tickets. Everyone had boarded, and Wolf was the last person to climb on when he heard a loud commotion from his right. He turned his head to look down the platform and realised that the noisy group walking towards the third-class carriages was the theatre company. He was keen that Kit not realise that Wolf's group was going to Devil's Dyke until it was too late to turn back, so he quickly climbed onto the train and followed everyone else to their carriages.

Lily and Tobias, Ashby, Bear, the children, and Dodo had taken one carriage, leaving the dowager, Lady Archibald, Langley, Tabitha, and Wolf in the other. Wolf closed the door behind him and pulled down the shades so that no one could see into the carriage.

"Is there a reason we are attempting to travel incognito, Jeremy Dear?" the dowager enquired.

"Kit Bailey and the company are on the train. I'd prefer he not realise we're also on. At least until the train is at its destination."

"I do love all this intrigue," the dowager exclaimed. "How very exciting."

It wasn't until they were all seated that Tabitha noticed that the dowager had a new cane. It was not uncommon to see the old woman using a walking cane, though vanity often compelled her to do without. But this one was definitely new. It was a highly polished mahogany stick with a finely engraved curling handle. "Is that a new walking cane, Mama?" Tabitha asked.

Tabitha hadn't meant this as anything other than a causal pleasantry to pass the time, but the dowager's reaction was highly suspicious; an incredibly guilty look momentarily flashed across her face, and she squinted her eyes and pursed her mouth as if considering her answer. The dowager's reaction was so brief that if Tabitha hadn't been looking straight at her, she might have missed it. But she hadn't.

Finally, the dowager answered with forced casualness, "Indeed, it is. I ran into a fine little shop in The Lanes when I was out shopping with Lily. The charming proprietor said he could make something up to my specifications, and he sent this over yesterday morning." Her nonchalant words belied her behaviour, and Tabitha knew there was more to this story; she just couldn't imagine what.

Lady Archibald pre-empted any further interrogation, "Well, it is quite fine, I must say that. I believe you will be glad for it when we are up on the Downs. While it is not a hard walk once we are up there, and if you stay just on the top, if you wish to explore any more of the area at all, it is wise to have such a cane."

The dowager seemed happy to use this interruption as a way of diverting the conversation and asked a few pointed questions of Lady Archibald about the history of the landmark.

"Well," she explained, "we will take a charabanc the short distance to the summit, at which point we will be able to see the entire Dyke before us."

"Why does it have such a dramatic name?" the dowager asked.

"Well, the story goes that the Dyke was dug by the Devil himself, who attempted to create a channel through the South Downs for some nefarious purpose or other. I can't remember why. Anyway, he was defeated, I don't know by whom, before he managed to finish, which is why the Dyke is incomplete. The surrounding hills are said to have been formed by the soil he flung away as he dug."

The train ride wasn't long, and the group spent the rest of it in idle chatter dominated by the dowager and Lady Archibald. Watching them gently tussle for control of the conversation, Tabitha decided that if their group's stay in Brighton lasted much longer, that unholy alliance would definitely come to an end; the two women both enjoyed the spotlight too much not to clash eventually. But for now, they were just about managing to share it, however awkwardly sometimes.

The train ride itself was just over three miles long, running on the Brighton to Portsmouth line before detouring at Dyke junction. Once it broke off from the main line, the train began to climb in altitude. Looking out of the window, Tabitha took in breathtaking views of the countryside below.

Dyke station itself was quite a humble affair, a corrugated iron building with a matchwood interior. Beyond this simple building, the other buildings comprised a house for the station master and a disused railway carriage that was used as a tearoom in the summer.

As their large group descended from its two first-class carriages, Wolf again spotted the theatre company, and this time, they spotted him. The first person to recognise their group was Merryweather Frost, who hailed Wolf. Realising that this was the moment to put their story into action, Wolf raised his hand in a return greeting but remained with his group. Out of the corner of his eye, he noticed Merryweather speaking to Kit and then pointing in their direction. There seemed to be some discussion, perhaps about who would come forward to acknowledge the aristocratic group. Finally, with what looked like a little shove in his back from Merryweather, Kit walked up the platform.

If the reason for their day trip had been to discomfit their culprit, it seemed that their mere presence had achieved some of that end. Kit approached Wolf with a look on his face that was far from the man's normal, affable demeanour.

"Lord Pembroke, what a surprise seeing you here," Kit remarked tersely.

"Mr Bailey, good afternoon," Wolf answered with forced friendliness. "I'm not sure if you know Lady Archibald. "At this, Arlene turned and inclined her head in greeting. Wolf continued, "She and I are old friends. It was, in fact, Lady Archibald who asked me to investigate Miss Mapp's murder."

The expression on Kit's face at this news was hard to read, and so Wolf just continued in the same sunny, casual manner, "Lady Archibald persuaded us that we must not leave the area until we took in the view at the summit of Devil's Dyke. Given that it is a reasonably sunny day, if a little cold, we decided this afternoon would be the perfect time. It seems your theatre company had a similar idea. What a coincidence!"

If Kit had any thoughts about just how coincidental it might be, they went unsaid and instead, he replied, "Lady Archibald? I don't believe I've had the pleasure. But I have heard Danielle mention your name on occasion. Well, enjoy your afternoon. There is a funfair at the summit, which I'm sure the children will enjoy," he added, nodding towards Melody and Rat, who was holding a very excited Dodo in his arms.

"Will the fair be open this late in the season?" Wolf asked with genuine curiosity.

"Probably not all the rides. But the funicular and the aerial cableway across the valley are still new enough attractions that people will continue to come up here, perhaps through the entire winter. So, they keep some of the rides going." As he said this, Kit gestured to the people who had spilt out of the other third-class carriages onto the platform.

Wolf wasn't sure if now was a good time to drop the news about Bobby Charles, but he was worried there would be no better time. He caught Tabitha's eye, and she nudged the dowager, who looked momentarily unsure of what she was being told to do. She looked at Wolf, who tried to make clear with his eyes, without being too conspicuous, that this was the time for her performance. Luckily, finally, the dowager seemed to remember what her self-nominated role was and said in her most high-handed of tones, "Mr Bailey, I wonder that your little outing doesn't include your stagehand, Mr Charles."

"And good afternoon to you too, Lady Bracknell," Kit said sardonically.

The dowager was a fan of Oscar Wilde and didn't miss the mocking subtext of this comparison to Wilde's imperious and rude character. However, she was too good a battle strategist to allow her defences to be breached by one paltry insult. In fact, this was just the kind of first move she most enjoyed, where the enemy showed their arrogance by overplaying their hand.

The old woman shifted slightly on the platform, so she was now facing Kit, her diminutive five foot to his more than six, doing nothing to diminish how intimidating she managed to look.

It was unclear to the rest of the group whether Kit was aware of the hornet's nest he had just stepped into. But those who knew the dowager well and had been on the receiving end of that look recognised the danger the man was in. "Isn't Mr Charles in police custody, suspected of murdering Miss Mapp?" Kit asked sarcastically. "Why would he be out day-tripping?"

"Are you not aware that Mr Charles has been exonerated by the testimony of a very credible witness?" That was probably pushing it a bit, Tabitha thought. However, the dowager continued, "He has now been released." The dowager conveniently forgot to mention that he had been released into their custody and was now residing with Lady Archibald.

Even though he'd had some warning of a possible alibi, it was amazing how shocked Kit looked at this news. An emotion washed over his face, but what emotion was it? Tabitha couldn't decide. It was more than surprise. There was no evidence of pleasure at hearing that one of his people was no longer imprisoned. But there was something else: fear? Guilt? What was the man feeling? If he was nothing else, Kit was a superb actor, and whatever the emotion was, it was quickly replaced with a very disingenuous smile. "Well, isn't that just marvellous news," he said. "I must tell everyone else that. They will be so happy to hear that Bobby is finally free. I'm surprised we haven't heard from him. I wonder where he is staying. I would have heard if he'd gone back to his rooming house."

As much as she could be outspoken to the point of rudeness, the dowager also knew when to keep her own counsel; if Kit thought his vague questioning statements would get him any more information, then he had no idea who he was up against.

When it was clear the woman would say no more, Kit nodded to the rest of the group and excused himself to go and herd his own people towards the exit.

"What do we make of that?" Wolf asked the group.

"Well, the news didn't please him. Let us see if it is enough to provoke him to action," Tabitha said.

"Now that goal has been achieved, is there any need to stay? Might we not just get the next return train?" the dowager demanded.

"We have achieved one of our goals," Wolf said. "Thanks to your masterful engagement with the man," he added somewhat obsequiously. The dowager was not easily placated. She thought too highly of herself and her achievements ever to assume anyone else ever thought otherwise. Wolf continued, "However, this is still a unique opportunity to attempt to engage with the theatre company in an informal setting. Also, it will be highly suspicious if we don't now appear at Devil's Dyke."

The trip from the station wasn't long, and they could have walked it, but in deference to Melody's little legs and the dowager's aged ones, Tabitha's group got in one of the horse-drawn, five-row charabancs that were waiting outside of the station. As first-class passengers, they were able to get the first ride, but Kit's group was seen taking one that was not far behind.

Wolf was a little worried that Kit might use this as an excuse to take the theatre company to another spot nearby, though he wasn't sure where else they might easily get to. But he discounted the sway of superstition; the company had to recreate the conditions of their first trip to Devil's Dyke to repeat the good luck that had supposedly been bestowed on the show. This meant going to the same spot. The company would have revolted against any other location.

CHAPTER 29

The trip from the station was quite a steep ride up to the Devil's Dyke estate. A pair of fine-looking pillars, each with an elephant head atop it, indicated the entrance to the estate. The whole area was more developed than Tabitha had expected. As if reading her thoughts, Lady Archibald explained, "About fifteen years ago or so, this estate was sold and began to be developed by the new owner. Five years ago, it was taken over by a Mr Hubbard, who by all accounts, is quite the innovator and has been responsible for much of the development here, including the funicular railway and aerial cableway." As she said this, Arlene pointed out over the valley below, which was spanned by thick cables strung between a pylon on their side and one on the other.

"Aerial cableway? Whatever will they think of next?" the dowager exclaimed. "I certainly won't be availing myself of that so-called entertainment this afternoon."

Lady Archibald laughed lightly and continued, "Mr Hubbard has built all manner of wonders here: an observatory, a camera obscura, and, of course, the fairgrounds themselves."

Those fairgrounds loomed on their right as they made their way down the driveway. Rat asked excitedly, "Lady Archibald, what kind of rides do they have? I've never been to a real fair."

"I have never visited the fair myself, but my understanding is that there is all manner of delights, including merry-go-rounds, bicycle railways, coconut shies. There is even a gipsy fortune teller." The young boy's eyes were round with excitement at this bounty of delights. Lady Archibald added a note of caution,

"However, I'm not sure that everything will be open at this time of the year." Seeing Rat's immediate disappointment, she added, "But I'm sure there will be enough to entertain you."

The charabanc was to drop them by the Devil's Dyke hotel, a fine-looking, white structure that seemed a little out of place in its formality for such a scenic countryside spot, because the scenery was the true attraction of Devil's Dyke. Descending from the charabanc, Tabitha took in the view before her. They were fortunate in the weather; while chilly, the day had cleared even more, and this allowed a wonderful view across the valley of the surrounding Downs. Below them, a patchwork quilt of farmland spread out in every shade of green and brown.

The rest of their group tumbled out of the charabanc, Melody giggling with almost as much excitement as Dodo was barking. But now what? Scanning the estate and surrounding area, Wolf realised that Devil's Dyke was a much larger attraction than he had anticipated. He tried to remember all the details of the theatre company's ritual, at least as they had been told to him.

"What is our plan, Jeremy?" the dowager asked with a certain impatience. However, the woman had cut to the heart of the issue; what was their plan? The charabanc pulled out, leaving his group standing in front of the hotel, unsure where to go next.

Wolf squeezed his eyes shut for a moment as he tried to recall all the details of the two conversations he'd had days ago about the company's planned trip to Devil's Dyke. What did the re-enactment involve? There was a picnic, he knew that. Had there been a mention of where? Wolf thought Merryweather had said something about near a cannon. He turned towards Arlene and asked if there was such a thing.

"There is. If you look over there, you can see it," she pointed off to the right. "Between the two bandstands, there's a model cannon. Why do you ask?"

"I'm trying to remember the details of that first lucky afternoon here that the company insists must be recreated. They had a picnic in front of the cannon."

"A picnic? In October? How absurd," the dowager proclaimed.

Under normal circumstances, Tabitha would agree with her.

"Did you see anyone carrying what looked like a picnic basket?" Langley asked the group.

"I wonder how literal this re-enactment has to be for the luck to hold?" Tabitha pondered. "I did see someone carrying something, but it didn't seem big enough to feed the entire group comfortably. But perhaps actually enjoying a picnic isn't the point. Maybe they feel it is enough to set up some sort of picnic and briefly go through the motions of partaking." Despite the dowager's dismissal of the sensibleness of a picnic, Ashby had been efficient enough to have rustled up a picnic basket for their group from the hotel. Given their early lunch, he had felt it prudent to at least have some light refreshments with them. If the theatre party set up for a picnic immediately, perhaps, Tabitha thought, their group could just seat themselves nearby.

The second charabanc, carrying the theatre company, pulled up at that moment, negating the need to guess where the group might go. As the theatrical coterie began their descent, it was Merryweather who was first down. Seeing Wolf, Tabitha and their associates standing rather aimlessly in front of the hotel, he approached them. Noting the basket Ashby was holding, the actor asked, "Are you planning to picnic here? We always head over there," he pointed in the same direction as Arlene. "Feel free to join us."

The man had answered their prayers. Relieved not to have to fabricate an excuse to impose their company on Kit's group, Wolf readily accepted the offer. By that time, Kit had joined them and seemed less than thrilled at their acceptance of the invitation.

The two groups made their way over to just past the cannon. While it was a dry day, given the rain before, Tabitha hoped the ground wasn't too damp. Luckily, Ashby came to the rescue again and pulled two blankets out of a bag that Bear had been carrying. The theatre company didn't seem to have any qualms about where they sat and merely arranged themselves in a loose grouping nearby.

Danny, the prop master, had been carrying the basket, but it seemed it was Mildred from the box office who was in charge of refreshments. With their basket, larger than it had seemed from afar, placed on the ground, Mildred began unpacking sandwiches and portable teapots with cosies, presumably filled with tea. In parallel, Ashby began unpacking their basket. It seemed the hotel had packed some more sausage rolls along with pork pies, some biscuits and even jam tarts. They also had tea.

While most of the theatre company seemed mildly interested in their illustrious companions, Kit sat as far away as he could, scowling. Merryweather, however, sat himself between the two groups and seemed happy to engage with Tabitha, Wolf and company.

Given that Merryweather had been one of the people to tell Wolf about this superstition, Wolf felt it wouldn't be suspicious to mention it, "Mr Frost, now that I see your group up here, I remember something about this being a lucky spot for your company."

"Indeed, it is, Blessings from Above," Merryweather replied with a smile. "As absurd as this may seem to lay people such as yourselves, theatre folks are a very superstitious bunch. Once the idea got hold that the interaction with the bird during the original picnic had made the show a success, Kit would have been foolish to do anything but attempt to recreate that day for the next production."

Tabitha was genuinely curious about this supposed re-enactment. They were outside in nature, and birds were everywhere. Surely, this was an entirely different proposition from the less likely scenario of a bird flying into the theatre. She posed this to Merryweather, who chuckled and said, "Well, you'd think so, wouldn't you? However, during that original picnic, Mrs Malloy, the costume mistress, had taken some crumbs from her sandwich and thrown them in front of her. A couple of small birds, maybe sparrows – I am no ornithologist – settled near her, pecking at the crumbs. One of the birds was particularly intrepid and came increasingly close to her as she threw her breadcrumbs a shorter distance. Finally, to the delight of the group, she held out some crumbs in her hand, and the little chappie settled there for a moment and then flew off with a breadcrumb. Quite an extraordinary sight, I can tell you."

Lily, momentarily distracted from entertaining Melody and Dodo, said, "Plants are my area of scientific interest, not animals, but even I know how rare it is for a wild bird to be lured towards a person. Surely that can't be something you've managed to recreate each year with random birds?"

Merryweather smiled and nodded his head in agreement, "Quite right, young lady. The second time we came back, we encouraged Mrs Malloy to attempt to recreate the circumstances from the previous encounter, but she was entirely unsuccessful."

The dowager, who had been busy pouring herself a cup of tea out of the flask, interrupted, "It's hardly surprising that anyone foolish enough to believe in such superstitions in the first place would continue to stretch the bounds of rational behaviour." Tabitha threw her a sharp glance; they hardly needed to offend the theatrical company and drive them away. Whether or not the old woman caught her meaning, she was distracted from any further comments by Melody's demands to open up the package of sweet treats.

If Merryweather had been offended by the dowager's comments, he was gracious enough not to show it. Instead, he continued, "It was actually Danielle, the deceased, who came up with the idea of recreating it as closely as we could. She suggested to the group that perhaps it was merely the intentional gathering of birds down from the skies to be near the group that had brought us good fortune and that if we could throw breadcrumbs to bring a bird or two as close as possible, that might suffice."

Tabitha couldn't help some scepticism creeping into her voice, "And has it always proven lucky?"

Merryweather sighed, "Well, to be honest, not always. But there is such an elaborate web of superstitions involved in bringing luck to a show that when a production is greeted with anything less than total enthusiasm, a rationale can always be found to explain that away. Regardless of how illogical that may sound, it has been my experience during a decades-long career in the business of theatre that, regardless of evidence suggesting their lack of efficacy, superstitions are never retired once they are established."

The actor paused and pointed to the understudy, now leading lady, Jackie, who was busy crumbling up some bread. "In poor Mrs Malloy's absence, young Jackie there has been designated as the bird mesmeriser for the afternoon. We will see how she does."

Given Merryweather's easy conversation on the topic, Wolf thought to gather as much information from the friendly man as they could, "Is this bird gathering the only ritual during this outing?"

"Ha! If only," Merryweather replied. "It's all Mrs Malloy's fault, really – and she's not even here today. The woman is rather given to spiritualism and the like. You know the stuff: seances, magical healers, those kinds of charlatans. But the woman is a fervent believer. So, after the sparrow interaction, the group wanted to visit the fairground. Mrs Malloy insisted on visiting the gipsy they have up there doing so-called fortune telling. So, we all troop up there, and Mrs Malloy goes first. It seems the gipsy woman somehow guessed that Mrs Malloy was part of a theatre company and predicted a good run for the new show."

Seeing the look on Tabitha and Wolf's faces, Merryweather said, "Oh trust me, I completely agree with you on this one; I'm sure this gipsy is a charlatan, and Mrs Malloy gave away far more than she realised. Once you know you have a theatre person in front of you, the only fortune that can be told is that a show will be a success. Anyway, after that, a visit to this fortune teller became an intrinsic part of this superstition. As if the woman now says anything other than some version of how successful the show will be. A total waste of time and money if you ask me, but I'm sure we'll do it again today."

Shortly after, Merryweather excused himself and went to sit near Mildred, who was busy doling out refreshments. Tabitha turned back to her own group. Melody was sitting next to the dowager, who was letting the little girl eat jam tarts at a rather alarming rate. Lady Archibald was in their little group; it seemed the unholy alliance with the dowager hadn't shattered yet. Rat was now holding a very excited Dodo in his arms and sitting next to Langley, with whom he seemed in deep conversation. Reflecting on this other rather unlikely pairing, Tabitha wondered if the taciturn, often quite humourless earl had actually found a kindred spirit in the rather serious, sometimes heartbreakingly mature young boy.

Looking further out at the edge of their little gathering, she saw Lily and Tobias huddled together, speaking in low voices. Was there something going on between these young people? As Lily's aunt by marriage and someone who had grown very fond of the highly intelligent, intellectual young woman, Tabitha was a little concerned. All the evidence so far was that Tobias was a wholly unserious young man who had a lot of growing up to do. While she didn't doubt that time spent with Lily would be good for the rakish viscount, would time with him be as beneficial for her? Glancing back over at the dowager, it seemed that the old woman was still blissfully unaware that there might be a growing attachment between her granddaughter and godson that went beyond mere friendliness. And if she did suspect this, it was unclear to Tabitha what she might feel about such a match.

Bear was sitting just to the side of Lily and Tobias and, Tabitha now realised, was sketching the pair. She made a mental note to remind Bear of his promise to show her his portraits of Melody when they finally returned home.

Between their group and the theatre company, there were a lot of people and quite a lot of noise. But suddenly, Kit stood and cleared his voice. Most of the talking ceased; the large, flamboyant man commanded a hilltop as well as he did a stage. "Good afternoon, everyone, friends," he nodded towards Tabitha and Wolf's group, "and new acquaintances. As we all know, we are gathered here this afternoon to confer the Blessings from Above on our upcoming show. Young Jackie here has kindly set the stage," at this, he gestured to the breadcrumbs scattered strategically a little way past the theatre group. Birds had already started to show some interest, occasionally swooping in to nab a crumb.

"I would ask that we try to keep quiet for some minutes in the hope that an intrepid bird in the group yet again bestows its Blessings." No sooner had he said this than Dodo started to bark and yelp. Kit looked accusingly in Rat's direction, and Langley, taking the hint, stood and indicated to Rat that they take Dodo for a walk away from the gathering. Melody jumped up to join them, and the little group made its way back up towards the hotel.

Seemingly satisfied, Kit continued, "As I said, let us keep quiet and hope we can tempt one of our little winged friends to join us." Tabitha wondered how low the theatre company had set the bar for the supposed blessing over the years. Was it enough for a brave little sparrow to land for a minute or two? It seemed it was. With Dodo gone, and a hushed silence finally falling over both groups, two little birds had started hopping over to the edge of the breadcrumbs and pecking. Once the birds had either had their fill or reached their tolerance for proximity to humans, they flew off. The entire spectacle had lasted less than a minute or two, but as the birds took flight, the theatre company broke out into applause. It seemed that, at least in their view, the Blessings from Above had been achieved. Tabitha shook her head in wonder at their collective willingness to believe in such an absurd superstition.

CHAPTER 30

The first part of the ritual apparently successful, both groups returned to chatting and eating. But as the dowager had pointed out, October was no time for a leisurely picnic, particularly in such an exposed spot. It was clear from the way people pulled their coats tight and, in some cases, visibly shivered, that it was time for some movement. In particular, Tabitha was concerned about the youngest and eldest in their group; both Melody and the dowager had very red noses from the cold.

It seemed that the theatre folk had similar thoughts because Mildred had started packing the remnants of their picnic back in the basket as people started to stand and then make their way up to the fairground. Taking that as their cue, Wolf suggested that their group do likewise. Keen to have Bear and Ashby stay close to Kit, that did leave the question of what to do with their blankets and picnic basket. Watching the theatre group, Tabitha wondered what they were going to do with their basket. This was answered when Danny picked it up and started to follow Mildred towards the hotel.

Straggling behind the rest of the group and seeing Tabitha watch the box office mistress, Jackie said, "Mildred feels the cold more than the rest of us. She has offered to wait in the hotel's coffee shop with our things while the rest of us enjoy the fair. I'm sure she'd be happy to watch your basket and blankets as well." Ashby nodded at this and made to follow the woman into the hotel with their belongings.

That issue dealt with, and Langley and the children still

nowhere to be seen, the dowager, Lady Archibald, Lily, Tobias, Tabitha and Wolf began to make their way towards the fairground. Tabitha was surprised that the dowager hadn't begged off visiting the fair and instead taken shelter in the hotel. If she had made a bet, Tabitha would have firmly put her money on the snobbish woman wanting nothing to do with such a plebian entertainment. Perhaps it was Lady Archibald's apparent enthusiasm that was persuading the dowager to put her own prejudices aside.

On entering the fairground, it was apparent that some of the entertainments were closed for the season, but there seemed to be enough open to keep everyone amused. Ahead to her right, Tabitha could see a carousel and caught sight of Langley standing by it, holding Dodo. Guessing that Rat and Melody were on the ride, Tabitha indicated to Wolf that they should walk in that direction.

The carousel was delightful; colourfully painted wooden horses were two deep and held in place by elaborately carved, equally colourful wooden poles. Cheerful music played as the carousel spun around and around. As Tabitha and Wolf arrived next to Langley, they heard a high-pitched, childish squeal of delight as Melody and Rat came into view. Melody was riding a very smart-looking horse with red, blue and silver decorations and a similarly painted pole. Her horse was on the outside of the carousel, and Rat was riding next to her on the inside.

As Melody caught sight of them, she yelled, "Tabby Cat, Wolfie, look at me. I'm riding by myself."

Melody's joy was delightful to behold, but Langley said apologetically, "I tried to persuade her to share a horse with Rat; she is only four, after all. But she is a very wilful young lady and insisted that she is almost five and could ride alone." He looked guiltily at Tabitha, "I apologise."

Tabitha laughed, "You have nothing to apologise for, Lord Langley. I am very aware of what a determined young lady Melody is and how hard it is to say no to her once she has her heart set on something." Langley looked relieved. He still felt as if he were walking on eggshells when it came to Melody and Tabitha's willingness to trust him. After all, it hadn't even been two months since he had abducted the little girl.

As they talked, Melody and Rat came around again, and this time it was Rat waving. It made Tabitha's heart glad to see the young boy being just that, young. He had spent far too much of his short life carrying the burden of responsibility for his sister, and it was comforting to think that perhaps he was now sure enough of her security that he could let his guard down and just be a ten-year-old.

The music played, and the carousel went around and around. The dowager and Lady Archibald appeared beside them, though Tabitha noted that Lily and Tobias were nowhere to be seen. Melody's horse came around again, and they heard shouts of, "Granny, Granny, look at me."

The dowager waved indulgently at the little girl. Lady Archibald asked curiously, "Melody calls you Granny, Lady Pembroke. I know that Lady Lily is your granddaughter. Is Melody her sister?"

The dowager laughed, "Melody isn't related to me by blood. She and her brother are delightful orphans that I have taken under my wing." Tabitha's eyebrows shot up at this inaccurate characterisation of how the children came into their lives, but she didn't comment. The dowager continued, "It pleases Melody to call me Granny, and I find myself quite in thrall to the child. And Matthew, who insists on being called Rat, is a highly intelligent young man whom Lord Langley is mentoring."

Langley looked very nervous at this last comment. He didn't want the dowager to go into any detail about what he was mentoring Rat in and why. He managed to catch her eye and give a subtle but sharp shake of his head. Whether she caught his meaning or not, the dowager didn't elaborate any further and instead said, "Unfortunately, my children are a greatly disappointing bunch. The only one with any spunk was my son, and he had other, not insignificant failings." As she said this, the old woman glanced at Tabitha. She continued, "Given the lack of pride my progeny inspire, I'm delighted to have two such worthy recipients for my beneficence in Melody and Matthew."

After one more trip around, the carousel came to a standstill. Melody looked inclined to beg for another ride, but, having handed Dodo to Wolf, Langley forestalled this by stepping up on the carousel and lifting the little girl off the horse and into his arms. Rat followed them off the carousel, a wide grin on his face. "Can we go and see if the camera obscura is open, m'lord?" he asked Langley. "And will you explain what it is and how it works?" the young boy asked shyly.

Langley put Melody down next to Wolf and placed a fatherly hand on Rat's shoulders, "That sounds like a wonderful idea, Rat." However, Melody scrunched up her nose. That didn't sound very fun to her. She had caught sight of a donkey as she was riding the carousel and had high hopes for a ride.

Seeing the little girl's lack of enthusiasm for the camera obscura, Tabitha suggested, "Lord Langley, why don't you take Rat, and Melody can stay with us." Langley nodded in agreement, and he and Rat set off.

Now that Melody was off the carousel, Dodo was squirming in Wolf's arms and yelping quietly, eager to be put down. Seeing her puppy eager to be reunited with her, Melody said, "Wolfie, can I take Dodo's lead?"

Wolf was happy to put the wriggling puppy down and hand the lead to Melody. "Hold it tight, Melly," he said. Dodo isn't used to so many people and so much excitement."

"What shall we do now?" Lady Archibald asked. She hadn't spent much time around children and had no idea what such tiny but demanding people might enjoy.

"Donkeys, donkeys!" Melody chanted.

"Do they have donkeys here?" Tabitha asked Lady Archibald.

Before the woman had a chance to answer, Melody sang out, "Over there. I saw some over there." She pointed off towards the west of the fair, at the other end from the entrance. With no better plan, Tabitha agreed, and the group made their way in that direction.

As a donkey came into view, Dodo seemed to have picked up its scent, and her excitement grew. She barked and pulled on the lead. "Melly dear, do hold on tight," Tabitha cautioned just as the little dog gave a particularly strong tug, which caused Melody to drop the lead. Dodo immediately made the most of her freedom and shot off in the direction of the donkey.

Melody cried out, and Wolf scooped her up in his arms, saying in a soothing voice, "Don't worry, Melly. She's headed towards the donkeys. We'll catch up with her there." Tabitha hoped he was right. As they quickened their pace towards the donkeys, they seemed to have lost sight of Dodo. Whatever the attraction the donkeys had held seemed to have been supplanted in the puppy's enthusiasm, and the dog was nowhere to be seen.

Arriving by the donkey, because it seemed there was only one, they looked all around, but Dodo was nowhere to be seen or heard. They asked the old man holding the donkey if he'd seen a dog, and he pointed out towards some tents on the outskirts of the fair. "It was headed this way to nip at my Daffodil's hooves no doubt, then it was distracted by something and went off in that direction," the old man said, his disdain for canines evident in the disapproving look he was shooting their way.

This was Dodo's first taste of freedom, and Wolf was nervous about how easy it would be to catch the puppy, even if they tracked her down. What was the best way of approaching this problem? By this time, Melody was crying.

Wolf said unthinkingly, "This estate is large; she could be anywhere by now."

At this, Melody started crying harder, and Tabitha glared at Wolf, who looked guilty and patted Melody on the back, saying gently, "There, there, Melly. We'll find Dodo. I'm sure she's having a wonderful time running around." This placated Melody somewhat, and she buried her face in Wolf's coat, and her crying subsided to sniffles.

Arlene watched Wolf deal with the little girl with amusement. Time had definitely mellowed the man. He seemed surprisingly suited to domesticity, she thought. Arlene's conjugal duties had been mercifully infrequent, but even then, she had taken her lack of pregnancy as an indication that she was not intended for motherhood. And she hadn't been unhappy at that prospect. Her deceased husband had been married as a young man and had two grown daughters. While he might have liked a son to pass his estate onto, he was fond enough of his nephew that he didn't hold her barrenness against his new young wife.

Looking at Wolf with Melody, Arlene had a momentary lapse into sentimentality as she considered what it might have been like to have a family with Wolf. Of course, it was not too late. But given both her disinclination towards motherhood and her apparent inability to conceive, perhaps she was not the person to give him the life that he now, surprisingly, seemed inclined towards.

Lady Archibald looked over at Tabitha. Was this the woman who might give him what he wanted? It was rare for Arlene to concede ground to another, particularly to another woman. But this Lady Pembroke, while undeniably beautiful, also had something else about her. Never one for false modesty, Arlene wouldn't allow that the other woman's beauty transcended her own. But she knew Wolf well enough to understand that physical beauty was never sufficient to get his attention. In the short time she had spent around Tabitha, Arlene could tell that her putative rival had intelligence, wit, and spirit. More to the point, this was the first time she had seen Wolf and Tabitha together. Watching them interact as naturally as if they were already a loving, married couple, their minds and hearts in sync, Arlene acknowledged to herself that this battle was truly lost.

Arlene was never one to cry over spilt milk. She roused herself from her reverie and said briskly, "Wolf, why don't you and the younger Lady Pembroke head off in the direction that the dog ran? The dowager countess can wait here with Melody in case the dog comes back. I will go and find Lord Langley and inform him of the search and then seek out Lady Lily and the young viscount and recruit them." This was as good a plan as any, and so everyone quickly dispersed as she had suggested.

Tabitha and Wolf stood at the edge of the fairground and looked around. They had been calling Dodo's name as they walked, but the little dog was nowhere to be seen. As they surveyed the area, they realised the puppy could be anywhere at this point. She might have run down the hill, away from the fairground, in the direction of the golf course, been distracted by a cow or a sheep in any of the surrounding farmland, or even set off down the other side towards the village of Poynings. Given the treats that Melody had been slipping the dog during the picnic, it was unlikely she would be hungry enough anytime soon to return of her own accord.

"She could be anywhere," Tabitha said despairingly. She was already considering how they would break it to Melody that her puppy might not be found that day, if at all. "There is too much area for us to cover in pairs," Tabitha decided. "You go towards the golf course, and I'll make my way over to that copse behind the hotel. With all those trees, I'm sure there are plenty of squirrels and even rabbits, and I could see Dodo happily chasing after them for quite some time."

Wolf couldn't argue. He hoped that the others would come to the same conclusion and suggested that if he or Tabitha ran across others in their group, they suggest they also split up to cover as much ground as possible.

CHAPTER 31

Tabitha followed the path from the fairground to the little wood off to the side of the hotel. She was glad the afternoon had warmed up somewhat, but even so, she was chilly. Sure that the dark, dank wood would be ever chillier out of the sunlight, she pulled her coat around her. As she walked, she called Dodo's name. Did the puppy even know her name? Tabitha wondered. She had played very little part in training the dog and had no idea what Dodo had or hadn't learned. She assumed the spaniel would come when called, but was that true?

Truth be told, despite her initial serious reservations about keeping the dog, Tabitha had become quite fond of the adorable, sweet-natured puppy. Even she might be sad if they were unable to find Dodo. Trying to scan the horizon in all directions as she walked, Tabitha clapped her hands to try to warm them up.

Arriving at the edge of the thicket, Tabitha wasn't sure which of the various paths to take. The ground was littered with dry, fallen leaves, and whatever animals lived in there were making a lot of rustling noises. She thought how exciting the sounds and smells would be to a dog. Tabitha could imagine Dodo happily running through the leaves and decided not to call Dodo for a while and instead listen hard for any noises that seemed louder and more urgent than the mere rustling.

The wooded area was larger than Tabitha had first thought, and she must have spent twenty minutes combing it before she heard something that sounded as if it were more than a squirrel or rabbit. And then she heard a yap that was definitely coming from Dodo. Tabitha hoped to take the little dog by surprise rather than have the dog see her coming and run away again. Tabitha walked as quietly as she could in the direction of the sound. She was almost at the other end of the small wood when she came upon Dodo busily digging through the leaves. Had the dog found a foxhole or the end of a rabbit warren?

Dodo was so preoccupied with her digging that she didn't hear Tabitha approaching. Realising she only had a few moments to act, Tabitha threw herself in Dodo's direction, managing to scoop up the surprised puppy. Surprise did not equate to unhappiness, at least as far as Dodo was concerned. The puppy greeted her captor with affectionate licks to her face that the still, far-from-dog-enthused Tabitha was not quite comfortable receiving. Tabitha was surprised to see that only a short scrap of lead was still attached to Dodo's collar and assumed that it had caught on something, and the dog had then chewed herself free.

As Dodo continued to greet her eagerly, Tabitha realised how muddy the puppy was from her digging and was grateful that she had chosen to wear her dark blue coat rather than her more stylish cream one. Tabitha had become so turned around during her hunt for Dodo that she wasn't sure which direction she had originally come from. It looked as if the trees thinned out ahead of her, so she decided to walk in that direction and then get her bearings once she was out of the wood.

Looking down at the dog in her arms, Tabitha realised that the puppy must have tired herself out with her escape and subsequent small animal chasing; the dog had closed her eyes and was snoring quietly. At least she wouldn't have to worry about the dog trying to escape from her grasp, Tabitha reflected gratefully. She walked as carefully and quietly as she could, eager not to wake the sleeping hound. Tabitha could only imagine what her mother would say if she could see her in that moment, walking through muddy woods with an equally muddy and rather stinky dog in her arms. She laughed to herself; there were many things about Tabitha's life recently that would appal her mother. Dodo was probably the least of it.

Just as she was about to exit the wood, Tabitha heard voices ahead of her. Familiar voices. As she sneaked closer, Tabitha thought she recognised Merryweather and Kit talking in hushed but angry voices. Tabitha wondered where Ashby and Bear were; the men were not supposed to be letting Kit out of their sight. Curious about what the two actors were arguing about, Tabitha crept closer, trying to move from tree to tree in case the men glanced in her direction. She was now even gladder that Dodo was asleep.

As she crept behind a large oak tree that she hoped was near enough to where the men were to enable her to overhear their conversation unnoticed, Tabitha wondered if this was another argument about the money Kit owed Merryweather.

"I wish I'd never even said what I did, Merry. I've always liked the lad, and I felt terrible that he was accused based on my word. Now that Bobby has been released, I refuse to do anything else, and I will just be grateful that I wasn't responsible for sending an innocent man to the gallows," Kit was saying in a low voice, his tone laced with acrimony.

Well, this was interesting, Tabitha thought to herself. It seemed that there was no doubt that Kit had intentionally and falsely sent the police in Bobby's direction. They had suspected as much, but it was nevertheless shocking to have it confirmed. While she had not found Kit as charming as others seemed to, nevertheless, she was happy to hear the man's evident regret at his actions and refusal to continue with the charade.

"You refuse, do you? Need I remind you that not only do you owe me money, a lot of money, but that I was prepared to forgive that debt in return for your help? Are you reneging now?" Merryweather asked in a sneering tone that seemed totally out of character for the hitherto friendly and genteel actor.

"I'm not reneging on anything. You begged me to lie, and I did. And because of my lie, Bobby was thrown into jail. It's hardly my fault if these busybodies have somehow managed to have him released. I still held up my end of our bargain," Kit protested.

"Exactly!" Merryweather said in a triumphant tone. "You said it yourself; these people are busybodies."

"When they told me they believed they had a witness who could provide Bobby with an alibi, I thought they were either bluffing or that they'd never managed to track this so-called witness down. How could I have known they would find him and convince the police to believe him?" Kit said in a self-pitying tone.

This caught Merryweather's attention, "Wait! You knew about this alibi and said nothing to me?" Merryweather complained. "What were you thinking? How long will it be before they turn their sights on me?" Now, this was very interesting, Tabitha thought.

"I have no idea. Actually, I believe they might think I'm the killer at this point," Kit said, confirming for Tabitha that he'd become aware of the directions of their recent suspicions.

"Do they now? That's interesting," Merryweather said in an all too gleeful tone. "I wonder how I might turn that to my benefit?"

"You can't possibly be suggesting that I throw myself on my sword to save your sorry neck?" Kit demanded in shock.

"I would never expect anything as noble from you, of all people," Merryweather spat.

"At least part of the reason I agreed to lie for you was because, with Danielle dead, I can't afford to lose my leading man as well. The company is struggling as it is. With no headliners, I might as well close up shop. But I don't care about the theatre company enough to go to the gallows in your place. I can tell you that!"

Kit had raised his voice at this point, and Merryweather was quick to shush him, "Keep your voice down, man. Do you want someone to overhear us? That's the last thing either of us needs."

In a now lowered voice, Kit continued, "I know that you didn't mean to kill Danielle, Merry. I realise it was an accident."

"It was an accident," Merryweather acknowledged. "When she told me she was leaving the Theatre Royal for the Hippodrome, I just saw red. I know that I'm a bit over the hill to play a leading man at this point. It was because Danielle couldn't afford to be picky that she hadn't moved on years ago. We both know that young Jackie isn't half the draw that Danielle was. It was self-defeating to kill her. I was just angry at that moment at the thought of what this would mean to my career. It's not like I ever complained once, did I?" Merryweather demanded. Kit didn't reply, and the actor continued, "I didn't! There are a lot of actors who wouldn't have played opposite a woman like her for all these years. But I recognised her talent, and so I accepted my lot gracefully. How dare she abandon me."

"You say this as if the ungrateful girl didn't also stab me in the back," Kit said sulkily. "I was the one who took a chance on her. I plucked her from obscurity and made her a star. A star who shone so bright that audiences looked past the colour of her skin and adored her. That was all me! But when she told me she was quitting, I didn't put my hands around her throat and strangle her. Did I?" Kit said in an accusing tone.

It seemed Merryweather had no good rejoinder to this. Instead, he said, "What's done is done. It seems Bobby is free, and the police have started looking for a new suspect. And even if they don't, I doubt that this so-called earl and his merry band of nosy parkers will give up so easily. So, what do you suggest I do?"

Merryweather sounded panicked and desperate, yet the question had been asked as a challenge. In response, Kit huffed and said, "I have no idea, Merry. You got yourself into this mess, and I'll be damned if I make it my responsibility to get you out. You're not the only actor in Brighton, you know. If I have to, I'll find a replacement leading man. I'm certainly not going to take the blame on your behalf." And with that final retort, Kit turned and stomped off.

Peeking around the tree, Tabitha could see Merryweather still standing in the same spot, fuming. Unfortunately, Dodo chose that moment to wake up from her brief nap. As she did so, a squirrel ran up the tree Tabitha was hiding behind, causing the dog to bark.

Hearing the bark, Merryweather spun around, "Who's there? Show yourself."

Tabitha stood very still and put her hand gently around Dodo's soft muzzle to try to keep the puppy quiet. She hoped that Merryweather would assume it was a dog walking by itself through the trees. But the man's suspicions had been raised, and instead of following Kit away, he turned toward the wood and started to follow the direction he thought the sound had come from.

If she'd been alone, Tabitha might have taken her chances and tried to steal away, but Dodo was wide awake now and chaffing at Tabitha's hold. It also occurred to Tabitha to make a run for it. It was hard to believe that she had walked so far from the others that she wouldn't quickly come upon someone, particularly if she yelled as she ran.

She had just made up her mind to run when Merryweather surprised her from behind. How had she not heard him creep up on her? "So, it's you, the queen of the nosy parkers," Merryweather said in a nasty, mocking voice. As he said this, he grabbed her with one arm while putting his hand over her mouth with another.

Tabitha was so surprised that she dropped Dodo. The dog was surprised as well and initially just stood in the leaves looking up at her with those soulful, chocolate-brown eyes. Then, with a sharp bark, Dodo launched herself at Merryweather's ankle. If the man had been wearing boots, he might have been okay. But Merryweather was too foppish to wear anything less than highly polished Oxford shoes, even for a picnic in the countryside. With his arms raised to hold Tabitha, his hem was raised, leaving his ankles nicely exposed to the sharp little puppy teeth.

Dodo must have taken a nice bite out of Merryweather because the man dropped his hold on Tabitha and instinctively bent to brush the puppy away. "Get away from me, you rat," Merryweather growled, trying to hit the dog. But Dodo was too quick for him, and, having achieved her goal, she ran off out of the wood. Realising the wisdom of the dog's actions, Tabitha took the opportunity to do her own sprint out of the trees. Cursing her and Dodo, Merryweather took off after them.

It had been many years since Tabitha had run any distance. And wearing a corset didn't make it easier. But she had youth and robust good health on her side, as well as a head start. Running as fast as she could, Tabitha tried to take in where she was without having to stop. She saw that she had come out the other side of the wooded area and was running towards the edge where the ground sloped steeply down towards the village of Poynings. Realising that if Merryweather caught up with her on the slope, she'd be in danger of falling or being thrown, she changed direction and started running along the ridge, back towards where they had picnicked.

Where is everyone? Tabitha thought. She wanted to yell, but she didn't have enough breath to run and shout at the same time. She just had to keep running until she saw someone, anyone. The hotel loomed up ahead, and she ran towards that. People were working there; someone would come if she called. Surely, Merryweather would stop his pursuit then. At this point, Tabitha was concerned less with apprehending the murderer and more with not being his next victim.

Suddenly, she heard barking. Looking up, she realised that Dodo was running back towards her, with Rat not far behind. And walking, if not fast, at least purposefully behind the dog, and boy was the dowager. Tabitha had wanted to encounter people, but not an old woman and a small boy. She was worried that, rather than being deterred, Merryweather might decide to hurt them as well. Unsure what to do, Tabitha stopped, turned, and looked around. There must be someone else within earshot. "Help," she yelled. Then yelled it again.

By this time, Merryweather was catching up with her. But so was Rat. "Stay back," she yelled at the boy. But he kept running. Tabitha yelled for help again, but her words seemed to get lost in the brisk breeze that swept over the Downs. For the life of her, Tabitha couldn't think how she might run from Merryweather, hopefully towards a more crowded spot, without Rat following her. She knew the boy was brave and a little foolhardy. Moreover, he was fiercely loyal. It was obvious that Tabitha was in trouble, and she was worried that Rat would believe he could save her single-handedly. Tabitha found that doubt had immobilised her suddenly.

Before Tabitha had a chance to consider her next move, Merryweather had caught up with her and grabbed her around her arms again. "Slippery little thing, aren't you, countess?" Merryweather snarled, not even noticing Rat and the dowager coming towards them. Merryweather continued, "But you won't escape again. Everyone will think that you fell over the edge here and tumbled to your death." Then he laughed, a bone-chilling sound. He tried to drag her towards the edge, but Tabitha struggled. Seeing Rat almost upon them, Tabitha yelled, "Go back, Rat. Go and find Wolf."

But Rat wouldn't be deterred. He realised that by the time he had found Wolf, the nasty old man might have already hurt m'lady Tabby Cat. Instead, the young boy ran as fast as he could and hurled himself at Merryweather's back. Rat wasn't large, but the momentum as he propelled himself was enough to knock the much older man off his feet, sending him flying to the ground and taking Tabitha along with him. The fall would have knocked the wind out of Tabitha even without the large actor falling on top of her. Now, pinned under her captor, Tabitha breathlessly struggled to get free from the weight on top of her.

Meanwhile, Merryweather was cursing and trying to catch his breath at the same time. As he attempted to sit up, try to keep hold of Tabitha as he did so, a voice behind him commanded, "Stay where you are, or I will be forced to wound you further." Tabitha took advantage of the distraction to roll out from under Merryweather's arm. Lying on the ground, now a safe distance away, Tabitha looked up in the direction of the familiar voice. The dowager was facing down Tabitha's pursuer with an intimidating look on her face and a terrifying, sharp-looking long blade in her hand.

Looking more closely at the blade, Tabitha realised that its handle was the same one she had admired on the dowager's walking cane earlier that day. It seemed the woman had acquired a sword stick at some point. But did she have any idea how to use it? The same thought must have occurred to Merryweather as he looked at the diminutive old woman and said dismissively, "Is that supposed to scare me, old lady?"

The dowager had now positioned herself closer to Tabitha so that if Merryweather tried to recapture her, he'd have to go through the dowager first. "Please don't make the mistake that so many do," she glanced momentarily at Tabitha, "of underestimating me. I know how to use this well enough, and it will give me a great deal of pleasure to have an opportunity to practice on a live subject." As small and aged as the dowager was, Tabitha had to admit that, at that moment, the woman seemed as ferocious as any mighty warrior.

Merryweather looked at the blade, then looked at Tabitha, and then looked back again. Then he looked around him. If he ran, how far would he get? Merryweather was not in the best physical shape. An excess of rich food and drink over the years had caused him to suffer from gout. Chasing Tabitha had been the most exercise the man had engaged in for decades. He didn't think he had it in him to stand up and run any further. He shook his head in despair and bewilderment. How had he been brought low by a chit of a girl, an old woman, a scrawny brat of a child, and a stupid dog?

Just as Merryweather Frost was contemplating his sad situation, it was suddenly made much worse as a large body landed on top of him and yelled, "Take that, you fiend. You will no longer hurt innocents, at least not on my watch."

Given that his face was now being squashed into the ground, Merryweather didn't have a chance to appreciate the bravery and gallantry on display as Viscount Tobias saved the day. Or at least that was the young man's view of his just-in-time rescue. To Tabitha, who had finally calmed her breathing and was sitting up watching the display, it looked as if the young man had come upon a situation that was now under control and had thrown himself unnecessarily into the fray at the final moments. But given how Tobias was beaming with pride and that Lady Lily was watching the scene with admiration shining in her eyes, Tabitha decided to keep quiet about her view of events.

However, neither Tabitha nor Tobias had counted upon the dowager, who exclaimed, "Your watch, Tobias? This fiend will no longer hurt innocents on my watch!" she was still brandishing her weapon and now came close to Merryweather, still struggling under Tobias' weight, and made a show of flourishing her blade in his face. "One move and I will happily skewer you with this," she proclaimed.

Worried about how the situation might escalate if the dowager and her godson were to continue in this battle for glory, Tabitha finally stood up, brushed herself down as best she could, and looked around for Rat. Having suffered no ill effects from his truly heroic part in Merryweather's capture, the boy was now standing nearby, his hands in his pockets. "Rat, go and find Wolf, Bear, and Ashby. Tell them what has happened," Tabitha explained. Now that she could think clearly about the situation, she realised that Tobias was helping somewhat by ensuring that their miscreant couldn't escape.

However, it seemed there was no need for Rat to alert the rest of their party; Tabitha could see Wolf running towards her, with Bear and Ashby bringing up his rear. In the distance, she could even make out Lady Archibald and Langley, who was holding Melody's hand.

Tabitha must have looked worse than she felt because Wolf's face showed more concern the nearer he came. He ran by the Merryweather and Tobias jumble and swept Tabitha into his arms. Holding her so tight that she could barely breathe, he said in a panicked voice, "Are you all right? We heard that you were attacked. I'm sorry I left you alone."

Pushing against his chest so that she could look into his eyes, Tabitha said, "I'm fine, Wolf. A little shaken, and I can only imagine what a state I look, but I'm fine."

Looking down at her mud-streaked, flushed face surrounded by hair that was mostly out of its pins, Wolf thought she had never looked more beautiful to him. But rather than telling her that, he bent his head towards her and kissed her. What started as a gentle touch of his lips took on more urgency as she moved her hands to wrap around his neck, pulling him towards her with a passion that surprised them both.

They were interrupted by a disapproving throat clearing, "Tabitha, Jeremy, please remember where you are and that there are children watching," the dowager scolded. Tabitha wasn't sure how long the kiss had lasted, mere seconds most likely. But she had been so caught up in the moment that time had seemed to stand still. As the dowager broke that spell, Tabitha pulled away from Wolf and realised that the crowd gathered now included many of the theatre company, including Kit.

There was lots of chatter as the crowd speculated as to what was happening. The drama of Merryweather's apparent apprehension by a young toff and a little old woman brandishing a long blade had now been intensified by the romance of the kiss. Several younger women in the crowd could be heard sighing over the dashing lord sweeping his leading lady into his arms. Even Mildred, the box office mistress, had her hand on her chest in reaction to her accelerated heartbeat.

Ashby had assessed the situation and had immediately run back to the hotel and now emerged carrying some rope. As he and Bear tied Merryweather's hands behind his back, with at least a worthy show of help by Tobias, Wolf tried to make sense of what had happened.

Tabitha explained, "I went to search for Dodo in the wood behind us. I found her and was carrying her out when I heard voices and realised that one of them was Merryweather." Tabitha caught Kit's eye. The man was clearly worried about what she might have overheard. She considered what she would say next. Wolf had shown her much about the difference between legal remedies and justice. In previous cases, the difference had been quite clear; now, it was murkier. There was no doubt that Kit had knowingly pointed the police towards Bobby Charles and had done nothing when it seemed the young man would be convicted and then hung for a murder that Kit knew he hadn't committed. Christopher Bailey was no innocent in this situation. However, from what she had overheard, his regret over his actions was genuine, and his refusal to compound his sin by continuing to shield Merryweather, despite the certain disastrous effects on his theatre company, should count for something.

And yet, as she looked at the desperately worried man staring back at her, Tabitha reflected that without his headlining leading lady or man, Kit's already significant financial concerns would be compounded. It also wasn't lost on her that if she turned Kit in, he might choose to stand by Merryweather's version of events rather than her own. They still had no concrete proof that Merryweather had killed Danielle; it was now her word against his. Sparing Kit would give him an excellent reason to validate Tabitha's story of overhearing Merryweather's confession.

This last point was the deciding one, and Tabitha said, "I hid behind a tree and heard Mr Bailey confronting Mr Frost with his suspicions that he had been the one to strangle Danielle. They fought, and Mr Bailey said he would be going to the police with these suspicions. Mr Frost then admitted to the murder and begged Mr Bailey to protect him, which he refused to do."

As she told this story to a mesmerised audience, no one's eyes were wider than Kit's. When it became quickly apparent that Tabitha had decided to skip over his complicity, Kit smiled gratefully in her direction. He then straightened up, threw back his shoulders, and strode out from the crowd, "It is true," he declaimed. "I had long had my suspicions about this man," he pointed an accusing finger in Merryweather's direction. If his erstwhile leading man had any thoughts about Kit's masterclass in turning one's coat, he was too busy being restrained to comment.

Kit continued, now getting into his stride and enjoying his moment back in the spotlight, "Yes, as Lady Pembroke explained, I confronted the man, and we fought. Others might have worried for their safety, but I had no such concerns."

Well, this was getting a little out of hand, Tabitha thought. It was one thing to spare the man; it was another to have him throw himself into the role of righteous saviour. As if intuiting her thoughts, Kit toned his performance down, ending with, "And so I turned and stormed off."

Tabitha picked up the story, explaining how Dodo had alerted Merryweather to her hiding spot but had then saved the day by attacking the man and enabling her to escape. Hearing her name, the puppy came up to Tabitha - it seemed she did know her name after all.

The dog looked up pleadingly, and Tabitha bent down to pick up the muddy but still adorable puppy. Without thinking about what she was doing, Tabitha planted a kiss on the top of the dog's head and said, "Dodo definitely saved the day." Catching a movement out of her eye, she quickly added, "And of course, I was saved a second time from Mr Frost's clutches by the quick-thinking and bravery of the dowager countess, Rat, and then Viscount Tobias. Thank you all."

CHAPTER 32

After the drama-filled trip to Devil's Dyke, the group seemed restless on the train ride home. Perhaps it was all the excitement of the afternoon. Perhaps it was because they had been in Brighton for almost a week, and most of them had been away from their own beds for far longer than that. It was time to go home. Even Lord Langley seemed happy enough at the prospect of returning to London.

As it happened, Langley had received a telegram from his mother that morning saying that there was some horse-related emergency at the family estate in Cornwall that necessitated her immediate return. She had informed her offspring that a decorator had been engaged who had strict instructions that were not to be deviated from. Fiona Sandworth, Dowager Countess of Langley, now felt that her duty towards the earldom had been discharged, and she was returning to her beloved estate near Delabole just in time for the start of hunting season. Langley would have begrudgingly returned home if his mother had still been in residence, but he was very happy to know she wouldn't be.

On the short train ride back to Brighton from Devil's Dyke, the dowager had expressed her firm conviction that Tobias should return with her to London. If she had been expecting resistance, she was pleasantly surprised by the young man's willingness, even happiness, to comply. It didn't escape the dowager's keen eye that her granddaughter seemed equally bright-eyed at the prospect.

During the trip, Tabitha and Wolf had carefully avoided each other. Neither regretted their kiss, but they each overlaid the spontaneous affection with so many complex emotions. Wolf feared he had pushed Tabitha too quickly and that, even though she seemed to respond with equal passion at the time, would come to regret such an overt demonstration. Tabitha's feelings were an intricate weave of worry, elation, uncertainty, and excitement. For all that she had been married two years, that might as well have been her first kiss.

Melody didn't really understand what had happened that afternoon, but she knew that her puppy and her brother had saved the day, and she was too excited to sit still. Instead, she ran back and forth between the two first-class carriages with Dodo. After a few minutes of this, everyone's patience had worn thin, and Langley had coaxed the little girl onto his lap, where he made up stories for her for the rest of the blessedly short train ride.

On their arrival back in Brighton, Merryweather Frost, who had made the trip in the custody of Bear and Ashby, had been handed over to Inspector Maguire. Tabitha's statement, backed up by Kit, ensured that Robert Charles was formally exonerated. If Wolf wondered about the completeness of Tabitha's story, he didn't ask. He had full faith in Tabitha's moral compass and judgement. He was happy to go along with whatever version of events she had decided to share with the police.

They had parted ways with Kit at the police station. However chastened the man had been briefly at Devil's Dyke, all shame at his false accusation of Bobby had now been conveniently forgotten. Always a firm believer in fully committing to a character during his years as an actor, Kit had wholeheartedly embraced the role of innocent bystander that Tabitha's lifeline had provided him. As the group bade him a wary farewell, Kit exclaimed, "Adieu. Parting is such sweet sorrow that I shall say goodnight till it be morrow."

The dowager was no great fan of Mr Shakespeare's plays, and hearing his words come out of such an irritating jack ass, compelled her to answer, "I find there to be nothing sorrowful about bidding you adieu, Mr Bailey."

"Ah, my dear Lady Bracknell," Kit exclaimed, happy to mock the dowager to the last moment, "but I feel sure you will miss me once you are gone."

Perhaps seeing the sharp retort about to be aimed at him, he added, "I will certainly look back on our time with nothing but the fondest of memories. Indeed, while I think on thee, dear friend, All losses are restored and sorrows end."

Realising how futile it was to waste her scorn on such a man, the dowager harrumphed, turned her back on him, and made her way into the waiting carriage. The rest of the group made somewhat less acrid farewells

Finally, Tabitha, Wolf and the rest of the group returned to the hotel. After a long soak in a hot bath, while being fussed over by Ginny, Tabitha finally felt more like herself. "You'll be covered in bruises tomorrow, m'lady", Ginny said in a stern voice, as if it was through Tabitha's negligence that she had found herself in such a state. Tabitha knew that this apparent sternness merely masked how worried Ginny had been to hear of the danger Tabitha had been in.

Tabitha would have happily gone straight to bed after her bath. But she knew that if she did anything but present herself at dinner looking well and cheerful, Wolf would worry. Despite the awkwardness that had suddenly sprung up between them, she did not doubt his genuine concern and had no desire to add to it.

For his part, having seen his companions off to their various rooms, Wolf had stayed behind in the lobby to bid farewell to Lady Archibald.

"Whatever doubts you might have had should be dispelled now, Wolf", Arlene said kindly.

Wolf didn't have to ask what she was talking about. But he also didn't want to discuss the kiss with anyone at the moment, particularly Arlene. Instead, he took her hand and said, "I wish you well, Arlene. I hope that you find love. Or whatever it is you are looking for." He stopped short of encouraging her to let him know when she was next in London.

"Thank you for all you've done. All of you. I will take care of Bobby. It's the least I can do for Danielle," Arlene said with unusual sincerity. "I assume you'll leave for London tomorrow."

They probably would, Wolf agreed. There was no reason to continue to stay in Brighton. They could easily take an afternoon train the following day. He was ready to be back home. As Wolf thought this, he realised that he did now think of Chesterton House as home. A home full of people he cared about. A home that he shared with Tabitha.

Arlene always had been able to read his thoughts. It seemed he was no less transparent to her now. "I expect an invitation to the wedding, you know," she teased.

Wolf blushed slightly, "Let us not get ahead of ourselves," he stuttered.

Arlene lay a hand on Wolf's arm, saying, "I have no doubt that by this time next year, you will be happily married and eagerly anticipating a new addition to the family." And with that final prediction, Arlene turned and left.

As it turned out, dinner that evening was a quiet affair; the dowager had sent word that she was exhausted from all the excitement and would dine in her room. Langley said he had some business to take care of and would also not join them. Bear told Wolf that he was going to spend the evening at the Cock and Bull, saying goodbye and thank you to Paddy and Jeanie. Having been given the evening off, Ashby was going to join him.

"Please give them my thanks," Wolf said. "Their help was invaluable."

Given the awkwardness still between them, both Tabitha and Wolf were glad for Lily and Tobias' company at dinner. Having agreed that there was no reason for them to remain in Brighton any longer and that they should all prepare to leave the following day, no one seemed inclined to linger over their meal or afterwards. Tabitha was more than happy to have an early night.

At breakfast the following morning, the rest of the group concurred with the decision to take an afternoon train. It was a short trip to London, and they could all eat dinner in their own homes that evening, with time to spare. While Wolf would have liked to have made good on the bet with Langley and taken the dowager to the fish and chip restaurant, it was clear that the group was weary and ready for home. Telegrams were dispatched to the various households, alerting their staff. Maids and valets scrambled to pack.

On their arrival back in London, the members of the group dispersed to their separate homes. Rat went with Lord Langley, and Tobias begged the dowager to allow him to return with her rather than going straight to his family's home. Whether it was because she felt the young man should face the parental music immediately or that she was concerned about having the two young people under one roof, she refused. She did, however, pat him on the arm and say with surprising kindness, "Tobias, you have behaved yourself quite well over the last couple of days, for the most part. And you were somewhat helpful with the investigation at the end. I will be sure to inform your father of the welcome shift in your attitude." The young man flushed with pleasure at the praise, albeit limited and conditional.

Tabitha, Wolf, Bear, Melody, Dodo and their servants made their way back to Chesterton House. Walking through the front door and being welcomed by Talbot, it felt as if they had been away for months rather than a few weeks. Even so, it was hard to believe that they had caught two murderers since they had been gone.

It felt as if their arrival back in London heralded a new season; winter was suddenly with them. It was late October, and Tabitha noticed how bare the trees in front of the house were compared to when they had left for Scotland. Suddenly, everyone on the streets seemed bundled up in their warmest winter clothes. She was happy to make her way into the cosy parlour where a fire was raging, and Talbot had ensured that tea and cake would be waiting for them.

Finally, alone, Tabitha took a restorative sip of tea while Wolf watched her nervously over the rim of his cup. For her part,

Tabitha felt very much as if the intensity of the last couple of days almost hadn't been real and that, now they were back in their own home, things might resume as they had been before. Was it naive of Tabitha to even consider that?

Realising that, of course, it was naive and unfair to Wolf, Tabitha put her teacup back in its saucer and said, "I know we must speak, Wolf. I want us to discuss what has happened and what this thing is between us. But I need a little bit of time to settle back into a routine and to consider everything without all the drama that has swirled around us recently."

Wolf was relieved to hear Tabitha say this. He was relieved because it meant there was hope, but also relieved because he wasn't sure he was ready to have this conversation. His feelings for Tabitha had been growing for months, but it felt as if Arlene's brief incursion into their lives had artificially accelerated things, and he didn't want either of them making life-altering decisions with anything but the clearest of heads.

"Take as much time as you need," he assured Tabitha.

EPILOGUE

When Wolf had said to take as much time as she needed, he wasn't sure what he'd expected. But Tabitha had very much taken him at his word. Everyone had fallen back into their routines, and a few days later, it felt as if their trips to Edinburgh and Brighton might never have happened. Any awkwardness between them had evaporated, and Wolf was starting to realise that he might have to face the possibility that Tabitha would never again raise the topic of that kiss.

The dowager had picked back up where she'd left off before departing London and telephoned to speak with Melody every morning at ten o'clock on the dot. The little girl's visits to "Granny" and Lord Langley also resumed. On the days that Melody didn't visit Langley, Rat would normally visit Chesterton House to eat supper with his sister in the nursery.

Wolf had considered the advice given to him by both Langley and Tabitha about how he might utilise his thief-taking skills in his new life as an earl. But having been away for weeks, there was so much to catch up on with estate business and the other commercial holdings he had inherited that he didn't have time to think about taking anything else on.

The days turned into a week and then two. Before they knew it, they were in November. As Wolf caught up with estate business and Tabitha caught up with household tasks and with the girls at the Dulwich House, they both began to feel different versions of the same feeling: restlessness. Wolf considered Langley's suggestion that he take an interest in politics and take up his seat in the House of Lords. Tabitha considered her suggestion to Wolf that he be more open to continued investigations. They both felt confusion and concern at the awkward state between them of important things left unsaid. But as they continued to circle each other warily, neither spoke of the agitation they were feeling.

On a perfectly normal Wednesday, Wolf was busy with papers in his study. Tabitha was sitting at the writing desk in the drawing room, having just finished going over the menus for the week with the housekeeper, Mrs Jenkins, when the telephone made its clanging, discordant sound. Glancing at the clock on the mantelpiece, Tabitha realised that it was long past the time for the dowager's morning call. And anyway, she was sure that had already happened. Few other people had telephones installed, so Tabitha waited expectantly for Talbot to find her with news of who was calling.

A soft knock on the drawing room door, and the butler entered with a rather worried look on his face. "I'm sorry to disturb you, milady," the man intoned in a tone that seemed peculiar to all butlers she had ever met. "That was Mr Manning, the dowager countess' butler, on the telephone. He is worried about the dowager countess and believes she might be in imminent danger. He has asked if he might call to speak to you and Lord Pembroke after luncheon."

Whatever Tabitha had been expecting, it wasn't this. The idea of a servant, even one as trusted and loyal as Manning, reporting on the behaviour of their master or mistress was bizarre enough. That the often particularly inscrutable butler wanted to disclose something about the dowager was intriguing. What trouble could the impossible woman have got herself into? Tabitha put down her pen and went to find Wolf. It seemed she should have enjoyed the peace and quiet while she could. It was possible that, yet again, her life was about to be anything but boring.

Note:

The train line to Devil's Dyke actually left from Hove station, not Brighton. But it suited my narrative better for it to be Brighton. For any train buffs in my readership, I apologise.

What was Tabitha's wedding to Jonathan really like? Discover exclusive short stories about your favourite characters, and more, by signing up for my newsletter.

Want a sneak peek at book 5, An Audacious Woman? Keep reading….

Prologue

The older woman heard footsteps behind her but thought nothing of it. But as she turned onto the quiet, dark street, the footsteps continued, perhaps even getting closer. Not normally faint of heart, the woman suddenly realised that she was being followed. There was only one person she had cause to fear, but she thought she had successfully neutralised that danger. She had never considered before how dark this street was. The woman was fully alert to her shadowy companion but still was not unduly worried; this was nothing more than an attempt to scare her into compliance. Those were the last words she thought before a hand grasped her around the waist, and another slammed across her mouth, muffling any screams.

Chapter 1

Monday, October 30, 1897

What was the protocol for receiving an apparently urgent afternoon visit from your mother-in-law's butler? When she was younger, Tabitha's mother, Lady Jameson, had drilled her in the appropriate etiquette for every conceivable situation, or so she had thought. But this one had escaped the attention of even the ever-vigilant Dowager Marchioness of Cambridgeshire.

Earlier that day, Tabitha & Wolf had received a telephone call. Given that the Dowager Countess of Pembroke, Tabitha's erstwhile mother-in-law, was one of the few people they knew with a telephone - in fact, she'd been the one to install it without permission at Chesterton House - Tabitha had assumed that it was she calling. Indeed, the call had come from the dowager's household, but instead of being from the woman herself, it had come from her butler, Manning.

There was no doubt that the dowager and Manning shared a closer bond than might be expected of an aristocrat and one of her household staff. This bond had been evident when Manning was arrested for murder, and the dowager had begged Wolf and Tabitha, by extension, to prove the man's innocence. Manning's devotion and loyalty to the dowager was beyond dispute - the man was willing to go to the gallows to protect his employer's reputation. However, Tabitha had wondered at the time if the dowager reciprocated his feelings or was merely unwilling to lose a well-trained servant. Nevertheless, even this recent evidence of their bond, whatever its motivation, had not prepared Tabitha to hear her own butler, Talbot, intone, "That was Mr Manning, the dowager countess' butler, on the telephone. He is worried about the dowager countess and believes she might be in imminent danger. He has asked if he might call to speak to you and Lord Pembroke after luncheon."

Unlike the dowager countess herself, Manning had never struck Tabitha as being given to melodrama and hyperbole, and she couldn't imagine what imminent danger an aged aristocrat could have managed to get herself into such that she would drive her butler to inform on her. Yet, as she sat in the drawing room waiting for Wolf to join her for Manning's arrival, Tabitha also reflected on what it would take for the famously discreet and normally stoic butler to break ranks and tattle on his mistress; was the dowager truly in peril?

AFTERWORD

Thank you for reading An Inexplicable Woman. I hope you enjoyed it. If you'd like to see what's coming next for Tabitha & Wolf, here are some ways to stay in touch.

SarahFNoel.com

Facebook

@sarahfNoelAuthor on Twitter

sfnoel on Instagram

@sarah.f.noel on TikTok

If you enjoyed this book, I'd very much appreciate a review (but, please no spoilers).

You can pre-order the next in the series, An Audacious Woman on Amazon.

ACKNOWLEDGEMENT

I want to thank my wonderful editor, Kieran Devaney and the eagle-eyed Patricia Goulden for doing a final check of the manuscript

ABOUT THE AUTHOR

Sarah F. Noel

Originally from London, Sarah F. Noel now spends most of her time in Grenada in the Caribbean. Sarah loves reading historical mysteries with strong female characters. The Tabitha & Wolf Mystery Series is exactly the kind of book she would love to curl up with on a lazy Sunday.

BOOKS BY THIS AUTHOR

A Proud Woman

Tabitha was used to being a social pariah. Could her standing in society get any worse?

Tabitha, Lady Chesterton, the Countess of Pembroke, is newly widowed at only 22 years of age. With no son to inherit the title, it falls to a dashing, distant cousin of her husband's, Jeremy Chesterton, known as Wolf. It quickly becomes apparent that Wolf had consorted with some of London's most dangerous citizens before inheriting the title. Can he leave this world behind, or will shadowy figures from his past follow him into his new aristocratic life in Mayfair? And can Tabitha avoid being caught up in Wolf's dubious activities?

It seems it's well and truly time for Tabitha to leave her gilded cage behind for good!

A Singular Woman

Wolf had hoped he could put his thief-taking life behind him when he unexpectedly inherited an earldom.

Wolf, the new Earl of Pembroke, against his better judgment, finds himself sucked back into another investigation. He knows better than to think he can keep Tabitha out of it. Tabitha was the wife of Wolf's deceased cousin, the previous earl, but now she's running his household and finding her way into his life and, to his surprise, his heart. He respects her intelligence and insights but can't help trying to protect her.

As the investigation suddenly becomes far more complicated and dangerous, how can Wolf save an innocent man and keep Tabitha safe?

An Independent Woman

Summoned to Edinburgh by the Dowager Countess of Pembroke, Tabitha and Wolf reluctantly board a train and head north to Scotland.

The dowager's granddaughter, Lily, refuses to participate in the preparations for her first season unless Tabitha and Wolf investigate the disappearance of her friend, Peter. Initially sceptical of the need to investigate, Tabitha and Wolf quickly realise that the idealistic Peter may have stumbled upon dark secrets. How far would someone go to cover their tracks?

Tabitha is drawn into Edinburgh's seedy underbelly as she and Wolf try to solve the case while attempting to keep the dowager in the dark about Peter's true identity.

An Audacious Woman

The Dowager Countess of Pembroke is missing!

While Wolf is contemplating whether or not he wishes to continue taking on investigations, it seems that the dowager has taken the matter into her own hands and is investigating a case independently. But why has she gone missing from her home for two nights and what mischief has she got herself into? Tracking down the elderly woman takes Tabitha and Wolf into some of the darkest, most dangerous corners of the city.

What on earth is the exasperating dowager caught up in that she seems to have become entangled with London's prostitutes?

A Discerning Woman

It seems Christmas will be anything but peaceful this year!

Tabitha and Wolf are hoping to spend a quiet Christmas at Glanwyddan Hall, the Pembroke estate in Wales. However, before they even leave London, they receive unsettling news of disturbing pranks happening on the estate. Is this just some local youthful mischief, or is something more sinister afoot? Moreover, why is the dowager countess so determined that they not cancel their visit? With the dowager guarding a secret, Tabitha and Wolf are thrust into a desperate quest to uncover the truth. As danger looms, they must navigate treacherous paths to safeguard their loved ones.

Will Tabitha and Wolf reveal the malevolent force lurking in the shadows before it's too late?

Printed in Great Britain
by Amazon